A Wrens' Wartime Christmas

Vicki Beeby writes historical fiction about the friendships and loves of service women brought together by the Second World War. Her first job was as a civil engineer on a sewage treatment project, so things could only improve from there. Since then, she has worked as a maths teacher and education consultant before turning freelance to give herself more time to write. In her free time, when she can drag herself away from reading, she enjoys walking and travelling to far-off places by train. She lives in Shropshire in a house that doesn't contain nearly enough bookshelves.

Also by Vicki Beeby

The Women's Auxiliary Air Force

The Ops Room Girls
Christmas with the Ops Room Girls
Victory for the Ops Room Girls

The Wrens

A New Start for the Wrens
A Wrens' Wartime Christmas

VICKI BEEBY

A Wrens' Wartime Christmas

CANELO

First published in the United Kingdom in 2022 by

Canelo
Unit 9, 5th Floor
Cargo Works, 1–2 Hatfields
London, SE1 9PG
United Kingdom

A CIP catalogue record for this book is available from the British Library.

Print ISBN 978 1 80032 427 5
Ebook ISBN 978 1 80032 426 8

Look for more great books at www.canelo.co

Printed and bound in Great Britain by Clays Ltd, Elcograf S.p.A.

1

For my family:

Mum

Duncan, Jana & Emma

Chris, Katka & Elena

Prologue

So this was Orkney. As Mary Griffiths trailed up the path leading from Stromness, she lagged behind the two other newly qualified visual signaller Wrens and Joe Pallant, the signaller who had been sent to show them around the signal station. The others were chatting, laughing over some comment of Joe's, and she was in no mood for merriment.

Had Owen ever strolled along this footpath? Had he gazed out to sea and thought of all the times they had walked hand in hand along the cliffs at home? It was two years since he had died, yet the pain of loss was as sharp as ever. Of all the places she could have been sent, she hadn't thought she would be sent here, only a few miles from Owen's final resting place. Yet she had joined the WRNS with a vague idea of making up for Owen's loss from the navy, so maybe an Orkney posting was appropriate.

'Penny for your thoughts.'

Mary jumped, not having noticed Joe drop back to walk beside her. 'Trust me, you don't want to know.'

Joe's brown eyes twinkled. 'Plotting a murder already? Orkney's been known to have that effect on people.' He wasn't bad looking, with his rumpled brown hair that was clearly never going to lie flat and his lean frame; had things been different, Mary might have enjoyed the banter.

Of course, had things been different, Owen would be alive and she wouldn't have ended up here. A fresh wave of misery struck, and she turned away, making a show of brushing hair from her eyes to give an excuse for the tears that threatened to spill down her cheeks. 'Keep on like that and you'll be the victim.' It was much easier to lash out and keep others on the back foot. That way no one could get close enough to realise how she was really feeling. She didn't want anyone's pity.

To her surprise, instead of striding off to catch up with the other Wrens, Iris and Sally, Joe fell into step with her. He shot her a grin. 'I'll risk it.'

Mary gritted her teeth. She had hoped for a moment to compose herself and be alone with her thoughts, not spend any more time than necessary with this annoying man who clearly thought he was God's gift to women. On the other hand, he had been in Orkney for some time and would be able to answer the question foremost on her mind. 'Actually,' she said, striving to keep her tone casual, 'I was thinking about the *Royal Oak*. I heard it went down in Scapa Flow. Can you see the place from here?'

He gave her a sharp look. 'Why do you want to know?'

'Oh, it's just that I remember everyone speaking about it at the time. It was awful. I don't like to think about looking out over a place where so many men died.' Great. Now he probably thought she was nervous. Not the best of first impressions.

'I wouldn't worry. You can't see it from here.' He pointed across the water. 'A large part of the south coast of Mainland is shaped like a wide M. We're near the foot of the western leg, with Stromness in an inlet about a third of the way up.' His finger traced the start of an imaginary letter M. 'The coast goes up to a point at the entrance to the Loch of Stenness, then back down to Houton at the lower point in the centre.' He pointed at some hills across the water to the east. 'The land you can see over there isn't another island but another part of Mainland. The *Royal Oak* went down in Scapa Bay, which is at the top angle of the eastern side of the M, about ten miles away as the crow flies. You can't see it from this part of the island because all those hills are in the way.'

'I'm glad.' It was bad enough knowing she was near the place where Owen had died; having to stand watch every day over the dark water that had stolen his final breath would have been agony. She looked east for a moment longer then tore her gaze away and turned back to Joe, suddenly conscious that he was studying her, not the view. She plastered a smile on her face. 'I mean, it's good to have a reminder of why our job is so important, but I wouldn't want to have to see the place every day.'

A sudden thought occurred. 'Were you here when it happened?' If she could find someone who could answer her questions about how Owen had died, maybe then she could move on with her life.

Joe shook his head. 'I only arrived in Orkney last year.' Then he pointed up the track at Iris and Sally, who were nearly out of sight. 'We need to get a move on. As much as I'm enjoying our walk together, I'm supposed to be showing you around the signal station.'

As she increased her pace, Joe caught her arm. 'I think you're the prettiest girl on the island. It would be nice to have another walk together. What do you think?'

How could she possibly enjoy herself when the man she would never stop loving was dead? She opened her mouth to say as much then caught herself. It was hardly fair to snap at Joe, who could have no idea of her loss, and she didn't feel like explaining herself. After drawing a steadying breath, she schooled her features into a bland smile. 'I don't think that would be a good idea,' she said, then hastened after Sally and Iris before Joe could say anything more.

Once at the signal station, Joe gave them a quick tour of the bunkroom, galley and living area downstairs before leading them up a ladder and through the hatch into the signal room. There he introduced them to the two signalmen on duty. Mary didn't pay them much attention, being too busy taking in the cramped room where she would be based for the foreseeable future. Her eyes were immediately drawn to the windows, occupying three sides of the room and leading out onto a balcony. Beyond, she could see the coastline stretching in a wide panorama, from the narrow strip of water between Hoy and the Orkney mainland on one side to the endless expanse of the Atlantic on the other. She was hit by the isolation of Kyeness and a sense of the immensity of the area she was to guard. When she was on watch, the safety of the fleet would be her responsibility. With a sudden sense of urgency, she dragged her gaze from the view and turned to the others, aware she mustn't miss any instructions.

To her frustration, she realised the signalman sitting at a wooden desk had been speaking, and she hadn't caught a word.

Sally, who had been studying the charts pinned to the wall, turned wide eyes on him. 'Are you all being transferred to ships?'

Mary relaxed. Whatever the man had said, it didn't seem to have been about their duties.

'The three of us are.' It was Joe who answered, warming his hands at the stove while he spoke. 'Andy and Ollie to destroyers, the lucky sods, while I'm stuck on a minesweeper here in bloody Orkney. Pardon my French.'

'You won't think us lucky if we end up in the Arctic convoys,' one of the duty signallers said with a theatrical shiver.

'True.' Joe gave Mary a wicked grin. 'And I can't deny there are compensations for staying.'

Mary felt a tightness in her chest. She didn't think she could handle it if Joe wouldn't take no for an answer. She was here to do her job. Nothing more. She narrowed her eyes in what she hoped was a discouraging expression. 'Since this is the last time we're seeing each other, perhaps you could describe the routine at Kyeness.' She placed careful emphasis on 'last time'.

'The main thing,' Joe stated, 'is to send the code of the day challenge to all naval vessels passing this point, and the unknown ship call to international vessels. Then there are the loops.'

'The what?' Iris asked.

Joe beckoned them to the window and gestured at the sea. 'This is Hoy Sound,' he said. 'One of the entrances to Scapa Flow. It's your job to make sure only friendly vessels go through. We can't afford a repeat of the *Royal Oak* incident.' He gave Mary a glance when he said that.

Mary swallowed, knowing he was referring to the U-boat which had somehow got past the navy's defences and torpedoed the *Royal Oak* in supposedly protected waters. Were they supposed to look out for U-boats too? 'But how are we supposed to see the subs?' she asked.

'That's where the loops come in. There's an anti-submarine indicator loop laid across the Sound of Hoy.

No idea how it works, but when a vessel crosses – either on or under the water – it sends a signal to the station at Lower Skaill.' Joe pointed at a phone connected to a box with a handle. 'They will then call on this phone to ask us to identify it.'

He had hardly finished speaking when the very telephone he had pointed out rang, making Mary jump. She watched with interest when one of the signalmen answered then went to the window to identify the ship that must have just crossed the loop. Not a submarine, then. Mary hadn't realised how tense she had become until she was aware of her shoulders relaxing after the signalman had identified a friendly ship and reported back.

Mary made a mental note of everything the signalman had done, buoyed up by a sense of purpose that had been lacking since Owen's death. What could be more important than making sure no more U-boats entered Scapa Flow? While it was too late to save the *Royal Oak*, she would do all in her power to ensure no other ships were lost while in Scapa Flow.

Chapter One

October 1942

Mary glanced at the open log book as she took her place at the start of the afternoon watch, and at the sight of the date, her heart contracted. The fourteenth of October.

'I'll make tea, shall I?'

Mary only vaguely heard Sally's question. It was nothing more than background noise that, along with the waves pounding against the cliffs and the wind whistling through the signal station windows, could be pushed to the back of her mind. Her vision had become a tunnel, with the date scrawled across the top of the page the only thing in focus. How could today have crept up on her like this?

'Mary?' This time Sally couldn't be ignored, because her voice was accompanied by a prod between the shoulder blades. 'What's the matter? Has somebody reported sighting a ghost ship in the log or something?'

'What? I was miles away. Sorry.' Mary dragged her gaze from the book. Gradually, Sally's earlier question sank in. 'Tea would be lovely. Thanks.'

Sally gave her a long look then disappeared down the ladder. A moment later the sound of clattering came from the little galley on the ground floor. In a daze, Mary took up her station at the window and gazed out across

Hoy Sound. How could she have forgotten? Well, not forgotten exactly – Owen's death was a constant weight on her mind – but she couldn't work out how the third anniversary of his death had crept up on her without her realising. On the first anniversary, she had still been at home, in the Pembrokeshire fishing village where she and Owen had grown up. She had gone to work at the nearby woollen mill as usual, but had been so tearful the kindly woman who oversaw her work had sent her home. Instead of returning to her parents' cottage, she had followed the winding path from the harbour to the cliff top where she and Owen had often used to walk together. In the absence of a grave, she had twisted a little wreath from heather and placed it on the spot where Owen had proposed to her. Last year, she had been at HMS *Mercury*, in the middle of her WRNS visual signalling course. She had marked the day by throwing herself into her studies with fresh determination. Oh, and she had probably been especially nasty to Iris as well. Despite her gloomy thoughts, she couldn't help a wry smile at how the past year had changed her. She would never have thought she could be friends with a spoiled rich girl like Iris yet here they were, she, Sally and Iris, inseparable friends, to the point that Iris had turned down a plum posting to Portsmouth only a few months ago. Although the presence of Rob Sinclair in Scapa Flow must also have been a strong inducement for her to stay.

She shouldn't be surprised the date had passed her by this year, though. As a visual signaller, she lived her life by watches; instead of the weekly pattern she had lived before joining the Wrens, her days were now measured out in an unrelenting rotation of five-hour shifts, with a nine-hour one overnight every third night. As such, Mary found she easily lost track of the day of the week. No wonder the anniversary of Owen's death had crept up on her this year.

The ringing sound of feet on metal heralded Sally's arrival. She deftly held the tea tray with one hand while holding the ladder with the other. Mary half-turned from the window, about to help Sally with the tray, when a ship coming around the headland caught her eye. 'Stand by for a call from Lower Skaill,' she said. 'There's a ship incoming. Looks like one of our minesweepers.' They were easy to recognise, being less than half the length of the other ships in the fleet.

Sure enough, the telephone rang a moment later. Sally put down the tray and answered while Mary picked up the Aldis lamp and sent the challenge.

'It's the *Kelpie*,' Mary said, swiftly reading the Morse signal that the signaller on the minesweeper sent in reply. She heard Sally relay the message and then replace the receiver with a clatter. Now the incoming vessel was known to be friendly, there would be no need to activate the minefield between Graemsay and Hoy.

'Iris will be glad to know Rob's back safe and sound,' Sally said.

Lucky Iris. But the brief flurry of activity had given Mary time to get her dark mood under control, and she held her tongue.

She was about to step away from the window when she saw another signal flash from the ship. 'Wait. There's another signal. Take this down.' Mary felt a twinge of apprehension. Sometimes ships would signal to let them know of medical emergencies. Today of all days, Mary was aware of the dangers faced by the men at sea. Without taking her eyes from the ship, she read out each letter, knowing Sally would be ready with notebook and pencil to write it down. 'C-I-N-E-M-A end word.' Mary used the Aldis lamp to send the signal to show the word was received, then sighted the ship again to read the next word. Again, she read out each letter to Sally. She was so used to communicating in Morse that she usually had no trouble putting together each word without needing to refer to the written notes. Today, however, she was too distracted by thoughts of Owen to do anything other than relay each letter to Sally as it arrived. '2-N-I-G-H-T, end word, M-A-R-Y end word, question mark.'

Sally giggled, then said, 'I think I'll leave that out of the log.'

'What?' Craning her neck, she squinted at the pad Sally held out for her. 'Cinema tonight, Mary?' She cursed under her breath. 'Bloody Joe Pallant. I keep telling him not to do that.'

'What – ask you out?'

'No. Well, that too. But he shouldn't send personal signals.' She sighted the *Kelpie* through the crosshairs of the Aldis lamp and sent: 'Take a hike, JP.' She lowered the lamp with a huff of satisfaction. 'That's told him.'

'He likes you. Why not give him a chance?'

'You know why. Especially today of all days.'

But Sally just shook her head, turning a puzzled expression on her friend.

'I can't believe you've forgotten.' Then Mary bit her lip and drew a steadying breath through her nose. She was going to have to stop taking out her spiky moods on her friends, or they would soon lose all patience with her. 'I'm sorry. That was uncalled for.' She was on the point of explaining what today's date was when the dawning realisation on Sally's face told her Sally understood.

'Oh, goodness, Mary. I'm sorry. You're right – I should have realised. Here. Have some tea.'

While Sally busied herself with the teapot and tea strainer, Mary returned to the window for another visual scan of Hoy Sound. To the east, towards Stromness, the water was thick with boats taking supplies to the ships anchored in Scapa Flow or liberty men ashore. However, apart from the minesweeper *Kelpie*, now steering a course around Graemsay, there were no other ships entering or leaving the huge protected bay that formed the anchorage for the Home Fleet.

Sally nudged her arm. 'Here's your tea.'

Mary took it, some of her good humour returning. 'What is it with you English and your tea?'

'As my mum always says' – Sally's Yorkshire accent became more pronounced – 'there's nowt like a proper brew to set you right.' Sally picked up her own cup. 'And this is real, strong Yorkshire tea, not that pond water that Iris makes.'

They sipped in silence for a while, making occasional sweeps out of the window. However, much as Mary would have welcomed a busy watch, all was quiet. Often on times like this, she and her oppo would take it in turns to launder their shirts, collars and smalls in the tiny galley. The Wrens stationed at Kyeness had got into the habit of lugging bags of clothes up from the Wrennery in Stromness to the signal station, and it was a rare day when the metal screen around the signal room stove wasn't draped with stockings, shirts and the much-reviled 'blackouts' – navy blue knickers that were so large, they could double up as barrage balloons. Today, however, both Mary and Sally were caught up on their laundry, and all there was for them to do was collect the items they had left to dry on their last watch and fold them away.

'What was Owen like? You never really speak of him.'

Mary paused in the act of rolling up a pair of stockings. 'I… you've never asked.'

'I know. It occurred to me that he must have been a huge part of your life, yet I don't know anything about him.'

'He was…' Mary swallowed. Even now, having to use the past tense when speaking of Owen was like a dagger through the heart.

'I'm sorry. If it's too painful, you don't have to—'

'No.' Mary's vehemence surprised even herself. 'I want to talk about him. Your question took me by surprise, that's all.' For three years she had only spoken of Owen in terms of what she had lost. It would be good to simply remember Owen, not his death. 'We grew up together.' She sank into a chair, gazing at the stove and the dancing flames within. She seemed to be able to see fleeting images in the fire of the times she and Owen had spent together, when they had felt as though they lived within a charmed bubble and life would go on that way for ever. 'We did everything together. When we were children, we would go fishing or look for adders up on the cliffs. You know – all the stuff you do as kids. As we grew older, we gradually fell in love. By the time we were fourteen and ready to leave school, we knew we wanted to marry. Everyone said we would grow apart when we left school and had to work for our living, but we didn't. I got a job at the woollen mill, and Owen went to work with his da on his fishing boat, and we knew it might be years before we could afford to marry. We never changed our minds, though, and we always managed to see each other every day, even if it was just for a few minutes.'

After a pause, while Mary relived walking hand in hand along the tree-lined lane to Middle Mill, it occurred to her that she hadn't answered Sally's question. She marshalled her thoughts and started again. 'He was really bright, the kind of person who succeeds at whatever he puts his mind to. He was happy working on his da's boat, but he had big dreams about building up a fleet. He was optimistic, always seeing the best in people.' Mary drifted off in thought, dreaming of a time when she, too, had been optimistic, had dreamed big dreams, had thought her future would always hold sunshine and laughter, not the storm clouds and tears that had been her reality for the past three years.

'Was he handsome?'

Mary shot Sally a glance. She, too, was gazing into the flames as though sharing Mary's visions of golden days. 'I thought so. He didn't have the perfect good looks of a film star, but when he smiled at me, it was as though there was a light shining behind his eyes, and I thought there was no one to compare with him.' It was as though she could see him in front of her right now, smiling that smile at her and calling her his treasure, just as he had done on the day he had asked her to be his wife.

'He sounds lovely. Do you have a photograph?'

The image dissolved, and Mary returned to the present with a painful jolt. 'Neither of us had a camera. I made a few sketches, though.'

'I didn't know you could draw.'

'I don't. Not now, anyway.' She used to enjoy sketching. Her father had bought her a diary every year for her birthday, and although sometimes she would jot notes in it, mostly she had filled the pages with little pencil sketches. Of boats in the harbour; of cottages; of flowers; sometimes Owen had let her sketch him. She had never been happy with the results, feeling that she always failed to catch the glint of humour in his eyes, yet she cherished them now, especially as time had blurred his features in her memory.

She found she was twisting the stockings she still held, and relaxed her grip lest she ruin the precious nylons. Sally was still looking at her, eyebrows raised as though waiting for her to continue. 'Would you like to see them?' she asked, thinking Sally was waiting for her to offer to do so. 'I don't have them here, but they're in our cabin.'

Sally nodded. 'It's funny. I didn't have you down as the artistic type.'

'Oh, I'm not really. It's just something I enjoyed doing.'

'Why did you stop?'

'I… I was always with Owen when I did my sketches. It brings back too many painful memories.'

Sally reached across and squeezed her arm. 'From what you say, you have some wonderful memories of him. You should treasure them.' Her face turned wistful. 'I don't remember my dad, but my mum often used to tell me of the good times they had together, and it helped make him real. Owen sounds like a wonderful man. You should remember that.'

Mary was saved from answering by the phone. By the time they had sighted another incoming ship – a destroyer this time – and exchanged a flurry of signals to identify and then send directions to their anchorage, the conversation had moved on. Mary wasn't sorry. While it had felt good to remember the happy times they had shared, she felt his loss more keenly than ever. Sally was wrong. She would never forget Owen, but it did no good to dwell too much on what she had lost. Maybe for a romantic like Sally, gilded memories made up for the loss. But nothing could make up for the aching void she felt whenever she had picked up her pencil to sketch.

Chapter Two

The remainder of their watch flew by. They had been invited to supper at the Heddles' – a couple in late middle age who lived a short distance around the headland from the signal station. Their home, Curlew Croft, was warm and welcoming, and now the nights were drawing in, they had got into the habit of spending the evenings there on the days when they only had five hours between finishing the afternoon watch and starting the night watch. It saved two forty-minute walks in the dark on the lonely path between the signal station and the Wrennery in Stromness.

'Will Iris be there?' Sally asked as they stumbled along the dark track by the dim light of their shielded torches. 'I can't remember what she's doing.'

'I don't think so. Rob was trying to get a forty-eight-hour pass. She said something about going to the cinema.'

The Garrison theatre had opened in Stromness in the summer, much to the joy of the servicemen and women who were based in Stromness. Until then, there hadn't been much in the way of entertainment in Stromness apart from the NAAFI. Mary hadn't minded, not being in the mood for dances and parties.

Sally stumbled and clutched Mary's arm. When she had recovered she said, 'Weren't you even a little bit tempted to take up Joe Pallant on his offer?'

Mary sighed. 'Just because you were right about Rob being the man for Iris, please don't start playing the matchmaker with me.'

Sally huffed a laugh. 'This is the twentieth century. You can go to the cinema with a man without having to exchange rings. You should go out and have fun once in a while.'

'I haven't noticed you going out with every man to ask you.' And Sally hadn't been short of suitors.

'That's different. There's only one man for me, and he's not here.'

Mary held her tongue. From what she could gather, the young man Sally had set her sights on hardly knew she existed. 'If he's not here, he won't know you've been out with anyone else. And as you say, you're not committing to a life together by agreeing to accompany a bloke to the cinema.' After walking a little way in silence, Mary added, 'Anyway, I don't think I'll ever want to go out with another man. No one can compare with Owen.'

'Ah well, it looks like we'll be spending Christmas knitting more socks for sailors, then, instead of going to parties with handsome sailors.'

'Christmas? It's only mid-October. Please don't tell me you're one of those people who starts getting excited about Christmas the moment the first leaves start to fall from the trees.'

She could only see Sally's dark outline, but she heard her sigh and knew her eyes would have that dreamy expression they always took on when she was lost in thought. 'I love Christmas. When we still lived on the farm, we would make paper chains and decorate the cottage with holly. It was so magical.'

'I suppose you used to hang up your stocking on Christmas Eve and go carol-singing.'

'Yes, didn't you? We didn't get much, of course, but we would always get an orange and some walnuts. Christmas smells of oranges and pine needles, don't you think?'

'It smelled of fish and seaweed, just like every other day.'

'Honestly, Mary, you've got no soul. How did you celebrate Christmas, then?'

'We didn't. Not really. We'd go to chapel, and my mam would make a nicer lunch than usual.' Mary didn't really want to talk about Christmas. It had never been a particularly happy time. The Griffiths had usually breathed a collective sigh of relief when the festivities were over and they could return to their daily routine. Mary did have dim memories of games and laughter when she had been a very young child, but then... well, she didn't want to think of it. Needless to say, most Christmases in her experience had been dark, grim times.

Soon the dim shape of Curlew Croft loomed ahead. They knocked on the door and were welcomed inside by Elspeth Heddle, shielding the golden light of the oil lamp until Sally closed the door behind them to prevent it from escaping into the night sky. They were enveloped by the smell of peat smoke and the savoury scent rising from the stove. Elspeth greeted them with her usual smile, although it seemed to Mary that her eyes didn't twinkle with their usual brilliance, and they were reddened and swollen as though she had been crying.

'Is everything all right, Elspeth?' Mary asked.

Elspeth batted aside the question with a wave of the hand. 'Right as rain. Don't bother yourself. Come in and warm yourselves by the range.'

If Elspeth didn't want to talk about whatever the problem was, Mary wasn't going to press her. She stepped into the kitchen, grateful for its warmth and light after the blustery walk. Once the girls had shed their greatcoats and boots, they sat at the large table in seats close to the range. Iris wasn't there, so Mary guessed Rob had been successful in his application for leave.

Mary's suspicion that all was not well in the Heddle household increased when Archie entered the kitchen. The lines on his weathered face appeared more deeply graven than usual and his broad, bear-like figure seemed somehow shrunken. When he reached Elspeth he paused and clasped her shoulder without saying a word. Elspeth reached up and gripped his hand, the tendons stretching her skin, standing out in white ridges on the back of her hand. Mary wondered if she should try again to ask what was wrong, but she hesitated to intrude on anything the Heddles wished to keep private. Then Archie released his grip and strode to the sink, pouring water from the bucket to wash his hands, and the moment passed. Seemingly recovered from her momentary weakness, Elspeth served hearty portions of fish pie onto each plate, and they passed a pleasant mealtime talking of the latest news from Stromness.

'You'll never guess who I saw when I was visiting the post office this morning,' Elspeth said, scooping the last of her carrots onto her fork. 'Dr Irvine.'

'Stewart Irvine?' Mary stared at Elspeth in disbelief. 'I thought he'd been suspended.'

'Aye, he was. I had no idea he would still be in Stromness. Didn't Iris say he came from Edinburgh? I'd have thought he would have gone back there.'

'I don't know how he would dare show his face around here after making so many mistakes,' Sally said, her eyes narrowed. Mary couldn't blame her for her indignation. Earlier that year she had suffered a blow to the head and been taken to hospital. There she had met an Italian prisoner of war whose appendicitis Stewart had dismissed as malingering. In the summer, he had failed to diagnose a dispatch rider's concussion. This had almost led to disaster when the dispatch rider had then collapsed at Kyeness Signal Station during a storm when she had been required to deliver an urgent message to prevent a British ship sailing into newly dropped mines. After that incident he had been suspended, and another doctor had taken over his practice.

The corners of Elspeth's mouth turned down. 'He was sweet on Iris at one point, wasn't he? I did wonder if he's stayed here in the hope of winning her back.'

'There's no chance of that,' Sally said. 'Nothing could separate her from Rob. They're perfect together.'

Elspeth's expression softened. 'They are at that. It does my heart good to see those two together. Especially after what happened to her father, poor mite.' For Charles Tredwick, Iris's father, had been lost at sea when his ship had hit a mine.

Mary gazed down at her plate, not trusting herself to speak as she was struck afresh by a sense of loss. It therefore took her a moment to notice that Elspeth had pressed her fingers to her quivering mouth, and Archie was gripping his knife and fork so tightly his hands were shaking.

Sally dropped her fork. Her eyes wide with concern, she leaned forward. 'What's happened?'

Elspeth gave another wave of the hand. 'You girls dinnae want to be bothered with our troubles.'

'After all you've done for us? Tell us. If there's anything we can do to help, we will, won't we, Mary?'

'Of course.' Mary's own sorrows faded in her worry for the couple who had shown them such kindness. 'Please tell us.'

'It's our son, Don.' Elspeth pointed at one of the framed photographs on the shelf above their heads, indicating the younger of the two men in the uniform of the Royal Navy. 'We got a telegram this morning.'

Mary's stomach gave a sick twist; with memory of that fateful day three years ago so clear in her mind, she knew all too well how it felt to get an unexpected telegram these days. 'Oh no.' Her voice was barely more than a breath.

Elspeth's face contorted. Sally sprang up and crouched beside Elspeth's chair, wrapping an arm around the older woman's shoulders.

Archie took up the tale. 'His ship was torpedoed. That's all we really know.'

'I'm so sorry,' Sally said.

Elspeth sat up straighter, making a visible effort to compose herself. 'I won't give up hope,' she said. 'According to the telegram, he's missing. He could have been picked up by another ship.'

Mary didn't say anything, although she was forcibly reminded of Iris after her father was reported missing. She had refused to believe her father was dead, despite all the evidence pointing towards the impossibility of his survival.

Sally asked, 'Do you know where he was based?'

'The Mediterranean. He couldn't say in his letters, of course, but last time he came home on leave he told us he had been based in Malta.'

'That's why we're hopeful he survived,' put in Archie. 'The water's not so cold as the Atlantic. Don's a strong swimmer, and there's every chance he could have hung on long enough to have been picked up.'

'He'll be fine, I'm sure of it,' Sally said. 'Mark my words – a letter from him is winging its way to you as we speak.' She stood and started to clear the table. 'But what were you thinking, cooking us a meal when you've been so worried? Leave the clearing up to us.'

–

Much later, when they were trudging back up the track to the signal station, Mary gave voice to the thought that had been forming ever since she had heard the Heddles' news.

'Christmas will be really hard for them this year.'

'You never know. They might hear that Don was rescued.'

Mary couldn't see Sally's face in the dark, but from her tone of voice, she could picture her friend's eyes wide in an expression of infuriating optimism.

'I don't think you should have encouraged them to believe Don could have survived. You know it's unlikely.'

'But not impossible. Anyway, what was I supposed to say – tell them to give up all hope because their son's probably dead?'

Mary winced. 'No, I suppose not. It's just…' She swallowed to ease the sudden ache in her throat. 'They never found Owen's body. I spent weeks… months… hoping against hope that he would turn up alive and well. It dragged out the pain almost beyond endurance, the not knowing. It took the longest time to accept he was gone.' Mary drew a shaky breath. This was the second time that day she had been forced to talk about Owen, and after the memories of happier times she had spoken of earlier that day, it seemed doubly hard to relive his death. 'I'd hate the Heddles to go through the same thing,' she said finally in a low voice.

'Why mention Christmas, though? It'll be hard for them all the time.'

'That's when it hits hardest.' Mary thought of all the strained Christmases with her family over the years. 'Christmas is a time for family. When you've just lost someone, the celebrations feel so empty.'

'Well, it's still over two months away. I'm going to hold on to hope that they hear their son is alive and well before then.'

But Mary couldn't forget the agony of not knowing whether Owen had survived and how it had been months before she could accept he was gone for ever. And that had been for a ship torpedoed in home waters. Surely it would be much harder to discover what had happened to the crew of a ship sunk in the Mediterranean. Elspeth and Archie were in for a long wait, she was sure. 'I wish there was something we could do to help,' she said. 'They've done so much for us. It's only right that we be there for them in return.'

'What else can we do – other than making sure we visit more often?'

Mary's thoughts had returned to Christmas. 'We're going to bring some light into their Christmas. You, me and Iris – we're going to wangle leave for Christmas and spend it with the Heddles. It's a time for bringing light into darkness, isn't it? Well, that's what we're going to do.'

Chapter Three

Mary's thoughts were so full of the Heddles in the days that followed that she completely forgot her promise to show Sally her sketches. She and Sally had told Iris about the idea of taking Christmas to the Heddles, and Iris had been enthusiastic in her approval. Getting leave had proved easier than anticipated, and they had been granted three days, starting on Christmas Eve. To avoid placing a financial burden on the Heddles, they had agreed to pool two shillings a week into a Christmas kitty, dedicated to funding the celebrations. Of course, they would need to use the Heddles' food coupons, but apart from that, they were determined to shoulder the whole responsibility for the day. Spending so much time discussing Christmas had pushed all thought of her sketches from Mary's mind.

It was only a week later, when they were in the Wren-nery common room, that Sally reminded her. Mary, Iris and Sally had a rare day off together. The arrival of more visual signaller Wrens over the year had taken the pressure off the duty schedule, allowing for more time off than they had had at the start. At first, they'd only had the day after a night watch off. On paper, it looked like that should have provided them with plenty of leisure time, having every third day free. However, in practice it had never worked out that way. Coming off night watch at eight in the morning, they would have the long walk back from the cliff-top signal station, over the hill to the Wrennery on the outskirts of Stromness. If they were quick, they could get there while breakfast was still being served. Full up with porridge and, if they were lucky, bacon and eggs, they would retreat to their freezing cabin at the top of the house and snatch a couple of hours' sleep. Then at midday they would get up and tidy the cabin before descending to the mess for dinner. This only gave them the afternoon to run any errands they might have in Stromness. Therefore the arrival of more Wrens had been most welcome, giving them the occasional extra day off. Of course, if anyone was off sick or on leave, they had to forego their time off to cover. Very occasionally, the three friends would get their extra day off on the same day.

That day, however, no one was on leave, and no Wrens were in sick bay, so Mary, Iris and Sally got their once-in-a-blue-moon day off together. They had planned to hitch a lift to see the Ring of Brodgar, a huge stone circle they had heard about but not yet had the opportunity to visit. Sadly, the weather wasn't cooperating. Rain poured down from clouds so low and heavy, they seemed to skim the rooftops. The wind rattled the windows, lashing the rain so hard against the panes, it sounded as though huge waves were breaking upon them. Having no desire for a soaking, the girls retired to the common room. Mary and Sally took up their knitting and Iris was sewing the hem of a tweed skirt she was making. Mary couldn't avoid casting the skirt covetous glances as they worked. The fabric was a black and white dogtooth check, cut in the new Utility style. It was narrow and shorter than pre-war skirts, designed to skim the hips and flare softly to the knee. All Mary's skirts, apart from her uniform, were threadbare and much mended. While she cast stitches onto her knitting needles, she imagined how it would feel to own just one skirt as beautiful yet practical as Iris's.

'How are the Heddles, Iris?' Sally asked as she wound grey yarn around a knitting needle. Iris had walked out to Curlew Croft the previous afternoon. 'Have they had any more news?'

Iris paused in the act of threading her needle, a furrow forming between her brows. 'No. They're putting a brave face on it, but I know they must be eaten up with worry.'

Her voice quavered. With a pang, Mary knew she must be thinking of her father.

'I wish I could think of an extra-special Christmas present for them,' Mary said. 'They've given us so much over the year, I'd like to get them something in return.'

'Don't talk to me about Christmas presents,' Iris said. 'My mother still won't budge over my allowance, so I'm stuck with what I can manage from my pay.' Her wrinkled nose showed exactly what she thought of the ten shillings that they collected every Friday.

'I know,' Mary said with a wry smile, 'I've had to really cut back on the caviar and champagne since I joined up.'

Iris gave her a haughty look that must have been honed over generations. 'As I've told you before, I can't stand caviar.' Then she flashed Mary a wicked smile. 'Although I wouldn't say no to champagne if you could get any on the island. Don't worry – I don't regret choosing Rob over money. He's worth more than a thousand bottles of champagne. It does make it harder to buy nice presents for people, though.'

'You could make something,' Sally said. 'Elspeth was thrilled with that coat.'

'But I made it on her sewing machine. I want her Christmas present to be a surprise.' She placed several deft stitches, looking thoughtful. 'I have got some colourful embroidery silks. I could always make her a pretty picture and get it framed. It would have to be a small one, given the time available, but it would look nice in their kitchen. Something bright and cheerful, like a sunflower. And I could embroider some handkerchiefs for Archie.'

'Good idea,' Sally said. 'I thought of making some lavender bags for Elspeth and a case for Archie's reading glasses. What about you, Mary?'

Mary had been listening to her friends' ideas in growing dismay. 'I don't know. I was never any good at sewing. I don't know how to make anything pretty.'

There was a pause filled with no sound but the click of knitting needles and the rain upon the windows. It was at times like these that Mary wished she had acquired more feminine accomplishments. Oh, she could sew and knit, but her skills were purely practical. She couldn't compete with the elegant cut and line of Iris's creations, and she had never learned to embroider. While she could gut a fish in a few seconds, that wasn't a skill she could use to make Christmas presents. Unless the Heddles included their cat in the celebrations.

'Wait a minute, Mary,' Sally said, putting down her knitting. 'You can draw.'

'You can?' Iris, too, dropped her work into her lap and regarded Mary with arched eyebrows. 'I never knew that.'

'You said you'd show me your sketches. I'd love to see them,' Sally went on. 'You could do drawings for them both.'

'I told you – I don't draw any more.'

'Oh, but I thought…'

'What – that just because I told you about Owen, I would magically rediscover my desire to draw again?'

Mary knew she was being needlessly harsh, but she couldn't stop herself. 'Life isn't a fairy tale, despite what you might think.'

Sally bowed her head, biting her lip. 'I know,' she said.

Mary could have kicked herself. Too late did she remember that Sally's life had hardly been a fairy tale, either, with her father dying when she was a baby and her uncle being seriously injured in an accident, meaning Sally's family had lost the farm where she had grown up. 'I'm sorry. Look, I don't mind showing you my sketches, and I'll think of something suitable for Elspeth and Archie.'

She didn't wait for a reply but left the common room and climbed up to her cabin. She rummaged through her drawer until her fingers closed over the hardback diary that was tucked right at the back. Once it was in her hands, she tenderly brushed her fingers over the cover, starting to regret her promise to show Sally her drawings. When she had mentioned them before, she had thought Sally wouldn't be interested. Now, having lashed out at Sally like a wounded cat, she wanted to make up for it. If only there was another way. This book of sketches felt like her last link to Owen, and was something she had shared with him alone. Once Sally and Iris had seen it, what would she have left? There was no going back, though, so she tucked it under her arm and headed back to the common room on dragging feet.

Sally and Iris had their heads together and were speaking in low voices when Mary pushed open the door. The way they stopped and moved apart told her they had been talking about her. Not that she really minded; Sally was probably filling Iris in on all she had said about Owen, so it saved her having to tell Iris herself.

She opened the book and leafed through the pages. Each one had once been a blank page with the date at the top, although now most pages contained at least one pencil sketch made on that day. She turned it to a random page – the sixteenth of May 1938 – and held it out to Sally, who took it eagerly. She and Iris bent their heads over the diary.

'This is wonderful,' Sally said. 'Is it your village?'

Mary craned her neck and saw they were looking at a sketch of Solva, drawn from the cliffs and looking back up the narrow inlet towards the harbour and the huddle of cottages that formed the lower village. 'Yes, I made several sketches from the same place. I could never get the light right on the water.'

'I think it's wonderful.' Sally traced one of the fishing boat masts with her forefinger. 'Look at the way the pennants are streaming in the breeze and the waves are breaking over those rocks. I can almost hear the gulls and the rigging clanking against the masts.'

Iris nodded. 'It looks a bit like a Cornish fishing village we stayed in one summer. It's a lovely sketch. You've got talent.'

Thankfully, neither of them suggested that she take up drawing again, so Mary relaxed a little as her friends leafed through the other pages. Most of her drawings were of the scenery, buildings or boats. However, she had attempted a few portraits, and soon Sally's hand paused. 'Is this Owen?'

Mary swallowed when she saw the well-loved face upon the page, his mouth curving in the half-smile that had always set her heart aflutter and the familiar lines of nose, brow and jaw that she had concentrated so hard on to get right. Unable to speak, she nodded.

'Judging from the way he's looking at you, he loved you very much,' Sally said, her voice gentle.

The room blurred as tears welled in her eyes. All she could do was mutter a husky, 'He did.'

After that, she found it easier to talk them through the other pictures that caught their attention and she found herself talking about her home, describing how, when the tide went out, it receded from the inlet, leaving the boats stranded upon the mud until the waters rose again. She told them about the woollen mill where she had worked, of the swift-flowing river that had once powered the huge waterwheel in one of her drawings, and of St Davids – the city a few miles along the coast that was barely bigger than her village, except for the cathedral, which had been built in a hollow so that it couldn't be seen until you were almost on top of it.

She was starting to enjoy herself, lost in happy memories, when Sally leafed towards the end of the diary, and paused at a page in the December section. 'Oh, this looks like you, only much younger. Have you got a younger sister? You never said.'

Mary felt her insides turn to ice. She hadn't meant to let them see that one, only she'd been too lost in memories to stop them turning to that page. 'No, I don't have a younger sister.'

She made a move to grab the book but before she could reach it, Iris had leaned across and studied the picture with narrowed eyes. 'That *is* you,' she said. 'There's no mistaking those dimples.' Iris tapped the date at the top of the page. 'The tenth of December.' She raised her brows. 'Did you spend the day thinking of Christmas and regretting your lost childhood, or something?'

'Something like that,' Mary replied.

'I suppose you drew it from a photograph. It's very good.' Iris looked from the drawing to Mary, her head tilted to one side as she compared the two. 'Although maybe you didn't get the shape of the eyes quite right. How old were you in the picture?'

'Around eight, I suppose. I was eighteen when I drew it.' Mary sighed. 'Owen had left to join the navy the week before, and I wasn't in the mood to celebrate—' She caught herself. The day had been her birthday, and she'd been on the point of saying she wasn't in the mood to celebrate the day. But she hadn't told them when her birthday was, not wanting her friends to make a fuss. She never celebrated her birthday. 'I was feeling low, and I wanted to remember happier times,' she finished, hoping the others wouldn't pick up on her blunder.

Thankfully, the conversation moved on, to discussing what had made Owen join up – the only argument she had ever had with him, but he had been sure war was coming, and had wanted to join up on his own terms. While those weren't particularly happy memories either, she much preferred talking about that than the picture showing all she had lost at such a young age.

Chapter Four

Joe climbed out of the tender, taking satisfaction in stamping his feet upon solid ground. It was good to be on land for a while instead of a deck that constantly tilted under one's feet. Although many members of HMS *Kelpie*'s crew chose to spend their rest days on board rather than face nearly an hour each way in a small liberty boat over choppy water, Joe liked to go ashore whenever he could.

Seeing his friend Rob Sinclair walking ahead, away from the pier, Joe hailed him. 'Fancy meeting for a bite to eat later?' he asked when Rob stopped and looked back.

'Sorry, I promised to help out at the Heddles' croft this morning.'

'The Heddles? How are they?' Joe had visited Archie and Elspeth Heddle several times while he had been based at Kyeness and had grown very fond of them.

'They're well.' Rob hesitated. 'I would ask you to join me, but they've had some bad news recently – one of their sons is missing. They might not welcome too many visitors at the moment. I'm meeting Iris there at the end of her watch, so they'll probably have enough to cope with.'

'I'm sorry to hear that. Send them my regards.'

With that the two parted, and Joe directed his steps to the post office, as he wanted to send some money to his parents. Thinking of Iris and Rob going to see the Heddles, he couldn't help wondering if Mary would be there, too. He'd been attracted to her ever since he'd shown her, Iris and Sally around the signal station the previous December. Mary's striking dark looks had reminded him of Hedy Lamarr, his favourite actress. No sooner had the thought crossed his mind than he caught sight of a petite Wren, unruly dark hair escaping from beneath her cap. His heart skipped, and he broke into a jog to catch her up.

'Mary, fancy seeing you here.'

Mary turned, her pretty face guarded. 'Hello, Joe. Not pestering the Wrens up at Kyeness with unnecessary signals today, then?'

'That's a treat I reserve for you.' He stopped. 'Not pestering, I mean. I hope you don't regard me as a pest?'

He could swear her lips twitched as though holding back a smile. 'Maybe not a pest.' Her accent had a pleasant musical lilt. 'But you have to admit, they're usually unnecessary.'

'When was sending messages to a beautiful woman ever unnecessary?'

'When they could get her into trouble for breaking protocol.'

'Ah, but it would be worth it.' He fell into step beside her. 'Where are you going?'

'The post office.'

'Me too! You see, we're fated to be together.'

'You sound like Sally.'

'Why, does she think we're fated to be together too?'

'Of course not. Why would she say that? We hardly know each other.'

'So you think we should get to know each other better? I quite agree. Let me see, here are some facts you don't know about me. I'm an only child, my favourite author is John Buchan and I like cricket. Now it's your turn. Or if you don't have time now, how about I take you out for dinner later?'

Mary paused outside the post office. 'Do you ever give up?'

'Not when I've found something I want. We belong together like… well, Mary and Joseph. Why would I give up on a treasure like you?'

Until that moment, Mary had seemed in good humour; Joe could swear she had been enjoying the banter. But when he called her a treasure, she bit her lip and turned away. Her next words sounded strangled. 'I can't go to dinner with you. I'm on watch later.' She pulled open the door and marched up to the counter.

Of course, he should have known Mary wouldn't want to go out with him. Why would she want to be with a boring signalman who had been a trainee accountant before the war? There were plenty of men more exciting than him.

He paused for a moment outside the door. His natural instinct was to give up. The heroes in the films never gave up so easily, though, and he really did want to get to know Mary. Anyway, he had to send the postal order to his parents. Straightening his shoulders, he marched inside. The trouble was, there was only one assistant at the counter, who was already busy with Mary. He couldn't help noticing she was also sending a postal order. When she finished, she marched straight out of the post office with only a brief glance and curt nod at Joe. Once he had finished his business, he left, doubting Mary would still be in sight.

In that, however, he was wrong. A little way down the street he could see her outside the bakery, counting coins in her purse. He broke into a jog and drew level just as she tucked her purse into her pocket and started to walk away, looking resigned. A mouth-watering aroma of cinnamon and freshly baked pastries emanated from the shop.

'Let me guess,' he said, 'you were longing for a bun even more than you were longing for my company, only you've discovered you didn't bring enough money with you.'

'It's too early to eat.' Mary's stomach betrayed her with a gurgle that could be heard even above the screaming gulls.

'That's the trouble with the odd hours we work, isn't it?' Joe said. 'We never get to eat at mealtimes, so we're always hungry. Allow me. I'm rather hungry myself, and there's something so dispiriting about eating alone.'

Mary shook her head. 'Thank you, but I'm really not hungry.'

'Then do me a favour, and join me, because I would rather not eat alone.' He drew a deep breath, and now his own stomach rumbled when he caught the tempting aroma of sausage rolls. When Mary still didn't reply, he said, 'I'm going to buy two sausage rolls and two cinnamon buns. I'll leave it to your conscience to decide whether you'll join me or force me to look like a pig by eating it all myself.'

Without waiting for a reply, he marched inside and made his purchases, then emerged feeling the sausage rolls warming his hands through the brown paper package. He'd half expected Mary to have made her escape, but she was still hovering outside, looking as though she wasn't sure why she was still there.

Juggling the packages into one hand, he offered her his free arm. 'Let's go and sit down by the water.'

Mary looked as though she was battling through some kind of internal struggle. Finally she gave a grudging nod and took his arm. 'But you must let me buy you something another time.'

'Really, there's no need. This is a gift.' The Wrens, he knew, were paid less than the men, even though they did the same work. He couldn't help feeling gratified that Mary implied there would be another time, however.

'I insist. I won't eat with you now unless you allow me to buy you something in return. I owe you.'

Mary let go of his arm and half-turned. Seeing that she really did intend to leave unless he agreed, Joe said, 'Fine. In that case, I look forward to next time.'

They found a perch on a step with a good view of the harbour and unwrapped their sausage rolls. Joe shot sideways glances at Mary as she tucked into hers. She cupped a hand under her chin to catch the flakes of pastry and closed her eyes after taking the first bite and gave a smile that made her eyes curve into crescents. She looked for all the world like a contented cat. 'Delicious. Thank you, Joe.' Then she looked at him, her eyes widening in surprise. 'Aren't you eating yours?'

He was so enthralled watching her eat that he'd forgotten his. He hastily took a bite, and they munched in silence until they were left with just empty wrappings and a few crumbs.

Mary folded the paper and brushed the crumbs from her skirt. 'That was almost as good as one of my mam's oggies.'

'Oggies?'

'A kind of pasty.'

'From Wales?'

Mary nodded and unwrapped her bun. She drew a deep breath, and Joe was sure she was savouring the wonderful scents of cinnamon and yeast that made his own mouth water. 'I suppose I'd better eat this before the gulls get to it.' Her tone of voice managed to convey the message that she wouldn't usually dream of eating such a thing, but it would be a tragic waste to leave good food to the gulls. After a while she said, 'Where are you from, anyway?'

'Ipswich.'

'I've never been there. What's it like?'

Joe took a bite from his bun and thought about it while he chewed. 'I like it,' he said finally. 'I don't suppose it's any different from any other English town, but it's not far from the sea, which I love. I can't imagine living a long way from the sea.'

'Me neither,' Mary said once she'd swallowed the last bite of her bun. Joe was amused to see that despite her outward reluctance to eat it, she had devoured it with a speed that would put many a hungry rating to shame. 'I feel sorry for people who live miles from the coast. How far is Ipswich from the sea, then?'

She seemed to be more at ease now. It struck Joe with a pang that they were getting on better now he wasn't trying to flirt with her. Final confirmation, if he needed it, that she wasn't interested in him in a romantic way. Too bad, because ever since he had taken her around Kyeness Signal Station on her first day on the island, he had been drawn to her, despite her abrupt ways and determinedly stern expression. Maybe it was because just occasionally he could see another girl looking out from behind her eyes. A girl with a quirky sense of humour and sense of fun who seemed to be caged within. He wished he could see the girl he was sure Mary truly was.

'Let me see,' he said, hurriedly gathering his wits when he realised Mary was still waiting for his answer. 'Well, the River Orwell opens out into an estuary just a couple of miles from the town centre, and it feels like being by the sea if you go somewhere like Nacton Shore. I can't tell you how beautiful it is, to watch the sailing boats going up and down the estuary on a sunny day. But for proper seaside, there's Felixstowe, about twelve miles away. When I started my job, I used to get a half day on Saturdays, and when the weather was fair, I would cycle out to Felixstowe and spend the afternoon at the beach.' As soon as he said it, he could have kicked himself. Pretty girls like Mary went for men with cars or a motorcycle at least. *Great work, Joe. Telling her your idea of excitement is cycling to the beach isn't going to get her heart racing.*

'That must have been nice.' At least she was being kind. 'What sort of work did you do?'

'I was training to be an accountant.' There. Now she would make some comment about how boring he must be and make an excuse.

Instead, she simply asked, 'Did you enjoy it?'

'It was all right, I suppose.'

She shifted her position so she was looking at him face on. 'I'm bowled over by your enthusiasm.'

He couldn't help laughing. 'I mean it. It was a good job. I was lucky to get it, when there were so many out of work.' While it hadn't been his first choice of career, he knew his parents had been right. It was better to have a job that gave you security than go chasing after dreams that could leave you penniless.

Mary glanced at her watch. 'I'd better go. I've got some more errands to run, and I'm on watch later.'

'I've got forty-eight hours leave coming up next week. Fancy coming to the Garrison theatre with me? They're showing *Valley of the Sun*.'

Mary hesitated. 'Well...'

She was looking for an excuse, Joe knew it, and he didn't want to give her the chance. He had enjoyed these few minutes just chatting, and he didn't want to lose her as a friend, even if she never saw him as anything more. 'Not a date,' he said hastily. 'But I thought you might like the chance to pay me back for the snacks.' He pointed to the empty bags. 'Bring Sally and Iris, too. The more the merrier.'

'I suppose it couldn't hurt. I'd have to ask them, but we could make next Wednesday.'

'Wonderful. I'll meet you outside the theatre at 1800.'

When he returned to his wanders around Stromness, it was with an extra spring in his step. Where he had been going wrong, he now realised, was coming on too strong. If it was friendship she wanted, then he would prove to her he could be the perfect friend.

–

A few days later, as she watched the sun disappear behind the horizon while on afternoon watch, Mary still couldn't work out how she had ended up sharing pastries with Joe and enjoying the experience. Until then, Joe had struck her as something of a nuisance, attempting to intrude into her life when she had no intention of letting anyone steal Owen's place in her heart. Yet just when Joe had seemed to get the message, she had discovered new depths to his character. Sitting side by side, getting pastry flakes down their fronts, she had been able to see past his annoying attempts to persuade her on a date and been surprised to find they had things in common, such as a love for the sea and an enjoyment of the simple pleasure of sitting beside the water and watching the world go by.

The telephone rang, jolting Mary from her musings. Her oppo was down in the galley making tea, so she sprang to answer it. 'WSS,' she said. She relaxed when it turned out to be a request to identify a vessel that had just crossed the indicator loop. Looking out of the window, she soon saw the ship in question. Her heart gave a little skip – from its compact size she could tell it was one of the minesweepers, and she thought she recognised Joe's ship, the *Kelpie*. Not being totally certain, however, she picked up the Aldis lamp, sighted the ship in its crosshairs, and sent the challenge.

Confirmation soon came back in the smooth, easy-to-follow Morse that she had come to associate with Joe. Sure enough, she hadn't long relayed the information back to the officer on the other end of the line and replaced the receiver when more flashes came from the *Kelpie*: 'Mary?'

She knew she shouldn't encourage him by replying to personal messages, but somehow she hated to think of Joe gazing up from the signal deck, waiting for a reply that would never come. She couldn't forget it was cold, wet and windy out there, whereas at least she was in the shelter of the signal station, with heat billowing from the little stove. 'Yes,' she sent.

'Looking 4ward 2 Wed.' He sent the signal with only a brief pause between words, not giving her a chance to ask him to repeat the ones she hadn't understood. What on earth did '4ward' mean? Had she missed a gap between letters? The Morse for 'four' was four dots and a dash. Separating it with a space into two separate letters, it could be HT or SA, although neither of those made sense either. Then it dawned on her: forward. The message had been: 'Looking forward to Wednesday.'

After a moment's thought, she sent: 'Me 2.'

She couldn't help it; she grabbed the telescope and swung it round on its stand and peered through. There was *Kelpie*, gilded by the setting sun, ploughing through the choppy water. She could see tiny figures on the deck and she swung the telescope to the left slightly until she could see the signal deck, just behind the bridge. There was a dark figure manning the signal lamp. Another series of flashes pulsed out as she watched. 'Sausage roll and parkin 4 me.'

She laughed and sent back: 'U will get what ur given.'

She felt a pang of disappointment to see the *Kelpie* sail out of sight before Joe had a chance to respond. As she updated the log, leaving out the personal messages, she was aware of a sense of warmth like being wrapped in a cosy blanket. She couldn't deny Joe brought some much-missed fun into her life. Perhaps she should discourage him, but there was no harm in him, and he was doing a dangerous job, out on a minesweeper. If by being his friend she could bring a little cheer into his life, then she couldn't see a problem with that. And since he seemed to have got the message that she was only interested in friendship, then she would enjoy spending more time with him. Yes, she was actually looking forward to the trip to the Garrison theatre on Wednesday.

Chapter Five

Mary found herself taking extra care over her appearance as she got ready for their evening out. She couldn't help casting covetous glances at the cherry-red lipstick Iris was applying. Noticing, Iris held it out to her. 'You're welcome to borrow it.'

After a brief hesitation, Mary took it. She had always turned down Iris's offers of make-up before although she had secretly longed to emulate Iris's stylish look. She wasn't quite sure why she took it now, although it might have been associated with the decision she'd made at the signal station to make more of an effort to return Joe's friendship. Even though this wasn't a date, and they were going in a group, she found that she wanted to look her best.

All three girls were free to go to the Garrison theatre that evening, although Sally was on night watch, so would have to dash off as soon as the show was over. The theatre had only opened in the summer, to the joy of the servicemen and women in Stromness, who had discovered that as Orkney counted as an overseas posting, they got to see films before they went on general release. Therefore the new theatre was hugely popular with the men and women serving in the forces, and it was usually packed. It felt appropriate somehow to honour the occasion by putting on make-up, and she frowned at her reflection as she applied the colour to her lips, taking care not to smudge it.

Iris eyed her with her head tilted once Mary had applied the lipstick. 'It suits you. With your colouring, you could get away with far brighter colours than me, like a pillar-box red.'

Mary looked in the mirror and decided the deep cherry-red was quite colourful enough for a first outing in make-up. She didn't take it off, though. She turned her face this way and that, enjoying the way the shade contrasted with her pale face.

'Pity Rob can't make it tonight,' Iris said as they left the Wrennery and headed through the town. The Garrison theatre was on North End Road, right on the other side of town, and it was a long walk in the dark. They walked arm in arm as much to support each other when they tripped as for a show of friendship. Iris's face, which had momentarily clouded on mention of Rob's absence, now creased in a wicked grin. 'Still, Sally and I will sit together, and we promise not to interrupt your tête-à-tête with Joe.'

'How many times do I have to tell you? It isn't a date. We're just friends. If it was a date, why would he have invited you two along?'

'Probably because he knew you would turn him down if he asked you on a date. It's all part of his master plan to get you into his clutches.'

'I don't know.' Mary thought back to the simple camaraderie of sitting side by side with him, eating pastries. 'I don't think he's got a master plan. He seemed genuine when he said it would be just as friends. He's a lot shyer than you'd think.' Then she paused. 'No, not shy exactly, but I don't think he's as confident as he'd have us believe. I think half his cheeky banter is just a front.'

'Sounds like you've improved your opinion of him. What do you think, Sally?' Iris asked. 'Are they destined to be together?'

'I haven't seen them together enough to know.'

Mary snorted. 'I think we can safely take that as a no, then. You were telling Iris she and Rob belonged together after the first time they met.'

'Yes, but that was because she fell into his arms. It was a sign.'

'Coincidence,' said Mary. 'And maybe they wouldn't have got together at all if you hadn't planted the idea in Iris's mind.'

'That's not true,' Iris said, her voice ringing with indignation. 'I'm in love with Rob because of who he is, not because I was persuaded into it.'

'I know. I take it back.'

'Anyway, they wouldn't have been fated to be together if they hadn't been right for each other.'

Mary couldn't argue with Sally's logic, however skewed it might be. 'Just as long as you don't start seeing signs whenever I'm with Joe, I can accept that.'

Sally, who was walking in the middle, stopped, forcing her friends to stand still as well. She pointed up at the sky. The clouds had cleared, and the darkness of the blackout made the stars shine with a piercing brilliance. 'How can you look up into that sky every night and not feel the magic?' Sally asked, her voice hushed, reverential.

'They're beautiful,' Mary agreed, 'but I don't see how balls of gas in the far distance can affect my life.'

'You know what?' Sally said, 'If I could have one wish right now, it would be for you to experience the wonder and magic of Christmas this year. You've got plans to help

Elspeth and Archie through this Christmas, but I want you to have a wonderful Christmas too.'

Mary swallowed, feeling a rush of gratitude for Sally's friendship. She knew Sally had been affected by her tale of loss, and she squeezed Sally's arm, not trusting herself to speak for a moment, but wanting her to know how much she appreciated the sentiment. Maybe she didn't believe in magic or wishes, or any of the superstitions Sally tangled herself in, but she could make an effort for her friends' sake to be happy this Christmas. Owen had been gone for over three years now. Perhaps it was time she stopped clinging to his memory and freed herself to new possibilities.

–

Joe was waiting for them outside the theatre, his naval uniform standing out among the mostly khaki uniforms of the people making their way inside. As they walked in, Mary fumbled in her bag and handed a package to Joe. 'You said you wanted parkin,' she said. 'I still owe you a sausage roll, though.'

'Thank you, but you really don't have to, you know.'

'I owe you.' Mary hated owing anybody anything, and she wasn't going to start with Joe.

She enjoyed the film more than she'd expected. It was a rousing Western made more entertaining by Joe whispering alternative dialogue into her ear. This made Mary laugh, especially in places that weren't supposed to be funny. On her other side, Sally dabbed at tears when James Craig swept Lucille Ball into a passionate kiss. Mary, too, wiped away tears but these were of laughter. It was a good thing Joe had agreed to stop his pursuit of her, for she was finding out how much fun he was to be with, now she could relax around him. She didn't think she had laughed this much since… well, since Owen had died.

When the film finished, they filed out, and it felt natural to take Joe's arm to prevent being separated in the crowd. Joe didn't make anything of it, which reassured her that he had meant what he said about just going out as friends. With his track record, she was sure he would have made a flirtatious remark or tried to take her hand if he had still been romantically inclined. Anyway, a squally drizzle had started up since the start of the film, and it felt comforting to lean against his side and take shelter from the wind.

Once they were clear of the press of people emerging from the theatre, Sally glanced at her watch. 'Goodness, it's later than I thought. I must dash or Shirley will wonder where I've got to.' Shirley was the Wren standing the night watch with Sally.

Mary turned to Joe. 'Iris and I have to go back, too. We didn't get late passes.' She regretted not doing so now. She had thought she would need an excuse to get away from Joe, not imagining that she would enjoy the evening so much she would want to extend it.

If Joe was disappointed, he didn't show it. 'I'll walk you to the Wrennery.'

'Oh, there's no need, really.' However, her heart wasn't in the protest, and she didn't object when he insisted.

Accordingly they all marched towards the town centre, setting a brisk pace, chatting about the film. When the road narrowed, it seemed natural to split into two groups, with Iris and Sally walking slightly ahead, and Mary and Joe in the rear.

Mary, remembering Joe had a forty-eight hour pass, said, 'What are you doing tomorrow?'

'Is that an offer to meet me?'

'Well…' Mary groped for an excuse out of force of habit before giving up and admitting she looked forward to seeing him again. 'I still owe you that sausage roll.'

'True. I can't let you get away with that. When are you free?'

'I'm on watch until 1300, so I could… oh, bother.'

'What?'

'I promised to go to Curlew Croft for lunch.' How could she have forgotten?

'Well, if you promised.'

Mary couldn't see his face in the dark, but from the tone of his voice, she knew his expression would be downcast. 'That's not an excuse,' she hastened to assure him. 'If it was any other time, I'd let Elspeth and Archie know I can't make it; they would understand. But they've recently had bad news, and I want to support them.'

'I understand. Really, I do. Rob told me about their son, and I was very sorry to hear it.'

Mary had forgotten Joe had known the Heddles longer than she had. Acting on an impulse she couldn't explain, she said, 'Why don't you come? I'm sure they'd like to see you.'

By this time they had drawn level with the piers, which, even at this hour, were thronging with people – mostly ratings catching the tenders back to their ships, Mary supposed.

'If you're sure,' Joe said. 'I'd like to see them again.'

'Of course. I—'

At that moment a tall figure dashed out of one of the passages linking Ferry Road with Victoria Street and bowled into Mary, knocking the breath from her lungs.

'Terribly sorry. Please excuse me.'

The voice sounded familiar, but before she could place who it was, the man sped away down the road.

'Bloody cheek,' Joe said, making a move as though to go after the man.

Mary caught his arm. 'Don't bother. It was an accident.'

'Are you all right, Mary?' Iris had seen the incident and turned back with Sally.

'I'm fine. But do you know, that sounded a lot like Stewart Irvine.'

'Stewart? He's still here?'

Mindful of the passing time, Mary started walking again as she answered. 'I forgot you weren't at the Heddles' when they mentioned him. Apparently he's still in Stromness.'

Here Joe put in, 'Stewart Irvine — isn't that the doctor who lost his job in the summer? Rob mentioned something or other about him.'

'That's the one,' Mary said. 'We all thought he'd gone home to Edinburgh. I can't imagine why he'd want to stay here, where everyone knows he's completely incompetent.'

'Elspeth wondered if he had deeper feelings for Iris than we thought,' Sally said. 'He might have stayed to try and win her back.'

Mary snorted. 'In that case, why hasn't he approached Iris? He can hardly win her back by ignoring her.'

'Anyway,' Iris said, 'he could ply me with all the diamonds and silk stockings in the world and I would still think him a useless waste of time. I'll never forget how little help he was when Sally was hurt.'

They spent the rest of the walk abusing Stewart Irvine and speculating on what could have induced him to stay in a place he'd frequently said he hated, where nobody respected him. Sally agreed with Elspeth's idea that he was in love with Iris and couldn't bear to leave. In her opinion, he was only waiting to pluck up the courage to approach her again. Mary shared Iris's opinion, which was that he must be trying to get his job back. While he was exempt from military service on medical grounds, she was unsure if losing his job meant he would have to do another kind of war work. If he was, she was sure he would try to get out of it.

'Let's face it,' she said in conclusion, 'he never gave any sign of wanting to help his country, so I don't believe he'll want to start now.'

'That's true,' Iris said. 'I was always a bit shocked by his cavalier attitude towards his fuel allowance. He never seemed to have a problem keeping it for personal use when everyone else had to take a bus, walk or hitch a ride from army transports when they wanted to get out of Stromness. Maybe he thinks it will be easier to avoid war work if he stays here and keeps a low profile?'

'I don't see how. It's difficult to hide in Orkney. Everyone knows everyone else's business.'

By this time they had reached the Wrennery, putting an end to their speculation. Sally hurried inside to get changed into her warm bellbottoms and seaman's jersey before finding her oppo and leaving for night watch. Iris mumbled something about being tired and followed Sally, leaving Mary alone with Joe.

Joe shifted from foot to foot. 'Thanks for coming out. It's been a lovely evening.'

'You're welcome. I enjoyed it too.' Unaccountably, Mary felt like a child after being invited to tea at a friend's house, dutifully thanking the friend's mother for having her. She would have words later with Iris for leaving her alone with Joe. It had been so obvious she wasn't really tired but was making an excuse to leave them alone. She might just as well have done with it and said something like, 'I'll leave you two lovebirds alone.' Ridiculous. She'd made it plain to Iris and Sally that they were just going out as friends.

'Did you mean it about going with you to see the Heddles tomorrow?' Joe asked.

'Yes, of course.' And she found she wasn't saying it to be polite; she actually looked forward to seeing him again. 'I'm sure they'll be pleased to see you.'

'I'll meet you outside the signal station at 1300, then,' Joe said.

'Fine.'

There was an awkward pause in which Mary both wanted to escape inside and wished she could extend these last moments with Joe.

'Well, I mustn't make you late,' Joe said in the end and started to walk back into Stromness to the lodgings he had secured for the night.

Mary watched his dark shape as he strode away. She hesitated then called after him, 'I really did enjoy the evening.'

Chapter Six

Mary felt a flutter of pleasure when she saw Joe waiting for her outside the signal station when she left after the morning watch the next day. Although it was a cold, blustery day, typical of Orkney in early November, Joe had waited for her, his collar turned up against the wind, instead of going on to the Heddles' and the warmth of their peat fire.

'It was kind of you to wait,' she said, tucking her hand into the crook of his elbow. 'You must be frozen.'

'I spend my days up on the signal deck, remember,' Joe replied. 'This is like a summer holiday compared to that.'

They set off, their feet crunching on the loose stones along the track. Far below them, the waves pounded against the cliffs, occasionally sending flecks of spindrift to settle upon the grass like cuckoo spit. The heavy clouds sagged low in the sky, threatening a downpour.

Joe peered over the cliffs with a grimace. 'I can't believe Rob and Archie were stuck down there the night they spotted someone signalling that enemy plane.'

'I know. It's a miracle they weren't drowned.' They had taken Archie's boat out to check his creels, and had spotted someone signalling to the plane, showing where to send mines into the sea. They had been stranded by a storm at the foot of the cliffs and unable to go for help. In the end, Rob had climbed the cliffs to send a signal to the signal station. Iris had been forced to make a hair-raising ride by motorcycle through the storm to raise the alarm. 'I wish they'd caught the man sending the signal, though. I'd have liked to know who it was.'

'I think he must have drowned. We haven't had nearly as many mines to deal with since that night.'

'I would have liked the satisfaction of knowing who it was, though. Sometimes I think…' She hesitated, then dared to put into words the suspicion she had harboured after that dramatic night. 'You're going to think me mad, but did you hear the rumour that an enemy agent in Orkney guided the U-boat that sank the *Royal Oak* into Scapa Flow?' Her pulse sped up. If Joe laughed at her idea, she didn't think she could remain friends with him, yet she had enjoyed their time together and hated to think of ending their friendship.

'Yes, I've heard people talking about it. It's awful to think that there might have been someone on the island responsible for so many deaths.'

'But what do you think?'

'I think it's possible. It seems so unlikely for any vessel, let alone an enemy unfamiliar with the waters, to steer around the block ships in the Sound.'

'That's what I think. And…' But Joe hadn't laughed at her first suggestion, so she had every reason he would hear her out without thinking her mad. She took a breath and said the thing she hadn't even dared to share with Iris or Sally. 'I think whoever signalled to the plane in the summer was the same man who guided the U-boat.' She paused, casting sideways glances at Joe. Joe, however, frowned at his feet, seeming deep in thought. 'What do you think?' she prompted.

'It does make sense,' he said finally. 'After all, it's bad enough to think of one traitor on the island, let alone two. Thank goodness he drowned, and there's an end to him.'

Mary nodded.

Joe looked at her, his eyes grave. 'You seem to have put a lot of thought into this,' he said. 'It's as though it's very personal to you.'

'It is,' she said. She had only told Iris and Sally about Owen, and she felt torn between confiding in Joe and reluctance to reveal something so painful. Yet she had come this far, it felt right to tell him the truth. 'I had a fiancé who was killed on the *Royal Oak*, you see.'

'How awful. I'm so sorry. No wonder—' He bit his lip, and a ruddy hue suffused his cheeks, which Mary was sure had nothing to do with the chill wind. No wonder she had bitten his head off whenever he had got over-familiar. That's what he had been about to say. She was glad he had stopped himself, and had had the sensitivity not to make his expression of sympathy about himself.

'It was awful. But thanks to friends like Iris and Sally, I'm starting to find joy in life again.' And thanks to him, as well. It might only be a short while since she had allowed the possibility of his friendship to enter her heart, but she found she valued it all the same. She could never tell him that, though.

—

No wonder Mary had rebuffed all his advances. Joe was glad he'd kept his wits enough to stop himself from saying so. She was still mourning her dead fiancé and must have thought him a complete lout. Now he came to think of it, he remembered Mary approaching Rob soon after she had arrived on the island, when Joe and some of the other signalmen had been celebrating being released from Kyeness Signal Station and transferred to ships. If Joe remembered rightly, she had asked him about the *Royal Oak*. At the time, Joe had thought Mary had been setting her cap at Rob. Now, he realised she must have been trying to find out how her fiancé had died, and his heart twisted with sympathy.

'I'm really sorry you've had to go through that,' he said eventually. 'I'm glad you felt able to tell me about it.'

'I kept it to myself at first until I saw it was eating me up on the inside.' Mary's beautiful face was sombre. 'I'm gradually learning not to hide away my feelings from my friends.'

'I'm amazed you can think of me as a friend after all my clumsy attempts at getting your attention.'

A small smile lifted the corner of her mouth. 'I think you'll find I took notice of you properly when you stopped pestering me and started to act like a human being.'

'Ouch.'

'Trust me, you would never make a convincing Romeo. You're far better as a friend.'

That was him put in his place. He supposed he had better resign himself to the role of friend, because it looked like Mary would never take him seriously as a suitor. In the distance, he could hear a curlew's plaintive cry rising and falling across the cliff top. If there was a sound in nature that could be said to express his feelings at Mary's pronouncement, it was that.

He shook off his melancholy as they approached Curlew Croft, the Heddles' cottage, mindful that their son was still missing. However, they hadn't even knocked on the door when it was flung open, and Elspeth dashed out, her face aglow.

'We've just had the most wonderful news,' she said, ushering them inside. 'We got a telegram this morning to say Don's alive.'

'Oh, Elspeth.' Mary dropped her gas mask case and grasped both Elspeth's hands between her own. 'I'm so happy for you.'

If he hadn't just heard about her fiancé, Joe probably wouldn't have noticed the way her smile didn't quite reach her eyes. Although Joe was sure she was genuinely happy for Elspeth, this must be a bitter reminder of how her own hopes had been dashed.

'It's not all good news, mind. He was picked up by the Italians and is a prisoner of war.' Elspeth took Mary's coat and shook it to brush off the raindrops. She carried on brushing it down long after the last of the rain was off it.

Mary took the coat from her and hung it up, patting Elspeth's hand as she did so. 'I'm sure you must be all at sixes and sevens, but at least he's alive.'

'Oh, yes. Please don't think me ungrateful. Don was one of the lucky ones, I know. I just wish I could write, tell him how delighted we are to know he's safe and well.'

Mary frowned. 'I think you can write via the Red Cross. Leave it with me. I'll find out for you.'

'You are a good girl. Thank you, dear.' Then for the first time, Elspeth turned to Joe. 'And it's good to see you again, young Joe. It must be getting on for a year since we've seen you here.'

'I wanted to come when Mary told me about Don. I am pleased to hear he's alive.' He glanced at Mary. 'I'll see what I can find out about how you can send a letter to him.'

'A letter.' Elspeth clasped her hands together, her eyes shining. 'It would be marvellous to write. And to think that it's possible, that he's alive. Well, this calls for a celebration.'

Joe sniffed the air. 'That wouldn't be your famous fish pie I can smell? I can't tell you how many times I've dreamed of your cooking since joining my ship.'

'You could have come at any time. You're on the same ship as Rob Sinclair, aren't you? He's managed to visit fairly often. Still…' Elspeth glanced keenly between Joe and Mary. '…no doubt you'll be here more often now.'

Joe cringed inwardly, and Mary gave Elspeth a sharp glare, her lips pressed tight. Joe grappled for an excuse to go out for a while, to give Mary the chance to put Elspeth right. Seeing the bucket beside the sink was nearly empty, he hastened to pick it up. 'You're out of water. Let me fetch some more.' He was out of the door before Elspeth could protest.

When he returned, hauling the full bucket, it was to hear Elspeth say, 'Well, you know your mind. I—' She stopped when she saw Joe. 'Really, there was no need. But thank you. I must say, these buckets seem to get heavier every day.'

Joe and Mary set the table, and presently Archie came in from the fields and scrubbed his hands at the sink. 'You've heard the news about Don?' he asked over his shoulder. When they nodded he went on, 'I said to Elspeth when we heard, we've got plenty to be thankful for. The farm's done well this year, so we can go into winter knowing we've got enough to see us through.' He dried his hands then joined them at the table. Elspeth started to dole out portions of the fish pie.

Mary leaned across the table. 'You know, Sally, Iris and I have been thinking. We're going to take some time off over Christmas. It must be so hard for you with your sons away, and we thought we'd like to organise a special Christmas for you.'

'You're kind girls but really there's no need. Besides, we don't make such a fuss about Christmas as you folks away south.'

'Oh, do say yes. We can't be with our families this year, but we've become a family, haven't we? We want to celebrate with you, and we want to take the organisation out of your hands. What do you say?'

'It would be lovely to spend Christmas with you, of course, but even if you can all get the time off—'

'We've already arranged it with the other V/S Wrens,' Mary said in a voice that brooked no argument. 'We were the first Wrens at Kyeness, and had to work through last Christmas. The other Wrens here were still in the middle of their training last year and had a break over Christmas. We've sorted it out between us to give us a full seventy-two hours off.'

Elspeth looked at Archie as though pleading with him to talk sense into Mary, and Archie cleared his throat. 'I can see you lasses have put a great deal of thought into it,' he said. 'It would make Christmas special to have you here when we can't see our sons, but we can't let you take on all the work. You work such long hours up at the signal station.'

'And you work all hours here.'

Joe had to admire Mary for sticking to her guns. When Mary, Iris and Sally had first come to Kyeness, he had been glad that their arrival enabled him to join a ship and make him feel like he was taking a more active role in the war effort. However, he had been uncertain how the girls would cope working in such a remote location, isolated from the Wrens at the main bases. Now he was beginning to see that they had coped so much better than the men. While he and the other men had carried out their duties with diligence, they had devoted what little free time they had to their own entertainment. From what he had heard from Mary and Rob, the girls had not only shone at their work, earning glowing praise for their performance back in the summer when the plane dropping mines had been spotted, but they had also flung themselves into life on the island, befriending Elspeth and Archie, and joining in with the drive to knit socks for sailors. No doubt they would know all about the work going on for prisoners of war now the Heddles' son had been captured. He was beginning to think that if women had been in charge of the country, the war would have been won in a matter of weeks. There seemed no limit to what they could do, given the chance.

'We would love to spend Christmas with you,' Mary went on, 'only we don't want to make any more work for you. Your livestock still needs to be cared for over Christmas just the same as any other day. It doesn't seem fair for you to do all the work for the celebrations too. Let us do this. We're looking forward to it.'

'You might as well give in now,' Joe said to the Heddles with a grin when he saw they were still going to object. 'Once Mary has made up her mind, there's no stopping her. Same with the other two, I'm sure.' He turned to Mary. 'You've got my help as well.'

'See,' said Mary to the Heddles, 'we won't take no for an answer. You're going to enjoy this Christmas whether you like it or not.' She flashed Joe a wicked grin that had him tugging at his collar, feeling as though it had suddenly got too tight. However, quite aside from the effect she had on his libido, he felt a spark of wonder at the easy way she had accepted him into her schemes. There was a lot to be said for friendship after all.

–

Elspeth flung up her hands. 'Very well. I can see there's no talking you young people out of it.'

'That's the spirit,' Mary said. 'You wait, we're going to make this a Christmas you won't forget.'

Gratitude towards Joe welled up in her heart. There had been no need for him to offer help – however busy the Wrens were, it could be nothing compared to the men on board ship who could not call their time their own unless they were on leave.

When Joe collected the empty plates from the table at the end of the meal, Mary joined him at the sink. 'Please don't feel you have to help with the Christmas arrangements,' she said, keeping her voice low so as not to be overheard by Archie and Elspeth who remained at the table. 'It was very kind of you to offer but you mustn't feel obliged.'

'I didn't offer out of obligation. I offered because I'm very fond of the Heddles and want them to have a good Christmas.'

'Oh. Well, in that case…' Mary put down the empty pie dish she'd been holding. Acting on impulse, she raised herself onto tiptoe and kissed Joe on the cheek. 'You're turning out to be a good friend.'

She had obviously grown unused to being in male company since Owen's death. The chaste kiss made her feel suddenly unsteady, as though she wasn't standing on the solid stone floor of Curlew Croft but on the deck of a ship that pitched unpredictably. She had to fight the impulse to put her hand to her lips which burned and pulsed as though she had touched her mouth to a live wire. Snatching up the teapot, she spooned tea leaves inside, keeping her face turned away from Joe so he couldn't see her confusion. Honestly, what was wrong with her? Perhaps it was time to go on a few dates with men just to help her regain her perspective when alone with a man.

While she was filling the kettle from the jug of fresh water that Elspeth always kept filled up beside the sink, Elspeth said, 'Do you still draw, Joe?'

Mary slopped some of the water onto the floor. 'Idiot,' she mumbled and swapped the jug for a cloth and stooped to mop up the puddle. As she worked, she strained to hear Joe's answer.

Joe had wandered back to the table. 'Yes, I can't seem to help myself really. I don't get as much time on the *Kelpie*, of course, but I still get my sketchbook out when I can.'

Mary wrung the cloth into the sink, then spoke, doing her best to make it sound like a casual question rather than something of burning interest. 'I didn't know you could draw. What sort of subjects?'

'He drew this cottage for a start,' said Elspeth, pointing to the framed picture on the wall.

'You drew that? But that's beautiful.' Mary crossed to the picture and peered at it. She had noticed it on her first visit and admired it, never imagining that it had been drawn by someone she knew. It was a pencil sketch of Curlew Croft that not only reproduced every stone and line of the house but also somehow managed to express its character, the feeling of welcome that exuded from the place. She looked at Joe with a whole new level of respect.

Joe looked pleased and a little self-conscious. 'I'm glad you like it. I couldn't get the chimney quite right and—'

'Don't talk yourself down. I love it. The way you managed to get the pale light of the sun behind the clouds is perfect. I could never—' She stopped herself. *I could never get sunlight right*, she had been about to say. She didn't want to reveal her own artistic leanings, though, not when her own desire to draw seemed to have died. 'I could never understand how artists convey light using just a black pencil,' she said instead.

'I would hardly call myself an artist,' he said. 'I just enjoy drawing.'

'What other subjects do you draw?' she asked.

'I started out with landscapes and buildings that took my fancy. But I've started sketching my crew mates now I'm on the *Kelpie*.'

'I'd love to see them.'

'Really?' His face shone with surprised pleasure. When she nodded, he said, 'I'll bring my sketchbook next time I get leave.'

'I'm surprised you didn't know Joe was an artist,' Elspeth said. 'That's how we met him.'

Joe grinned. 'Yes, I was exploring the area not long after I was posted to Kyeness and fell in love with this cottage. The next time I had a free day and it wasn't pouring with rain, I perched on a rock just up the track and set to drawing. That's where Archie found me. He was tickled pink that I was drawing Curlew Croft, so he invited me in.' Joe gestured towards the framed picture. 'I gave them that as a present.'

Mary laughed. 'I'm beginning to wonder if there's a single sailor or Wren on the island that you two haven't adopted.' And the conversation moved to discussing the various young people Elspeth and Archie had befriended over the years. Mary found her gaze drifting to Joe's picture every now and again, however. How had she not known that he liked to draw? More than that, was a talented artist. She knew why, of course. She hadn't been interested in finding out. Her first impression of him had been that he was a brash young man with about as much depth as a rock pool. She hadn't bothered to look past the exterior to see that it was little more than a façade to hide his inner self from the world. Because his outer confidence was a form of defence, she could tell. She had built enough barriers of her own to recognise them in another. And what he seemed to be hiding was that he was a rather sensitive young man with artistic leanings. Nothing like the man she'd thought he was, and infinitely more interesting.

Chapter Seven

After a while the light started to fade, and Archie rose to light the lamps. Mary glanced at her watch with a start, having lost track of time. 'Goodness, I'm back on watch in half an hour. I'd better go.'

When Joe offered to walk her to the signal station, she agreed without hesitation. Funny, she reflected, as they said their goodbyes and bundled up into their outer wear, how her opinion of someone could change in such a short while. She had known Joe for as long as she had been in Orkney, yet it was only now that she had really noticed him or regarded him as anything other than a nuisance, even if an amiable one.

The sun had set by the time they left Curlew Croft, although there was a lingering golden glow in the sky and upon the sea and it lent enough light to show them the track. Still, even though she didn't need to hold onto him in case one of them stumbled, it felt natural to take Joe's arm.

'Have you always enjoyed drawing?' she asked, unable to get over her surprise at his artistic ability.

'Yes, it was my favourite subject at school,' he replied. 'In fact, promise you won't laugh?'

'Of course.'

'I wanted to do a degree in fine art when I left school.'

'Why would that make me laugh? You've clearly got talent. What stopped you?'

'My parents said it wasn't a secure career, and as they were funding my education, I had to go along with them. Anyway, I'm sure they were right. I was good at maths, too, you see, and I'm sure I'd earn more as an accountant than I would ever earn as an artist.' Then he snorted. 'Anyway, all thought of my future turned out to be moot when war broke out, and I ended up in the navy.'

'I know,' Mary said, a tightness in her throat strangling her voice. 'The war put an end to a lot of hopes and dreams.'

There was a painful pause, where Owen was an almost physical presence between them.

Maybe the silence would have lasted all the way to the signal station if nothing else had happened. Mary could have kicked herself for raising Owen's ghost. Just because he was a constant presence in her heart, it didn't mean she had to bring him into every conversation. In the event, however, Joe stumbled over a protruding lump of rock in the path, and he hopped, clutching his foot, releasing a string of oaths that Mary feared might reduce the stones to molten lava.

Mary couldn't help it. She giggled. 'They obviously teach you some interesting language in Suffolk.'

'Good heavens, no. You can't use bad language there; you'd set fire to all the thatched roofs.' He lowered his foot and tested his weight with a couple of tentative steps. 'Nothing broken. I do beg your pardon. Blame the influence of my shipmates. What must you think of me?'

'Trust me, nothing you say can embarrass me. You wouldn't believe the language I overheard when I used to play near the harbour when the fishing boats were coming in.' She seized the opportunity to steer the conversation back to Joe's drawings. 'Anyway, you were telling me about your sketches. How did you manage to get hold of enough paper for drawing out here?' The wartime paper shortage meant good quality paper was scarce, and even some newspapers were reducing the number of pages in each edition.

'Oh, when I got here I asked my parents to post me my old sketchbooks. I had quite a collection before the war. Enough to keep me going for another couple of years.' His eyes took on a faraway look. 'I can't imagine how I would feel if I couldn't draw. It's a compulsion. Like...' He appeared to grope for the right words.

'Like an itch at the back of the skull,' Mary supplied, unable to help herself.

'That's right. How do you know?'

She hesitated then decided to tell him. After all, it was something they had in common, and if Iris or Sally told him, he would be rightly hurt that she hadn't told him herself. She explained about the sketches she'd made in her diary.

It was too dark by this time to see his expression, though she could tell from his voice that it would be alight with enthusiasm. 'That's wonderful. We can go out sketching together. You're welcome to use one of my sketchbooks.'

She had to put a stop to this before it went too far. 'I can't. Not any more.'

'But what about that itch in the back of the skull?'

'I don't feel it now. It died when Owen, my fiancé, did.' She released a shaky breath, regretting the seeming impossibility of having any conversation without having to bring Owen into it. 'I tried a few times but there was nothing. No spark.'

'Maybe if—'

'No.' She put all the force she could into the single word. Then, not wanting to discourage him, she said, 'I'd love to see your work, though.'

By this time they had reached the signal station, and after she'd let him know her watches for the next two weeks, she escaped inside.

–

'Urgh, I hate these dark mornings,' Sally said a few days later as she stood beside Mary in the signal room, gazing out into the darkness. 'To think we've got several weeks of it getting darker still.' Then her face brightened. 'Although the stars are beautiful on clear nights, and there's a chance we might see the Northern Lights.'

Mary bit back the teasing comment she'd been about to make along the lines of Sally being a hopeless romantic. Maybe there was something to be said for looking on the bright side. After all, they had months of darkness ahead of them, and she might as well make the best of it. She, Iris and Sally had arrived on Orkney just before Christmas last year, so they had endured the darkest part of the year when everything was still new and exciting. Now life felt very routine, and facing up to the prospect of the long dark nights to come was bleak indeed.

'I'd love to see the Northern Lights. I always managed to be asleep when they could be seen last year.'

'Me too.' Sally's face shone. 'I'm sure it would be good luck to see them. They're so magical.' Her fingers crept automatically to the St Christopher medal that she had slid onto the chain with her identity tags. Mary noted the gesture with amusement. Sally had been given the medal by an Italian prisoner of war after her accident in the summer, and she often seemed to touch it when she wanted to ward away bad luck or had a particular wish.

However, maybe it was a lingering good mood from discovering a new friend in Joe, but she felt less inclined to tease Sally than usual. Instead she just smiled and said, 'I hope we all see them this year.'

Although the sun still wasn't up, the sea was now lit with a soft pearly light. A movement on the water caught her eye, and she saw a group of four minesweepers heading out of Scapa Flow, obviously on their way to the channel they were sweeping that day. Just as she was wondering if one of them was the *Kelpie*, the flashes of a signal light caught her eye.

'Get ready to take down a message,' she said to Sally and picked up the Aldis lamp. It was, indeed, the *Kelpie*. Once the signalman had successfully responded to the code of the day challenge, a further message arrived. She spelled it out to Sally before realising what it said: 'Good morning Mary.'

Sally laughed. 'That has to be Joe on watch. Don't be too hard on him.'

Funnily enough, it hadn't crossed Mary's mind to discourage him. Instead, she was aware of a spreading warmth in her chest. While Sally telephoned the station monitoring the indicator loop to let them know four minesweepers were about to cross, Mary sent back: 'Have fun.' She wanted to say, 'Stay safe,' but maybe some of Sally's superstition was rubbing off on her, because it seemed like tempting fate.

A minute later, Joe sent another message. 'Shore leave Sat. Can we meet?'

Mary felt a wave of elation. Saturday was in two days, and after coming off the night watch in the morning, she would have the whole day free. Remembering how Joe had puzzled her before with his abbreviations, she sent back: 'C u by n pier at 1000.' Anyway, their shorthand saved time and, with *Kelpie* pitching on the water, meant Joe was less likely to miss letters.

'Not so disapproving about sending personal messages now, are we?' Sally's arch voice made Mary jump, and she cursed the fact that Sally could have deciphered the message by listening to the clicks of the lamp's shutters.

'I've decided there's no harm in it,' she said. Then before Sally could make any idiotic remark about her and Joe, she said. 'What's a couple of signals between friends?'

Sally gave her a significant look but said nothing. She left Mary at the window and went to the desk to make a note in the log book.

Another signal from the *Kelpie* demanded her attention. 'Have a good day, Mary. C U Sat.'

She sent back: 'Look 4ward 2 it. Bring sketches.' And she watched the *Kelpie* sail around the headland feeling an odd lightness in her chest. She only tore her gaze away when it was time to go outside and hoist the ensign.

–

The sun rose on a rare cloudless day, and when their watch ended at one in the afternoon, Sally suggested walking back along the cliffs for a short way before heading back to the Wrennery. Mary breathed deeply as she gazed out to sea, enjoying this glimpse of sunlight and distant views after days of misty low cloud and drizzle.

'On a day like today, I feel like anything is possible.' Sally stretched out her arms as though about to launch herself in the air to join the birds.

Mary resisted the impulse to grab the back of Sally's coat like a mother restraining a toddler. 'If you leap off the cliff, I think you'll find that's not true.' Although Sally's euphoria must have been contagious, because Mary had to admit to a feeling of well-being that had been absent from her life for years. 'It is a good day for a walk, though. I hope Iris doesn't mind us being a bit late – I don't feel like rushing back.' As all three were off duty that afternoon, they had arranged to meet in the Wrennery common room to start their Christmas plans. Mary wished they had decided on another day now. Who knew when another sunny day would come along?

It seemed as though all the fishermen of Orkney had decided to make the most of the day as well, for several fishing boats were sailing through Hoy Sound, no doubt making a lot of work for the V/S Wrens on duty when they crossed the indicator loop.

'Look – there's the *Puffin*,' Sally said, pointing to a fishing boat they were both familiar with. She glanced at her watch. 'Making perfect time as ever.'

The Wrens of Kyeness had learned to recognise several of the larger fishing boats that plied the waters around Hoy Sound. They had soon discovered that the *Puffin*'s skipper had an uncanny knack of always rounding Kyeness at half past one in the afternoon, as long as the weather was in his favour. As one of the largest fishing boats in these waters, it never failed to trigger the indicator loop, so they had quickly become accustomed to its appearance.

'I reckon we could set our watches on her,' Mary replied with a grin.

They walked on until the Ness Battery came into view. At that point they had to turn away from the cliffs and pick up the path back into Stromness. They had just turned their backs on the sea when they heard someone sneeze. Curious, Mary looked around the cliff top until she saw a man dressed in tweeds sitting on a rock a few yards off the path. He had a notebook perched on his lap, and he was scribbling something with a stubby pencil. He looked up at that moment and met Mary's eyes, and she saw with an unpleasant jolt that it was Stewart Irvine. He looked as reluctant as she felt to engage in conversation. The trouble was, it was impossible to ignore someone when you were otherwise alone on the cliffs. He rapidly closed his notebook and stuffed it in his pocket.

'Oh, hello,' he said.

'Hello,' Mary and Sally chorused. Neither of them moved closer to him.

'What are you doing up here?' he asked.

'We thought we'd return from the signal station via the scenic route,' Mary replied. 'What are *you* doing here?' She really wanted to ask him why he was still on Orkney when no one wanted him there, but that seemed a trifle rude, even for her.

'Oh, watching the fishing boats.'

Mary couldn't resist glancing at the pocket containing his notebook; Stewart moved his hand to it as though in an unconscious gesture to hide it. 'I've got work writing articles for the *Orkney Herald* and thought of an article about the local fishing industry.' He glanced past Mary at Sally. 'Good to see you made a full recovery from your injuries.'

Sally gave him a tight smile. 'Thank you.'

Mary was amused that Sally's general propensity to believe the best in people didn't seem to stretch to the disgraced doctor.

'Well, we'd better get on. Things to do. I'm sure you know how it is.' Sally had already taken the first couple of steps along the path by the time she had finished speaking. 'Come on, Mary.'

Mary nodded a curt goodbye, not at all reluctant to leave. Once they were out of earshot, she released a breath and said, 'That was awkward.'

'I know. I suppose it's a good thing he's got a job with no possibility of hurting people.'

'I can't imagine why he wants to stay, though,' Mary said. 'Surely he'd be more likely to get work in a practice away from here. And did you notice how embarrassed he seemed about what he was writing?' A sudden thought struck her, making her snort. 'What if he was writing poetry? You did say you thought he might be trying to win Iris back. Maybe he was writing her a love sonnet.'

'Oh, goodness. That would explain why he was in such a hurry to hide his book.' Sally flashed Mary a look, her eyes alight with laughter. 'If Iris gets an anonymous book of love poems for Christmas, we'll know who they're from.' After a brief pause, Sally added, 'Talking of Christmas, have you any idea what to get Iris for a present?'

'I'm not sure.' Actually, Mary had thought of something. It had occurred to her when she was showing Iris and Sally the sketches in her diary. One of her drawings featured a view out to sea from a cliff top, with a fishing boat in the distance against a stormy sky. Iris had been particularly struck by it, possibly because it made her think of watching for the *Kelpie* and Rob from the signal station. While Mary didn't have much money to spare for Christmas presents, she thought she could stretch to a frame. There was another picture she thought Sally would like – the picture of Solva harbour – as the mass of fishing boats had reminded Sally of Whitby. She didn't want to tell Sally about her idea for Iris as it was too close to the present she had in mind for Sally. 'What are you getting her?'

'That's just it – she's already got so many lovely things. What can I get that wouldn't look shabby in comparison?'

'She doesn't have much money now, not with her allowance being cut off. Is there anything of hers that needs replacing?'

Sally walked on in silence for a while then she grabbed Mary's arm, her eyes alight. 'Of course – a needle case. Have you noticed how tatty hers is? If I can get some felt, I've got enough embroidery silks to make a really pretty one.'

'She'll love it. That's a great idea.'

As they walked on, discussing presents for various family members and friends, Mary's thoughts drifted to Joe. She was struck with the thought that she'd like to get him a present. Surely they were good enough friends for that. But what should she get him? The answer came to mind immediately. There was a little shop selling art supplies in Stromness which she often visited; despite having lost her urge to draw, there was still something about art shops that she found irresistible – the tins of watercolours; the tubes of oil paints displayed in rainbows upon the shelves; the boxes of pastels and charcoal and the endless array of pencils, india rubbers and sheaves of papers of all colours. She could spend hours in art shops.

She could easily discover if there were any materials he lacked and get them for his Christmas present.

For some reason, her dreams of art shops turned into imagining the expression on Joe's face when he opened her present. It occurred to her that for the first time in years, she was looking forward to Christmas.

–

'Poor you, having to speak to Stewart.' Iris wrinkled her nose. 'Did he say why he was still in Orkney?' Mary and Sally had found Iris in the common room as arranged and had hardly sat down before regaling her with the tale of their meeting on the cliffs.

'He said he was writing for the *Orkney Herald*,' Sally said. 'Although as he hid what he was writing, Mary thought he was writing you love poetry.'

Iris gave a dramatic shudder. 'Urgh! Spare me. Why couldn't he have got work with the *Penzance Post* instead?'

'What, and miss his literary outpourings?' Mary said with a grin. 'How would they go?' She thought for a moment until inspiration struck. 'How about this?' She struck a dramatic pose.

'I'm a poor doctor
And a bit of a dope
But if you'll forgive me
Please can we elope?'

Iris gave her a withering stare then picked up her notebook and waved it under Mary's nose. 'I won't dignify that with a critique. If you've quite finished, I thought we were going to start planning Christmas.'

Feeling like a naughty schoolgirl who had been disciplined by her teacher, Mary sat back in her chair and tried to concentrate on the matter at hand. 'Right. Let's start by making a list of everything that needs to be done. What makes a good Christmas?'

'A tree and decorations,' Sally said.

'Christmas dinner,' Iris said. 'Oh, and we must have parlour games. It's not Christmas without a game of charades.'

Watching their faces light up as they recalled the Christmases of their childhood, Mary felt a pang, remembering how magical Christmas had seemed when she had been very young, before tragedy had struck her family. She scribbled down the ideas, feeling downcast, wondering if it was worth the bother. How could they celebrate when there was precious little peace and joy in the world?

'What about you, Mary? You're being very quiet. What makes Christmas special for you?'

Mary gave a start, finally realising Sally was speaking to her. 'What? Oh, the same as you.' She shot a glance at the list. 'Decorations, food, games. The usual.' All accompanied by the sound of her mother sobbing when she thought no one could hear. She went on in a rush, 'Anyway, we ought to start with the food, work out how many coupons we're going to need so we can start putting them by.'

'Good plan,' said Iris.

But Sally didn't remove her gaze from Mary, concern clouding her expression. 'I think it's a wonderful idea of yours, to celebrate Christmas together,' she said, her voice gentle. 'With so much tragedy in the world, we need to remind ourselves that Christmas is about bringing light into the darkness. That's why my mother and I always paid extra attention to Christmas after my uncle's accident.'

Mary stared at her for a moment, lost for words. When she recovered herself, she said, 'You're a marvel, Sally. Everyone should have a friend like you. I'll never know how you manage to stay so unfailingly optimistic.'

Sally looked away then, mumbling something inaudible. Not wanting to embarrass her further, Mary turned her attention back to the food. Her spirits felt lighter, though, and she knew Sally was right. Sally was usually so cheerful, Mary often forgot she had experienced her own share of tragedy. Well, she wouldn't forget again, and she would follow her example. She needed to remember Sally's words – Christmas was about bringing light into the darkness. Sometimes you had to look hard for the light, but it was always there. She would remember that next time she was tempted to abandon their plans. In her case, the brightest part of her life was her friends, and she was luckier than many people this year because she would be spending Christmas with her closest friends. She had much to be thankful for.

They returned to the list, and soon had a menu planned that wouldn't stretch their budget and kept the ration coupons required to a reasonable amount. Of course, much of the food would be taken from the produce grown by the Heddles, although the girls were determined to reimburse them for it.

'My mouth's watering just thinking of roast gammon,' Mary said, stretching to ease her aching muscles after being bent over her notebook. 'I don't know how I'm going to last until supper. Has the post arrived yet, Iris? My mam promised to send me a fruitcake, and a slice would go down a treat right now.'

'I nearly forgot. It came just before you got back. Nothing for you, I'm afraid, Mary, but this came for Sally.' Iris fished a letter from her pocket and handed it to Sally.

Sally glanced at it then ripped it open. 'Thanks. It's from my mum.' She read it quickly, smiling or chuckling in places. Then she gasped, clapping her hand to her mouth.

'What is it?' Iris asked.

'You'll never guess. Adam's coming to Orkney.'

Adam was the young man Sally had convinced herself was the love of her life. While Mary had never met him, she wasn't convinced her feelings were returned. Or even if Adam had properly noticed Sally.

'My mum met his mother in the greengrocer's. Mum can't say much in a letter, obviously. Only that Adam's being posted somewhere near me.' Sally's eyes were shining. 'Isn't that wonderful? We'll be able to spend some time together at last.'

All Mary could do was agree. Exchanging glances with Iris, however, she saw her fears reflected in Iris's expression. Mary hoped Sally wouldn't get hurt. She could only resolve to observe Adam carefully when she met him and do her best to warn Sally if she thought Adam was going to break her heart.

Chapter Eight

Joe rubbed his fingers as he stood at his station. High above his head the wind whistled in the rigging, and the halyards knocked rhythmically against the foremast. While the weather might still be mild on shore, you didn't have to go far out to sea before the cold seemed to make its way through the many layers of your kit. He stamped his feet in an effort to get the blood circulating. It didn't help being up on the signal deck, which was one of the highest points on the ship; only the navigating bridge and gunnery rangefinder were higher. On the other hand, he thought with a wry smile as the ship plunged into a trough, sending spray over the breakwater, there could be worse places to stand. The poor sods manning the four-inch gun down on the main deck in front of the bridge were getting a soaking. Even so, at times like these he envied Rob, whose duties kept him below decks, keeping the ships electrical units in working order.

A flash of light from HMS *Levington* – one of the other minesweepers in the group – caught his eye. His stomach tightened when the message sank in, and he called up to the bridge. 'Message from the *Levington*. Submarine detected bearing red oh–four–five. Range two thousand five hundred.'

Lieutenant Commander Gamble – *Kelpie*'s skipper and the officer in charge of the group of four minesweepers that *Kelpie* was part of – drew a hissing breath through his teeth. A restrained reaction considering there was a U-boat only two and a half thousand yards away from the *Levington's* port side. Joe's every muscle was tense, and he dreaded seeing a plume of black smoke rising from the *Levington*. He caught himself feeling relieved that the *Levington* was between the *Kelpie* and the U-boat and felt a rush of shame. Anyway, what if there were other U-boats out there, undetected? As he strained his eyes so he wouldn't miss another signal, he half expected to feel the jolt of a torpedo strike. Now being out on deck didn't seem so bad, and he spared a thought for his friends below decks who might struggle to escape if the ship went down.

Gamble, however, remained calm. He ordered a change of course then instructed Joe to signal to the other ships in the group, directing them to converge on the U-boat. Being busy helped dispel Joe's nerves, despite the knowledge that the only way they could destroy the U-boat would be to get above it and drop a depth charge. Once Joe had sent the signals, he saw Gamble glance towards the Mainland. Joe looked too, knowing that the skipper was looking to see if there was a signal station in sight so he could alert the powers that be of the U-boat's presence. Where possible, ships used visual signals to avoid sending wireless transmissions that could be intercepted by the enemy. As luck would have it, Kyeness was just in view to the south, although it was at the limit of visual range. With the ship bobbing up and down on the waves, it would be difficult for the signaller at the station to view the complete signal.

Gamble must have decided it was worth a try, for he said, 'Yeoman of signals – make to Kyeness: "Am attacking submarine bearing red oh-two-five from *Levington*, two thousand yards".'

Joe sighted the signal station through the crosshairs of his Aldis lamp and set to work, cursing each time the waves knocked his aim off. At this distance, even a slight movement made a large difference to his line of sight. He released a breath of relief when the flash returned, showing each word had been received. He thought he recognised Mary's style. Certainly she was on watch today, and after their frequent signals to each other, they were accustomed to one another's quirks by now. Mary tended to signal a little faster than the others, and while some of the newer signalmen found they had to concentrate to keep up, Joe appreciated the speedy exchange of information. She rarely made mistakes, and it was a comfort to know she was up there, watching out for him.

Several times she had to request he repeat a word, but finally she sent the signal that the message was received and to stand by. He knew she would be on the telephone to their base, and he could imagine the wires humming as urgent messages were relayed to and fro. The report that a U-boat had got this close to the Home Fleet would be causing a great deal of concern.

By the time another light flashed out from Kyeness, Joe's nerves were stretched to breaking point, expecting to feel the impact that heralded a torpedo at any moment. He read the message and called up to the bridge. 'Message from Kyeness: Backup from RNAS Hatston coming.'

That was good news. Royal Naval Air Station Hatston would probably send a flight of Fairey Swordfish, which would be more than a match for a submarine. While submarines might be able to hide from ships, they were clearly visible from the air and were vulnerable to bombers armed with depth charges. How long would it take the pilots to get into the air after the scramble order, though? He had no idea. He was also not sure how long it would take to fly from Hatston, near Kirkwall. Not long, but every second was vital when the U-boat could fire a torpedo at any moment. It was too soon to relax his vigilance, and he waited with bated breath as the four minesweepers converged on the U-boat's estimated position. Now the hunter had become the prey.

–

Mary watched the minesweepers with her heart in her mouth. Beside her, Iris stood, white-faced. They had arrived on watch that morning still discussing their misgivings about Sally's news from the day before. Now their worries that Adam would break Sally's trusting heart seemed trivial compared with the drama playing out in the waters below. Mary's concentration was fixed on Joe, and she knew Iris's thoughts would be similarly turned to Rob. It was one thing to know someone you cared about was in danger in a general way – every time the *Kelpie* went out on sweeping operations there was the possibility of being struck by a mine it had failed to detect. Right now, however, knowing a U-boat was in the vicinity and dreading the sight of a plume of smoke that indicated a torpedo strike, it was a whole new level of fear. The telephone from the station monitoring the indicator loop was silent, meaning that the U-boat had not attempted to cross Hoy Sound into Scapa Flow, which was surely its aim. Had it already changed course in an attempt to evade the minesweepers?

'This is horrible,' Iris said, picking up the binoculars and training them upon the *Kelpie*. 'The odds are in their favour now, aren't they? Now they know the U-boat is out there.'

'They'll be fine.' Mary spoke with a confidence she didn't quite feel. Inwardly, she was praying, *please don't let it happen again*.

She was so focused on the scene out to sea, she didn't notice Iris had moved closer until she felt her squeeze her arm. She jumped and found Iris watching her with concern.

'This won't end like the *Royal Oak*,' Iris said. 'The tables have turned now there are four minesweepers on the U-boat's tail.'

Mary was struck by Iris's empathy, especially considering how frightened she must be for Rob. That Iris could spare a thought for Mary's feelings spoke volumes about the changes the past year had wrought in her friend. The Iris she had first known would have been oblivious to Mary's fear. 'Thanks, Iris. You're right. I'm sure the U-boat will be making its escape now.'

She jumped when a roar heralded the arrival of the promised aircraft from RNAS Hatston. The noise rose to a crescendo as they flew directly over the signal station then faded as they homed in on the group of minesweepers out to sea. 'Here comes the cavalry,' she said, holding herself back from releasing a whoop of joy and relief.

Beside her, she heard Iris release a long, shaky breath before muttering a fervent, 'Thank God.'

Now the Swordfish were on the prowl above the minesweepers, Mary's fears eased. The U-boat was outnumbered, and its crew would be focused on escape, not attack. The knot in her insides eased with every passing minute as no plume of smoke or water indicated a strike on either side. Finally, not long before her watch was about to end, another signal from the *Kelpie* came through. 'All contact lost.' The U-boat had escaped.

Their heads full of the chase, it was all Mary and Iris could talk about on their walk back to the Wrennery. 'I can't help wishing they'd managed to torpedo it,' Mary said. 'Now I'll worry that it will be back.'

'But what could it have been trying to achieve?' Iris said. 'The Germans must know about the loop, and about the anti-submarine nets and the minefield.'

Mary shrugged. 'Perhaps it was trying to intercept shipping coming out of Scapa Flow.'

'I suppose so.' Iris's brow was creased with worry. 'I hate to think it might try again.'

'Unless it was a false alarm,' Mary said. 'The *Levington*'s Asdic operator might have misinterpreted the reading. Who knows, it could have been a shoal of fish or even a whale.' She wasn't sure how Asdic worked, having only the vaguest idea that it involved listening to signals reflected off submerged objects. She had no idea how the operator interpreted these signals.

'Possibly.' Iris's face brightened. 'Let's hope so.'

'Even if it was a submarine, we've seen it off once and we can do it again.' Mary injected all the confidence she could summon into her words, as much to reassure herself as Iris. Scapa Flow had far greater defences than it had had at the start of the war. It was inconceivable that a U-boat could cause the same damage as it had done with the *Royal Oak*.

She was also fast coming to realise that losing Joe would cause her almost as much pain as losing Owen.

–

The next day she had to restrain herself from dashing up to Joe and pulling him into a hug when she saw him stroll towards her from the pier. He raised an arm and gave her a jaunty wave as though he'd done nothing more exciting than a fishing trip since they had last met.

When he got closer she saw he had something flat and rectangular under his arm. In her worry about the U-boat, she had forgotten all about his promise to show her his sketch book. Nothing seemed important apart from reassuring herself he was well.

There was an icy nip in the air, and the wind blew in strong gusts, so when Joe suggested going to a cafe, Mary accepted with alacrity.

'You said you wanted to see my sketches,' Joe said once they were seated in the Beehive – a cosy cafe located in one of the narrow alleys leading from the main street.

'Hang the sketches! I want to know what happened yesterday.'

'You know I can't talk about it,' Joe said, casting mean-ingful glances at the other tables.

Mary's cheeks burned. She had never forgotten the 'Careless lips sink ships' warning before. Yet now, when the words could be taken all too literally, her worry for Joe had overridden her common sense. 'Not even in general terms?' she asked, lowering her voice.

'I suppose it can't hurt to say we found nothing after the first… indication.'

Mary knew he meant Asdic blips.

'Either it was a false alarm or…' He finished with a shrug.

It was the same thing she and Iris had concluded. If the Asdic blips hadn't been a false alarm then the U-boat must have escaped once it detected the British ships had changed course to hunt it down. She wished she could ask if he thought it would be back, but decided it was best to keep quiet. Instead she said, 'I really would like to see your sketches.'

'Now that I *can* do.' Joe moved a vase containing a delicate arrangement of dried lavender aside and placed the sketchbook on the table between them, turning it so it was the right way up for Mary. 'Be my guest.'

Mary reached for it, feeling as though she were about to open a box containing unimagined treasure. She turned to the first page. On it was a charcoal drawing of a pub beside a wide river with Thames barges moored by the banks. It was beautifully done, and Mary found that the more she looked, the more detail she could see. She could almost feel the texture of the furled sails and marvelled at their contrast with the smooth masts. The water was choppy, and every tiny wavelet reflected the light perfectly. She could see the direction of the wind from the waves and the sense of movement in the long grass on the banks, and could swear she heard the creak of the pub sign as it rattled on its chains. 'This is amazing. Where is it?'

'Pin Mill near Ipswich. I did it in the spring just before the war.'

Mary leafed through the pages and saw that Joe had been prolific in the months before he'd joined the navy. There was a sketch of a high tower that Joe said was Orford Castle, several drawings of sailing boats, thatched cottages and flint churches. It was the details that struck her in each one. One picture that particularly caught her eye was an adder coiled around the roots of a gorse bush. Not only had Joe captured the soft sheen of its scales perfectly, he had also conveyed a sense of the snake's muscular power.

There was a change in the drawings that followed. For a start, the locations had changed. Although Mary had never visited Suffolk, through Joe's drawings she had begun to get a feeling of a rolling landscape, pretty villages with thatched cottages, wide skies and the land merging gently with the coast. None of the dramatic cliffs that Mary was used to in her native Pembrokeshire, yet with its own beauty. The drawings further on didn't have the sleepy, cosy feel of his earlier ones. 'Is this where you joined the navy?' she asked, pointing to a picture of an imposing civic building with a high central clock tower.

Joe craned his neck to look. 'That's Portsmouth, where I did my training. That building's the Guildhall.' He grimaced. 'It won't look like that now – I heard it was bombed. Sad to think of so many beautiful buildings gone for ever.'

Mary studied the drawing. While it managed to convey the grandeur of the building, with its impressive portico and domes, it lacked the minute detail of Joe's earlier sketches. She supposed it was because he would have had less time to pursue his hobby once he had joined up. Still, she had to admire the way he managed to hint at greater details with a few spare strokes of his pencil. This ability became more obvious in later drawings. Now she recognised the scenery. On one page was a sketch of the hills of Hoy rising beyond Hoy Sound; on another, a stone circle. There were also several sketches of boats crowding the piers in Stromness. The most detailed drawing was a view from the cliffs not far from Kyeness Signal Station, taking in Hoy Sound. 'I see you've missed out the gunnery placement.' She pointed to the place in the drawing where Joe had drawn just a section of rocky, grassy cliff instead of a concrete pillbox.

'I didn't think that was a good idea.' He flashed her a lopsided grin. 'Or are you looking for a way to get me arrested to get me out of your hair for good?'

'Of course not. I—' She broke off when his laughter made her realise he was teasing. The truth was, she had ceased to think of him as a nuisance, and even looked forward to seeing him.

She lowered her face over the book to hide her confusion. On turning to another page, Mary was arrested by several sketches dotted around the paper, depicting men who must be Joe's shipmates. There were men playing cards, others huddled around a wireless and another sailor smoking a cigarette. While the man's features were merely hinted at, the smoke was rendered in intricate detail, rising from the glowing end of the cigarette first in smooth, linear streaks then coiling and dispersing into chaotic spirals.

'These are amazing,' Mary said. 'I feel as though I was beside you in the mess. How you've managed to convey so much detail in a few pencil strokes is a real talent. If anything, I think these are better than the pictures at the start of the book.'

Smiling at Joe's expression of gratified surprise, she turned the page, still looking at Joe's face rather than the paper. As she watched, his eyes went wide.

He tried to snatch the book from her. 'No, wait,' he said.

Instinctively, Mary clutched it harder and looked at the new page only to see her own face gazing up at her. It was a startling likeness, and Mary gazed at it with the feeling that her soul had been laid bare for all to see. The eyes looked straight out of the page, managing to convey both a challenge and a hint of wary defensiveness. The lips showed not the barest suggestion of a smile. It was not a comfortable picture to look at.

'I didn't mean you to see that.' Joe tugged at the sketch-book, but Mary gripped one corner, preventing him from taking it back.

'Is that how you see me?'

Chapter Nine

Joe released the book and slumped back in his chair. 'Not any more. I know you now.'

'But at first?' Mary couldn't seem to drag her gaze from the picture. The expression of the girl in the sketch seemed to say she wanted to be left alone. She couldn't imagine how she had made any friends if that was the impression she gave people.

'If it makes you feel any better, I was never happy with that drawing. You never looked as fierce as all that.'

But that meant she *had* appeared somewhat fierce. It was not a comfortable thought. While she had wanted to be left alone, she hadn't wanted to be unfriendly. Her thoughts drifted to the lonely weeks of her signalling training. She couldn't deny being downright rude to Iris at times – Iris's obviously privileged background and air of superiority had rubbed her up the wrong way – yet she hadn't intended to keep the other Wrens at arm's length. If she had looked as unwelcoming as she did in the drawing, she couldn't blame them for staying away. No wonder she hadn't had any friends.

Then another thought struck her. 'When did you draw this?'

'Must have been early February.'

'But you hardly knew me then.' They had only met a couple of times at that point – once when he had shown her, Iris and Sally around the signal station when they had arrived on Orkney before Christmas and again at the WVS party a few days later. January had been such a dark month, and the girls were still getting accustomed to their new routine, so that they hadn't socialised much outside the Wrennery. It was only in the spring that she had bumped into Joe when out and about in Stromness with her friends.

–

Although Joe wasn't easily embarrassed, he could feel his face colouring. 'I have a good visual memory.' Which was true, although not the whole truth by any means.

Mary turned two more pages and looked at more pictures of his shipmates, a furrow forming between her brows. 'I was always with Iris and Sally the first few times you met me, yet you haven't drawn them.'

Because although he had liked Iris and Sally, their faces hadn't been burned into his memory like Mary's. He didn't say that, though. He knew it would send her running out of the cafe, and he would lose her. Telling Mary the truth at this stage would be a bad move. He could picture her expression if he told her everything. If Mary were more like Sally, he would have no trouble. He wouldn't need to hide the truth. He knew exactly what he would say. *If you must know, a few days before I met you, I saw H.M. Pulham, Esq. at the cinema and was transfixed by Hedy Lamarr. When I met you, you reminded me so much of her, I couldn't stop looking at you. I thought it must be some kind of sign that we should be together.*

He'd wanted to ask her if she believed in fate or magic, only Mary had made it all too clear that she wasn't interested in him, so he dismissed the whole thing as coincidence. Even so, he couldn't get her out of his thoughts, and the knowledge of her being up at Kyeness had sustained him through many a cold, cheerless watch on board the *Kelpie*. He had promised himself that he would get to know her, and now, almost a year since that first meeting, he would do nothing that might damage the fragile friendship between them. All he could do was hold onto the hope that one day their relationship would be secure enough for him to tell her.

Now was not the time, however, and she was looking at him, eyebrows raised, waiting for his response. He wouldn't lie to her, even if he couldn't tell her the whole truth. He could only pray this fragment of truth wouldn't scare her away. After all, he had never tried to conceal his admiration. 'Your friends are pretty, but they can't compare with you. Yours is the only face I wanted to draw.'

Mary raised her cup to her lips and took a drink, lowering her gaze and hiding the expression in her eyes. Only the slight tremor of her fingers gave any hint of discomposure. When she placed the cup upon the saucer, she finally looked up at him. By this time she had her expression under control, and it bore a remarkable similarity to his drawing. 'Are you saying you're friends with me because you like my face?'

'No. Your face was the first thing that caught my attention, but I'm friends with you because of who you are. You might not have made it easy to get to know you, but you are well worth the challenge.' And it had been a challenge. Her prickly exterior made it difficult for anyone to get close to her, but he sensed it concealed a big heart. She had clearly loved her fiancé deeply and feared to be hurt again, and now her defences were up to protect her wounded heart from further injury. However, her friendship with Iris and Sally showed that she was willing to open up to anyone prepared to make the effort to get to know her.

Her frown lines smoothed. 'I suppose I should be grateful I've found friends willing to rise to the challenge.' Mary leafed back to her portrait. 'I don't think I made it easy for anyone.'

'Ah, but the best things in life are worth fighting for.'

And he would fight for her. Not just for her friendship, but for her heart. Because the more he knew of her, the more he yearned for her to return his ever-deepening feelings.

–

Their duties kept Mary and Joe apart for the next three weeks, and Mary found she missed him. Not that she was able to forget him even had she wanted to, for Joe had made a point of finding out when she was on watch, and sending signals to Mary from the *Kelpie* whenever he could. Now they were only a week away from December, and the days grew ever darker and colder. Last year, Mary had found it depressing; this year, she found herself watching for signals from the *Kelpie*, and each time Joe sent her a message, the tiny sparks of light kindled a glow deep within that continued to warm her long after the minesweeper sailed out of view.

She thought long and hard about the portrait. While her reserve was deliberate, she had never intended to come across as unfriendly as she'd appeared in the drawing. She had sensed Joe was trying to be kind when he'd said he couldn't get the expression right. Her thoughts returned frequently to the antagonism she had directed at Iris throughout their training and how she often scoffed at Sally's superstitions and her over-romantic views. She had kept these thoughts to herself all this time but now, sharing an interminable night watch with Iris, she felt the need to talk them over. The *Kelpie* had been working in another part of Scapa Flow all day and would have returned to its anchorage hours ago; she could see nothing but inky blackness through the windows and she couldn't keep her thoughts to herself any longer.

'Why are you and Sally friends with me?'

Iris, who was huddled beneath a blanket in a chair beside the stove, cradling a mug of tea between her hands, started and looked up. 'What kind of question is that?'

'One I want an honest answer to. I was awful to you when we met, and you obviously didn't like me, so what made you change your mind?'

Iris put her mug upon the desk, wrapped her blanket more closely around her shoulders and rose. She approached the window where Mary stood, her brows drawn together. 'What's brought this on? Yes, we had a rocky start, but I've put it behind me and thought you had, too.' Her frown deepened. 'At least, I hope you have. I can't bear to think of the snob I was back then.'

'That's just it – you've changed. Anyway,' Mary added hastily, 'you weren't as bad as all that. But I haven't changed at all, and why would anyone want to be friends with me when I'm always rude to them?'

'You *have* changed. I don't think you're rude to anyone any more. You were rude to me at the start, but honestly, looking back I can understand why. You tease us now, but you're not insulting.'

'Do you really think so?' Mary longed to believe Iris. While Iris could be almost as outspoken as Mary, often blurting out the first thing that came into her head, she had learned to consider her words more before speaking, and Mary wanted to be sure she wasn't just trying to be kind.

Iris put her hands on her hips, her blanket slipping off her shoulders. 'You asked for an honest opinion, and I gave it. I wouldn't lie. But you still haven't told me what's brought this on. Have Sally or I said something that made you doubt us?' Then Iris tilted her head on one side as though listening to an inward voice. A slow smile crept across her face. 'Or is it Joe? You've been seeing a lot of him recently. Did he say something?'

Clearly it was impossible to keep anything to yourself in the Wrens, especially when confined to a small island where everyone knew everyone else's business. 'It's not what he said, but what he drew.' Realising it was pointless trying to hide anything from Iris now she had come this far, Mary drew a deep breath and explained about Joe's portrait and how its fierce, hostile expression had made her feel. 'So you see,' she said in conclusion, 'it really shook me up to be confronted with that... that *harpy*. Is that really how you all see me?'

'Of course not.' Iris shivered and pulled her blanket back up around her shoulders. She scowled at Mary. 'Why aren't you as cold as me? It's perishing in here. How can you survive in just your uniform?'

'Probably because I'm a cold-hearted ice queen.' Despite herself, Mary felt her lips twitch. It was impossible not to find the sight of Iris funny, wrapped as she was in her warmest jersey, bellbottoms and greatcoat beneath her blanket. 'Aren't you glad I advised you not to get rid of the blackouts?' When Iris had first seen them, she had been horrified and declared nothing could induce her to wear them. Mary, used to how cold it could get on a cliff top in the winter, had advised her to keep them.

'There you are,' Iris said. 'Even when we were at loggerheads, you gave me good advice. I must have been intensely annoying, yet you were good-hearted enough not to let me freeze to death.' Iris shivered again. 'Despite the best attempts of the navy.'

As if to emphasise Iris's statement, an icy gust of wind tore through the gaps in the window panes. Mary had to admit the signal station wasn't designed for warmth. Most of the heat generated by the stove flew straight out of the windows. Even when they were all closed, as they were now, the huge panes which occupied three sides of the signal room seemed to suck the heat right out of the room.

Iris shrugged the blanket and her multiple layers of sleeves clear from her wrist and glanced at her watch. She wrinkled her nose. 'Anyway, it's gone 0100 hours. Your turn to take the stove seat.'

'It's okay,' Mary said. 'Your need is greater than mine. I don't mind keeping watch a while longer.'

'Are you sure?' Iris was halfway to the chair before Mary assured her she was. 'You're an angel.' She sank into the chair and rubbed her hands together briskly, holding them out to the warm stove.

Mary turned back to the window and did another scan of the dark sea, seeing nothing but blackness. Behind her, she could hear Iris's teeth chattering. Mary was cold too – there was a bite to the air that numbed her fingers and the tip of her nose – but she supposed she had learned to push it to the back of her mind. Iris, who had been pampered and used to the luxuries of life, had never grown accustomed to hardship. Admittedly it was easier to forget about the discomfort when you were busy. On a quiet night such as this, Mary found it harder to ignore the cold that stabbed through her many layers of uniform, slicing through flesh and piercing her bones. There was something about an Orkney winter that nothing could prepare you for.

'That's what I'm talking about, you see,' Iris said after a long pause. 'You might try to hide it but your actions give you away every time. If you truly were a bad friend, you would never give up your turn by the stove. As far as I'm concerned, that's the greatest act of kindness anyone could perform.'

'Perhaps I'm being selfish. The worst thing about sitting by the stove is having to move back into the cold.' Mary was grinning, though, feeling lighter than she had since seeing the portrait. Iris could be almost as blunt as her, and Mary knew she could rely on her to tell the plain truth.

'You're right.' With a groan, Iris rose, shedding her blanket and joining Mary at the window. 'The longer I stay there, the harder it will be to leave. If you don't want the stove seat, the least I can do is join you here.'

'You don't have to.'

'I know, but I'm in danger of falling asleep if I sit there any longer and we were supposed to be using the time to plan for Christmas, remember?'

'True. That blasted picture made me forget completely. What's left to do?' She attempted to gather her thoughts and spoke rapidly, hoping to bury the memory of those hostile eyes beneath an avalanche of words. 'We still haven't decided on the decorations, and I thought it would be a good idea to get some board games from—' She broke off when Iris put a hand on her arm.

'Mary, you really shouldn't let yourself get upset about that picture. I can't deny you were difficult to get along with at first, but so was I. And even at your worst, I could always see the hurt girl looking out from behind your eyes. You told me about your fiancé early on, and if I'd bothered to think about it, I would have worked out that you were trying to defend yourself from more hurt. Once I got to know you, I soon learned what a true and loyal friend you are. And Joe can see that too. It's obvious he thinks the world of you. Anyway, didn't he say he hadn't got the expression right in the drawing? You can't put too much weight on a sketch he drew from memory.'

Something about Iris's earnest expression got through to Mary where her words had failed. Examining her friend's face, Mary could see nothing but concern and affection. The last of the burden fell away, and she felt as though she could breathe easily for the first time since seeing the picture. 'Thank you,' she said. 'You must think me a complete idiot for letting a silly drawing get to me like that.'

'Not at all. You know what I think?' Judgeing from the mischievous sparkle in Iris's eyes, Mary didn't want to know.

'I'm sure you're about to tell me.'

'I think the real reason you got upset was because you didn't like Joe thinking badly of you.'

'That's a load of hogwash.'

'Admit it, you like him more than you're letting on, and you can't bear to know he found you intimidating at first.'

'I won't dignify that remark with a response.'

'But I'm right, though, aren't I? You wouldn't have been so upset if Sally or I had drawn that picture. You're wound up about it because it was Joe. You want him to think well of you.'

'I… that's rubbish. We're friends, that's all.'

Iris arched an elegant dark-blonde eyebrow. 'I don't remember you putting on make-up to go out with Sally and me. Yet now you've started to go around with Joe, you're suddenly interested in borrowing my lipstick.'

Heat flooded to Mary's face. Iris didn't know yet, but she had liked how the lipstick made her look so much she had dashed to the NAAFI between watches yesterday when she'd heard a new batch of Gala lipsticks had arrived and had queued with other Wrens, WAAFs and ATS girls in the hope of buying one of the precious refillable lipsticks. Not only had she been one of the lucky few, managing to purchase one in a gorgeous shade of wine red, she had also picked up a powder compact which matched her skin tone perfectly. 'You know I never wore make-up until I came here. I like it. I'll probably wear it more often now I know how it looks.'

'Now you know Joe likes it, you mean.'

'No! I like it for myself. I never wore make-up for Owen.'

Iris threw up her hands in a gesture of surrender. 'Keep your hair on. I was only teasing.'

There was another pause while they both did another visual sweep to check for signal lights. Then Iris said, 'I think you and Joe would be perfect together, though.'

'Honestly, Iris, can't a girl be friends with a bloke without her friends planning what to wear to the wedding?'

'Think about it, though. You're perfect for each other – you've got so much in common. You're both visual signallers, you enjoy one another's company, and you are both artists. If I were Sally, I'd say you were destined to be together.'

Mary started to wish she hadn't told Iris about the portrait. Now she'd never hear the last of it. She still couldn't shake off the strange feeling that she must have made a huge impression on Joe for him to be able to draw her so accurately after such a short acquaintance. 'I admit we've got a lot in common. That's why we're friends. But I think we're too alike for anything more. Look at you and Rob – you're completely different.'

Iris tilted her head. 'We might come from very different backgrounds, but we still have a lot in common or I don't think we could have made it as a couple. We want the same things in life.'

On pondering Iris's statement for a moment, Mary realised that it was true. Iris had changed in the year Mary had known her. At first she had been a spoiled girl who thought she needed a wealthy husband to support her. However, a lot had happened to her in the past year – not only her relationship with Rob but also getting to know her estranged aunt and the tragedy of her father's death. All these events had taught Iris about who she was deep down and had helped her work out that she would enjoy the challenge of making her own way in life. However successful Rob's dream of owning his own boatyard would turn out to be, Mary knew Iris wouldn't be happy living off Rob's earnings and would be determined to make her own contribution.

'Maybe you're right.' All this was not helping her argument, though, and she clutched at the first objection that came to mind. 'But anyway, I'm not an artist, so we don't have that in common.'

'I've seen your drawings. You're an artist. You might not be inspired to draw at the moment, but who can blame you with all that's happened?'

Mary hadn't looked at it that way before. She'd considered her ability to draw gone forever, yet Iris seemed to regard it as a temporary loss. Was Iris right? Even though Owen was never coming back, would she one day regain her urge to draw?

It was only then that another thought struck. She had been able to consider Owen's death without the sense of suffocating desolation that had always assailed her before. The ache of loss was still there, and she didn't think it would ever completely go, but she seemed to be able to think of him without the giddy sensation that she was about to plunge into a deep, black chasm. Maybe there was hope for her after all.

Chapter Ten

As the *Kelpie* sailed through Hoy Sound, Joe couldn't resist a glance up at Kyeness where he could just make out the boxy concrete outline of the signal station. Time had dragged since he had last seen Mary, and he had missed being able to signal her. Even before their friendship had developed and she had returned curt, discouraging responses, he had enjoyed the challenge. Now his duties had returned him to the west side of the Mainland, it felt good to be back in this part of Orkney where he could at least signal to Mary when their watches coincided, even if he couldn't see her on shore.

In fact, if he remembered correctly, she should be on watch now. He had memorised her schedule the last time they had met. Even as the thought occurred to him, a light flashed from the signal station, sending a routine challenge. There was a chance it would be Mary's oppo, of course, although he thought he recognised Mary's speedy, fluent style. He had also noticed that Mary always seemed to do the signalling when she knew Joe would be on watch.

He aimed his lamp and sent back the standard response, naming his ship. When the signal came back showing his message had been received, he took a chance and sent: 'Mary?'

'Yes,' came the reply, and Joe's heart leapt. 'How r u?'

This was new – Mary had always answered his unofficial messages before, but never initiated one of her own. Could it be that Mary had missed him? Aware that his messages could be read by anyone watching, he didn't like to ask. Anyway, he didn't want to do anything to spoil their friendship. However, he raised his lamp again and sent, 'V well. Glad 2 b back.' He hoped she would read between the lines and realise he was glad to be in contact with her again. Then he sent, '48-hour leave from 2morrow. Can we meet?'

He awaited her reply with bated breath. The island was shrouded with dark grey clouds that seemed to skim the roof of the signal station, and a bitter wind froze his fingers, making it difficult to press the lamp shutter. Nevertheless, he felt as though he were bathed in warm sunlight when Mary replied, 'C u at 1400 2morrow. Bhive.' That was easy to work out – the Beehive cafe in Stromness.

He looked across at the other three ships in the group with a fresh sense of purpose. The cold and tedium of standing watch no longer seemed so unappealing, even when the clouds did look as though they were poised to release snow at any moment. The prospect of seeing Mary's face again after nearly four weeks apart made it all worth it.

He thought about his reply for a while, then sent back, 'Will have t 4 2 w8ting.' He would see what she made of that.

While he tried to think up some other coded comments for Mary to decipher, he idly tracked a fishing boat approaching Hoy Sound from the north. It was the *Puffin*, belonging to Malcolm Spence from Stromness. He knew the man by sight and waved when they passed, so close the *Kelpie's* wake made the smaller vessel pitch violently and veer a little from her course. Thinking to save Mary the trouble of identifying the fishing boat herself, Joe sighted the signal station and was about to let her know the boat's name – any excuse for another exchange of signals – when he saw a light flash from the *Levington*. He immediately called to his oppo to take down the message.

When he saw the signal, his mouth went dry. Another possible U-boat. He relayed the message to the bridge, praying it was another false alarm. Otherwise there could be a U-boat somewhere beneath them, perhaps about to fire a torpedo at this very moment. It had to be a false alarm, though. They were just within the invisible boundary created by the anti-submarine indicator loop, and Mary would have signalled if a U-boat had been detected crossing.

There was a flurry of activity on the bridge, and the skipper snapped out commands to attempt to intercept the U-boat, if U-boat it was. Then came the call to Joe that he'd been expecting. 'Yeoman of signals, make to Kyeness: "Submarine detected. Request air support. Group moving to intercept."' He then gave the bearing and range.

With the *Kelpie* being tossed about on the waves, and her distance from Kyeness approaching the maximum range for visual signals, Joe was grateful to have Mary on the receiving end of his message, for they were attuned to one another's styles. With some of the longer words, he was able to use the shorthand he and Mary had developed between themselves, knowing she would understand. As had happened the last time they had encountered a U-boat, some of his fear drained away knowing that she was watching out for him, which was illogical, seeing as there was nothing she could do. Or maybe it was just being able to communicate with her that made him feel less alone. That and the fact that the skipper kept him busy sending signals to *Kelpie*'s sister ships.

Joe knew time was of the essence. The U-boat crew must know that it had been detected and would surely be trying to evade the minesweepers. Even if the Germans didn't know the precise location of the minefield located at the other end of Hoy Sound, they would guess it was there and would only attempt to get through to Scapa Flow if they were feeling suicidal. The question was, would its captain attempt to sink one of the minesweepers before making its escape? The hairs on the back of Joe's neck tingled as he worked, expecting at any moment to feel the deck shudder beneath his feet as a torpedo struck. He knew that the Asdic operators on each ship would be desperately listening for pings to indicate the location of the U-boat or, heaven forbid, a torpedo. He gazed across the water separating the *Kelpie* from the other minesweepers. Was that a light slick of oil, betraying the presence of a U-boat, or was it his imagination?

Even as that thought crossed his mind, the skipper ordered a hard turn to starboard. Joe staggered as the ship turned. What was happening? Then a cry came from a crewman, pointing over the starboard rails: 'Torpedo tracks!' And Joe knew the skipper must have ordered the manoeuvre in response to a report from the Asdic oper-ator.

The skipper ordered another direction change, and Joe strained his eyes, trying in vain to see the trail the crewman had reported. In the background he could hear the skipper shouting more orders.

Time slowed. Joe clung to a rail to steady himself. The ice-cold metal burned his fingers, and his pulse hammered inside his throat. He counted out the seconds. Five… ten… fifteen. How far away was the torpedo? How long until it hit? Thirty seconds… forty-five. The skipper was still shouting orders and listening to a report from the lieutenant in the Asdic compartment. Surely the torpedo should have struck by now?

Another course change, and now the voices on the bridge were edged with grim determination rather than desperation. Time returned to its normal speed, and Joe discovered his fingers were turning white. He released his grip and massaged the life back into his hand, drawing deep breaths. The torpedo must have missed, and now the minesweepers were moving in on the U-boat. Joe guessed that between Asdic readings and the torpedo's course, the skipper must have pinpointed the submarine's location. Sure enough, he called to Joe to send course changes to each ship, and Joe set to work. As he sent his signals, he spared a thought for the *Puffin*, which he had seen only moments before the U-boat had been detected. Much to his relief, he spotted it entering Hoy Sound, well away from danger.

The minutes stretched out, and the tension built up to almost unbearable levels. Joe was glad to be on watch and busy; the concentration required to send and interpret signals helped keep his mind off the possibility of a torpedo strike at any moment. Even so, when it became clear the skipper had managed to close in on the U-boat's position, the muscles in Joe's chest became so tight he couldn't seem to draw enough oxygen from the air.

Then came the report from the Asdic compartment: the latest reading put the U-boat only a short distance in front of the *Kelpie*. The skipper ordered them to sail on for a moment then snapped the order to release a depth charge. All the noises around Joe faded as he waited for the explosion. A moment later, a fountain of water shot up from the depths to their stern. Joe's heart sank when he saw it was white with no trace of smoke or oil. They had missed. A second later there was another explosion in the distance. Joe looked around, confused, looking for signs of oil or debris that indicated they had struck the U-boat after all. Then he saw smoke rising from the HMS *Snow Queen*'s stern. While they had been attempting to hit the U-boat, the enemy had managed a strike of their own, and this one had succeeded.

The skipper ordered another course change, this time to go to the *Snow Queen*'s aid. From the way it had started to list in the water, it was clear it was going down. All they could do was pray as many of her crew made it to the life rafts as possible. His thoughts flew to the *Snow Queen*'s yeoman of signals, Matthew Parkins. They had met a few times and got on well. Where was he – scrambling for a raft or trapped below, surrounded by icy water? It was a horrible, helpless feeling to see men jumping overboard and knowing there was nothing he could do to help. As he watched, the lifeboats splashed into the sea. The *Snow Queen*'s stern was now beneath the water, tipping at an ever increasing angle; he doubted anyone left below decks would have time to escape.

Lieutenant Commander Gamble called to Joe. 'Make to Kyeness: "*Snow Queen* lost. Location of U-boat unknown".'

As Joe hurried to obey, he could only pray the U-boat was now making good its escape rather than lying in wait for the rescue ships. Although they would all be on the alert, it would be easy to miss the signs in the confusion.

–

Up in Kyeness, Mary had watched the drama unfold with bated breath, and when black smoke had erupted from one of the minesweepers she had felt sick. She had swung the telescope around, heedless of the icy gale that flew in through the open lights, and focused on the stricken ship, blinking to clear her suddenly blurred vision. But at that distance, she still couldn't make out the identity of the ship. Watching the minesweeper tilt and slide beneath the waves, she both wanted to look away and couldn't tear her eyes from the sight. Was that how it had been for Owen?

Then light flashed from one of the other ships: 'Kelpie to Kyeness,' the message opened. She sagged with relief, and heard Iris, who had been taking down the message, give a little sob. There was no time for exclamations, for the body of the message needed to be recorded and reported. Even so, it was a comfort to recognise Joe's signalling style and know that he was safe.

'I can't believe I wanted to work in a big base like Portsmouth,' Iris said in a breathless voice when there was nothing more they could do again but watch. 'And if I ever complain about being bored on watch, remind me about today. The thought of Rob being in the engine room, out there with a U-boat on the prowl…' She put a hand to her chest and blew out a shaky breath.

The telephone rang, making both the girls jump. Iris answered. Mary, who was concentrating on the sea, couldn't see her face, although from the tone of her voice she knew Iris must be frowning. 'Nothing's crossed in either direction,' Iris said.

After another pause she said, 'Yes, sir.' There came the clatter of the receiver being replaced, then Iris joined Mary at the window. 'Nothing's crossed the loop in the last five minutes, has it?'

Mary shook her head. 'Not so much as a fishing boat. I'd have seen.' A shiver went down her spine. 'Why, has something crossed the loop?'

'Yes, but they couldn't tell which direction. It could be the same U-boat leaving.'

Or it could be a second one arriving to join the fight. Neither of them said it, although Mary could see her own horror reflected in Iris's eyes.

Iris took the Aldis lamp. 'I have to signal the *Kelpie* to let them know.'

Mary listened to the rapid clicks of the lamp shutters opening and closing, able to follow the message from the sounds: 'Kyeness to *Kelpie*: loop signal detected. Watch for 2nd U-boat.'

'I really hope it was the first one leaving,' Iris said when she'd finished.

Mary gazed out to where the minesweepers were little more than a blur on the horizon. Looking through the telescope, she said, 'The other ships have reached the *Snow Queen*. They're bringing in the survivors.' Even as she watched, the last of the *Snow Queen* disappeared beneath the waves.

'There are more boats coming from Stromness,' Iris said.

Mary glanced in their direction. 'They'll be too late for anyone in the water,' she said. 'No one could survive long in the water when it's this cold.'

Iris went pale, and Mary was instantly contrite. She'd been so caught up thinking about Owen, Joe and Rob that she'd forgotten Iris's father had been killed in the spring when his ship had been struck by a mine. Iris had had a hard time accepting it at first, because no one had known exactly how he died. There had been no ships nearby to rescue survivors, though, so Charles Tredwick's last moments must have been spent in the icy cold water. Mary squeezed Iris's arm. 'I'm sorry. That was thought-less. I forgot about your father.'

From Iris's expression, Mary could tell Iris wished she could forget about his fate. She recovered herself and gave Mary a tight smile. 'I try not to think about what might have happened, because it would drive me mad. Let's think about something else.'

Mary could sympathise with that and peered back through her telescope at the minesweepers. There was no trace of the *Snow Queen* now, and two life rafts were on the water, obviously searching for all the survivors. 'I think the signal Lower Skaill picked up must have been the U-boat getting away. It couldn't have missed the minesweepers now they're all clustered together.'

'I think you're right,' Iris said, making an obvious attempt to push her father's fate to the back of her mind. 'What gets me, though, is how it got across undetected in the first place.'

'I know. That's worrying me. You don't think they've found a way to disable the loop?'

'In that case, why did it set off the signal when they crossed again?'

'Perhaps it was a beam or something they had to switch on and they were in too much of a hurry when they were escaping to disable the loop again.'

'You could be right.' Iris went to pick up the blanket she'd left discarded on her chair and threw it over her shoulders before returning to the window. 'Anyway, in case the U-boat is still out there, I'm going to keep my eyes peeled. I'd never forgive myself if another ship was torpedoed as a result of my inattention.'

A roar overhead made Mary look up in time to see four biplanes swooping down over the minesweepers and start circling. The Swordfish sent from RNAS Hatston had arrived at last. If there were any U-boats still out there, the Swordfish would either destroy them or, at the very least, chase them away from Hoy Sound.

Mary could relax, although she didn't let her vigilance slide. Together, she and Iris spent the remainder of their watch scanning the waters, looking for the slightest sign of a vessel lurking beneath the water. As the minutes passed with no further attacks, it became clear there had been only one U-boat, which had triggered the signal on the loop when it escaped. Eventually the aircraft abandoned their hunt and returned to base. Nevertheless, Mary and Iris remained on full alert until their shift ended.

Chapter Eleven

'White rabbit!' Sally's voice tore Mary from a pleasant dream she'd been having. The next moment she heard the click of the light switch, and a golden glow flooded the room. Mary groaned and scowled at Sally, who flung open the wardrobe door and pulled out a warm jumper.

'What did you wake me up for? It's our first day off together for ages.' Not to mention that Mary had been so wound up following the events of the previous day that she had been unable to get to sleep until the small hours.

'It's the first of December. That means we've only got twenty-four days left to organise the Heddles' perfect Christmas. Anyway, after the day you two had yesterday, I think we need to make it a special day and do something to put us in the Christmas spirit.'

A moment later, Sally bounded to Mary's side, and before Mary could gather her wits to work out what was about to happen, Sally pinched her arm, albeit gently, then thumped her just below the shoulder. 'Pinch, punch, first day of the month and no returns.'

'Do we have to do this every month?' Mary rubbed her arm, although Sally had not put much weight behind her blow.

Sally looked wounded. 'Don't you want good luck this month?'

The Mary of a year ago would have snapped that saying 'white rabbit' hadn't saved her from losing her fiancé. Now, however, she had learned to tolerate Sally's superstitions and even take amusement from them. They were part of who Sally was, and much as Mary teased her for it, she wouldn't have her friend any other way.

With another groan, she swung her legs out of the bed, sucking in a hissing breath as her feet hit the cold lino. 'Well, if I wasn't awake before, I am now. I swear this floor could double as an ice rink.'

Iris was still only visible as a mound under her blankets. Grinning, Mary grabbed the blankets and tore them back, then, deciding to get there before Sally, did her best to pinch Iris's upper arm through the layers of her pyjama top, a jumper and a cardigan. 'Pinch, punch, first day of the month. White rabbit, no returns.'

Quick as a flash, Iris's fist shot out and caught Mary on the shoulder. 'A punch and a kick' – Iris swung her right foot out of bed, catching Mary above the knee before she could jump aside – 'for being so quick.' She staggered to her feet, pushing her feet into her slippers and squinted at the windows. Even covered in their blackout blinds, it was obviously still pitch dark outside. 'What's the time?'

Mary glanced at her alarm clock. 'Seven.' She scurried to the wardrobe and pulled out her warmest clothes. Drifting up from the lower floor, she could hear the voices of the other Wrens as they left their cabins and headed for the ablutions.

Washed and dressed – something they did as quickly as possible in the freezing conditions – they were soon in the ground floor mess, with bowls of porridge and steaming mugs of tea in front of them. Mary stirred the lumpy porridge, scowling. When they had first arrived in Orkney, there had been no shortage of eggs or even bacon, and the Wrens on Orkney had enjoyed a far greater variety of food than their counterparts in other parts of Britain. Now, however, even though Mary knew food was still in plentiful supply in Orkney, they had to do without the luxuries more often. Today was a case in point, and there was nothing but porridge, without even any fruit to liven it up. It was only the knowledge that people were going hungry elsewhere that enabled her to force down the bland mess.

'What are the plans for the day?' Iris asked after finishing the last spoonful with a shudder.

'Christmas preparations, of course,' Sally replied. 'Have you forgotten – we arranged to make decorations.'

Mary squirmed. 'I told Joe I'd meet him at 1400 hours. I'd lost track of the date and forgot we'd arranged to work on the Christmas decorations today.' She went on in a rush before the others could object. 'After yesterday I really want to see him. It was bad enough watching the *Snow Queen* go down from the safety of Kyeness. It must have been terrifying for the crews of the minesweepers, not knowing if the U-boat was still on the prowl; expecting a torpedo at any moment.'

The light faded from Sally's face, and she leaned across the table. 'Of course we don't mind. Do we, Iris?'

Iris shook her head. 'I'd see Rob if I could, but he hasn't got leave.'

'That's settled then,' Sally said. 'We'll work on the decorations this morning and Mary will be free to see Joe this afternoon.'

The others agreed and there was silence for a while as the girls sipped their tea. Then Sally said, 'The most important thing to arrange is a Christmas tree. It's not Christmas without a tree. Any ideas?'

'Before the war, my father would take me for a walk in the woods, and we would collect holly and ivy and other greenery to make garlands,' Iris said. 'Our gardener always used to order our Christmas tree, though.'

'Look around you,' Mary said, resisting the urge to tease Iris about having staff to decorate the house. 'Orkney isn't exactly famous for its woodlands.'

'What did you do, then? You can't have had many trees in Pembrokeshire.'

'There were trees inland along the river, and up by the woollen mill, where I worked.' Mary tapped the rim of her cup while she thought. 'I know. Driftwood! If we can scavenge enough pieces, we could make a model tree from it.'

'That's a wonderful idea,' Sally said, her eyes shining.

'You'd have to put it together at Curlew Croft once you'd collected the wood, though,' Iris said. 'It'd be too fragile to carry it over the cliffs already made up. It's a shame, because it won't be a surprise.'

'Not a problem,' Sally said. 'I think it would be nice to have the tree up as soon as possible. It'll brighten the place up. We can bring the decorations as we make them, so the tree will fill up as the month goes on.'

'That's sorted, then. We'll go on a hunt for driftwood this morning. What can we use for decorations?'

'We could crochet some snowflakes and stars with string,' Iris said. She glanced at her watch. 'There's still over two hours before the sun comes up, so we can't go out searching for driftwood yet. Let's make a start on the decorations once we've tidied the cabin. I'm sure I've got some red and green ribbons, too. They'd add a lovely splash of colour to the tree.'

Accordingly, once their cabin was neat enough to satisfy the eagle eye of Second Officer Wendleton, they collected string and crochet hooks from Iris's sewing supplies and made a start on the snowflakes and stars under Iris's guidance. At first Mary kept losing count and had to unravel her first attempts. However, by the time the sun had risen, she had three snowflakes beside her that she felt were good enough to hang on the tree. Sally had managed five and Iris eight.

'That's a good start,' Iris said, gathering up the completed decorations. 'All we need now is a tree.'

'Any ideas where we can find driftwood?' Mary asked, rotating her shoulders to ease their stiffness after being hunched over her task.

'I don't know – a beach, maybe?' Iris's cut-glass accent dripped with sarcasm.

'Yes, I know, but we need somewhere where any driftwood won't have been grabbed within thirty seconds of it reaching dry land.'

Mary saw comprehension dawn in Iris's expression. On an island where wood was in short supply, driftwood was a precious commodity and didn't linger on the shore.

'We could try Kye Geo,' Sally said, naming the inlet where Archie kept his boat. 'I'm sure I've heard him mention making driftwood fires sometimes when he works down there.'

'Good idea.' Mary glanced at her watch. 'It's 0945 now, so that gives us plenty of time to get there and back before lunch.' Not to mention her meeting with Joe. After yesterday's fright there was no way she was missing that; she needed to reassure herself Joe was whole and well.

After bundling up in their warmest clothes, they set out. At Sally's insistence, they sang Christmas carols as they marched up the path over the headland to get themselves in the mood. 'We have to do it properly,' she'd insisted, as though there were a special formula you had to follow for bringing Christmas to the Heddles. Although Mary had been sceptical when Sally had introduced the idea, by the time they had finished their first two carols ('God Rest Ye Merry, Gentlemen' and 'Hark! The Herald Angels Sing'), all her inhibitions had disappeared, and she launched into 'Ding Dong Merrily on High' with gusto. She had, after all, been brought up in a chapel-going Welsh family to whom singing was almost as vital as breathing.

It probably helped that it was one of those rare days on Orkney when, although dark clouds gathered on the horizon, the sky overhead was blue and the view was crystal clear. The hills of Hoy, whose tops had been shrouded by low cloud for the past three days, towered tall, touched with gold from the low sunlight. There was even a slight frost shining silver on the withered grass by the side of the path.

'What next?' Sally asked as their arrival at the top of the winding path that led down into Kye Geo coincided with the end of another song.

'"I Saw Three Ships",' Mary said, without hesitation. What could be more appropriate on a day like today, when the sea sparkled, reflecting the deep blue sky? She drew a deep breath of the crisp, clean air and launched into the song. Looking out to sea as they trooped down the path, she half expected to see three sailing boats skimming across the waves, loaded with costly treasures from exotic lands.

A movement in the long grass further along the cliff caught her eye, and she paused, looking back. Nothing.

Probably a bird or a rabbit. A little farther down the path, however, there was a clump of heather; a scrap of paper was snagged upon it, flapping in the breeze. It couldn't have been there long; Mary guessed the movement she had seen had been the paper fluttering down from the cliff top. She reached out to pluck it from the branch, only for a gust of wind to whip it from the shrub just as her fingers had been about to close upon it. She caught a brief impression of a list of words and figures before it was gone, fluttering out to sea.

'Did you see that?' she asked the others, who were ahead of her.

Iris turned, brows raised. 'See what?'

'The paper. It must have been dropped by someone up on the cliffs.'

Iris shook her head and walked on. Mary turned and gazed back to the cliff top. She thought she caught the briefest glimpse of a dark shape in the corner of her eye but when she looked in that direction it was gone.

Chapter Twelve

Sally's voice floated up from the bottom of the path. 'Hurry up. There's loads of driftwood down here.'

Giving herself a mental shake, Mary hurried to catch up. There was no law against walking on the cliffs, and whoever it was had every right to be there. Yesterday's events had clearly made her jumpy; that was all. If she allowed herself to be suspicious of a mere piece of paper floating in the wind, she would never get another wink of sleep. She should forget about it and trust the powers that be to ensure there were no further U-boat incursions. In the meantime, what better way to cast off the jitters than a day spent preparing for Christmas with her friends?

Down on the shore, there was indeed a good supply of driftwood. In places it had been stacked out of reach of the tide, probably by Archie.

'Should we take it, do you think?' Iris asked. 'It seems a bit of a cheek to rob him of his supply of driftwood.'

'He can have it back after Christmas,' Mary said. 'It's not as if we're burning it. And it's for him and Elspeth, so it's better to take it from here. If we go to a different beach, we could be denying someone else of wood they desperately need.'

'I suppose you're right.' Iris picked up a stick and brushed away the sand, grit and seaweed. Once cleaned, it was revealed to be pale grey and smoothed by the action of the sea, its grain clearly visible, displaying every twist and knot in the wood. Iris frowned. 'It doesn't look very Christmassy. We should be collecting holly.'

'Where from?' Sally spread her arms wide, taking in the coastline and the distinct lack of trees. 'Anyway, I've got an idea. If we collect sticks varying in length, from this' – she flourished one that was about the length of her arm then picked up another much shorter piece – 'to this, we can stack them in a kind of cone shape. I'm sure the Heddles will be able to lend us a hammer and tin tacks to hold it together. Then we can hang our decorations on the end of each stick.'

'I suppose that would work.'

They bent to their task, chatting merrily, not caring about the cold or that the clouds swept in to shut out the sunlight. Soon, they had enough driftwood to make a tree about three feet high.

'We could stand it on a stool, draped with some pretty fabric,' Iris said, seeming more enthusiastic now. 'It would look perfect next to the fireplace.'

Sally glanced at her watch. 'We need to get a move on if we don't want to miss dinner.'

'I don't fancy lugging this lot all the way to the Wrennery,' Iris said. 'Should we take it to Curlew Croft?'

'How about the signal station?' Mary said. 'It will dry out properly there and we can clean it up during our watches. That way we won't be cluttering up the Heddles' kitchen with a load of driftwood. We're supposed to be cheering them up, remember, not filling their house with rubbish.'

The others agreed and after a short detour to the signal station to drop off the wood, they hurried back to Stromness.

'I feel all Christmassy now,' Sally said as they left Kyeness behind. 'I think that was the perfect start to December.'

Mary, on the point of replying, stopped when something cold and soft brushed her nose. Looking up, she saw white flakes tumbling down from the clouds.

Sally saw it at the same time. 'Snow!' she cried, spreading her arms wide and turning in a circle as though trying to catch as many snowflakes as possible. 'Now it really does feel like Christmas.'

Mary couldn't deny a thrill of excitement. Snow rarely fell on the Pembrokeshire coast, and the sight of it sent her back to her early childhood, when a fresh snowfall seemed a work of magic and her life was untouched by sorrow.

'I think it's a sign,' Sally said. 'A sign that this is going to be the best Christmas ever.'

And instead of scoffing, Mary linked arms with her friends, and they scampered down the path, laughing and squealing as the increasingly heavy snow clung to their coats and stuck to their eyelashes. Maybe Sally was right, and this year would be the first Christmas she had enjoyed in a long time.

-

Perhaps it was the lingering Christmas spirit, but Mary felt a flutter of excitement when she left the Wrennery after lunch to meet Joe at the Beehive. No, not excitement, she told herself. It was simply that after the scare of the day before, she was anxious to see for herself that Joe was whole and well. She also wanted to know his thoughts on how the U-boat had managed to get into the protected waters of the Home Fleet without triggering the loop.

Reaching the Beehive involved a steep climb up stone steps, and this afternoon the climb was made more hazardous by the layer of snow. Although the snow had stopped, it had fallen thick and fast on the walk back to the Wrennery, and the streets and roofs were blanketed in a good inch. Heedless of the ice, she took the steps two at a time. No matter that she would be pink in the face when Joe saw her, she needed to see for herself that he was unharmed.

The absence of pubs in Stromness meant the Beehive was popular with the many servicemen and women in the town. Today was no exception, and Mary entered the room to see all the tables occupied. She was on the point of leaving, thinking she would have to wait for Joe outside and find somewhere else when she saw him waving from a corner table.

'Good job I got here early,' Joe said as Mary shrugged off her coat and hung it on a nearby coat stand.

Once Mary had sat down and placed her order, she leaned across the table. The room was filled with the buzz of conversation and the clatter of cutlery, so there was little chance of them being overheard. Nevertheless, Mary was careful to pitch her voice low. 'It's such a relief to see you after yesterday. Are you all right?'

'Right as rain.'

Mary studied Joe's face. Was she imagining it, or was he paler than usual? There was also a tightness around his eyes and mouth that hinted at strain. 'Something's wrong, though,' she said. 'I mean, obviously something's wrong – a U-boat sank one of our ships. I meant you, though. Are you sure nothing's wrong?'

'There's nothing wrong with me. But one of my friends was on the *Snow Queen*, and he was one of the ones that didn't make it.'

'I'm so sorry.' Mary felt like an idiot. She'd watched the desperate rescue effort, yet had been so relieved Joe's ship had been undamaged, she had forgotten to ask if any of the *Snow Queen's* crew had been lost. It should have been the first thing she'd asked. 'How many were…' She couldn't say 'killed'. 'How many didn't make it?'

'Only three. At least with the other minesweepers nearby, we were able to pick up the survivors before they all succumbed to the cold.'

'It's still three too many, though. What was your friend's name?'

'Matthew Parkins.' Joe picked up the sugar tongs and twirled them between his fingers. 'He'd just got married. Last time I saw him, he was about to go on leave, and he married his sweetheart while he was home.'

'How awful. His poor wife.'

'I know. I've spent the morning writing her a letter. It's the least I could do.'

That explained his distress. Young men Joe's age should be enjoying time with their friends, looking forward to what the future had in store, not writing letters of condolence to a friend's widow. A helpless anger swept through Mary as she thought of all the lives the war had cut short. How many more before it was finally over?

She reached across the table and pressed Joe's hand. 'It must have been hard, but it was a thoughtful gesture, and I know Matthew's wife will appreciate it.' She thought of the dearth of communication after Owen's death. 'After Owen was killed, no one could tell me exactly how it happened, and the not knowing nearly sent me mad.'

Joe nodded. A moment later, he returned her grip, clutching her hand as though grasping a lifeline. Mary made no effort to extricate herself, instead pouring all the comfort she could muster into the touch, hoping Joe wouldn't read more into it than intended. Although it had been intended purely as comfort to Joe, she felt oddly comforted herself. Thinking of poor Matthew Parkins' wife and all those lost in this terrible war, brought home to her that she was not alone. She wasn't the only person grieving the loss of a loved one. Of course, she had supported Iris through the loss of her father, and she had been aware of other deaths since coming to Orkney, yet this was the first time the knowledge seemed to reach her heart. Perhaps witnessing the sinking of the *Snow Queen* made the deaths of Matthew Parkins and his two shipmates seem more personal. Gradually, however, her focus homed in on her hand where it touched Joe's. His hand was warm and strong around hers and she was struck with the crazy thought that she didn't want him to let go. Where had that come from? She and Joe were just friends; she had made that clear from the start and didn't want anything to change between them. Why, then, did she have a heightened awareness of the exact places where his fingers pressed the back of her hand, the faint pulse beating in time with hers between their joined palms? She should pull away, yet a strange heaviness weighed down her limbs, and she couldn't seem to find the strength. Or the will.

'Here's your tea, my dears.'

The waitress placed the tray upon the table between Mary and Joe, the teacups rattling. Mary jumped, snatching her hand away from Joe's. She felt sure her hand must be glowing scarlet and was surprised to see it looking the same as ever. Somehow she managed to smile at the waitress and thank her in a voice that betrayed only the slightest quaver.

Once the waitress had left, Mary struggled to pick up the thread of the conversation. She had been holding Joe's hand – there was no problem recalling that – yet she couldn't remember whose turn it was to speak or what exactly had just been said.

Thankfully, Joe spoke, saving her the awkwardness of repeating herself unintentionally. 'I thought of you when the *Snow Queen* went down. After you told me how your fiancé was lost with the *Royal Oak*, I remembered how when you first arrived, you tried to find out more about the *Royal Oak* from Rob.'

Mary winced. 'Don't remind me. I made a complete idiot of myself.'

'That's not true.' Joe poured milk into each cup then continued in a gentle voice. 'It's perfectly understandable you would want to find out all you could about your fiancé's last moments. I can't imagine what it must be like to get such terrible news delivered in an impersonal telegram.'

Mary blinked back tears, overcome by Joe's perception. While it had been Owen's parents who had broken the dreadful news to her that day, the fact remained that they'd had no more information than the few stark words in the telegram. 'It was torture,' she said, her voice husky. 'I would lie awake at night, imagining all the ways Owen might have died. If only someone could have told me it was quick and painless, it would have helped. But of course, I'll never know.'

'That's what I thought.' Joe fiddled with a teaspoon, apparently unaware he was doing it. 'It made me realise that, painful as it might be for Matthew's wife, she would appreciate more information about the *Snow Queen*. Although I don't know what Matthew's last moments were like, at least I could tell her what his life had been like on Orkney.'

'I'm sure that will help, even if she can't bear to read about it at first.' Mary realised she had been staring at Joe's hands, transfixed by his long, strong fingers as they twisted the spoon. She tore away her gaze and poured the tea while she framed her next words, remembering how the people around her had treated her after learning of her loss. 'When Owen died it seemed as though everyone was afraid to talk about him in my hearing, as though they didn't want to keep reminding me he was dead. Ridiculous, considering that was literally the only thought in my head most of the time. I would have loved to have heard from his friends about happier times. Although, of course, his close friends were killed at the same time.' Maybe that was why she had turned in on herself for so long after Owen's death. Those who, like her, had known him as a boy, seemed afraid to mention his name in her company while the only men who could have told her more about Owen's time in the navy had also been killed when the *Royal Oak* had gone down. It was as though his entire existence had been erased.

Then Mary's thoughts strayed to Mr and Mrs Thomas, Owen's parents, and she felt a twinge of guilt. While she had written to them a few times since joining the WRNS, communication with the Thomases had been deeply painful and she had kept her letters brief. Perhaps she should follow Joe's example and tell them more about her life in Orkney – or as much as the censors would allow, at any rate. They might appreciate anything that would help them build a picture of Owen's time in the navy. On the other hand, if she told them more about her life, she would have to tell them about her friends, including Joe. She didn't want them to think she had forgotten Owen.

Another silence stretched out between them, and Mary, not wanting either of them to sink into morbid thoughts, changed the subject. 'I still can't get over how a U-boat managed to escape detection.' She glanced around to be sure they couldn't be overheard. 'I mean, how did it get across the loop without setting off a signal? It was picked up when it crossed again. At least, we have to assume it was the same U-boat – there was no other vessel in the vicinity to create the signal.'

'No idea. It was all anyone could talk about last night.'

'I wonder if the Germans have developed a way to evade detection.'

'I suppose it's possible. I mean, we've developed a way to stop ships setting off magnetic mines.' Joe looked grim. 'God, I hope you're wrong. Imagine what would happen if the whole wolf pack got into the anchorage.'

'Too hideous to contemplate. What if yesterday was a test run to see if they could get through?'

Joe tapped the spoon against his teacup, his expression one of deep thought. 'But we picked it up pretty quickly on Asdic, so in a sense the U-boat failed, even if it did get the *Snow Queen* before it left. Anyway, if they'd tried to get through to Scapa Flow, they would have hit the minefield.'

Some of the crushing weight of dread lifted from Mary's shoulders. 'True. And it set off a signal when it crossed back across the loop, remember, so whatever they might have used can't be infallible.'

'Let's hope the Germans decide the risk is too great.' Joe's mouth set in a determined line, and he appeared to study the fern pattern on his teacup for a while. Then he looked up. 'Whatever they decide, I'm going to work extra hard to keep my wits about me when we're at sea. A signalman might only play a small part in tracking U-boats, but as it's the job I've been given, I'm going to do all in my power to make sure we catch the next U-boat before it strikes.' He drained his tea. 'Anyway, that's enough doom and gloom for one day. Let's do something to clear our heads.'

A desire to get out of the stuffy tearoom overtook Mary. She grabbed the coat from the back of her chair. 'Come on. We've still got over an hour of daylight left. Let's go for a walk. I want to see the view before it goes dark again.'

'Speaking of the view, I nearly forgot.' Joe picked up a leather satchel Mary hadn't noticed until that moment. He fished inside and pulled out a sketchbook. He handed it to her. 'This is for you.'

Mary opened it, expecting to see more of Joe's drawings. However, apart from a rough sketch of a church on the first page, the rest of the book was empty. 'What's this for?'

'It's a sketchbook. You use it to make sketches.' He grinned. 'It's not a complicated concept.'

'I know that. I mean, why are you giving it to me?'

'I thought you might find it useful, what with paper being in short supply. I'm sorry I couldn't find one that was completely empty, but this one's only got one drawing in it.'

'You know I don't draw any more.'

'You stopped for a while and that was hardly surprising. Doesn't mean you won't want to start again.'

'But I haven't felt the slightest urge to draw for ages, and you could use this.' She held the book out to Joe, although she felt strangely reluctant to give it up. Probably because she had never had the money for a proper sketchbook and had been forced to do her drawings on the thin paper of her diaries. She surreptitiously slipped a finger inside the book and felt the thickness of each sheet and the high quality rough surface that would take watercolours and pastels as well as pencil. She had always wanted to try watercolours but the paper she had would have fallen apart if she'd tried to paint on it.

Joe shook his head. 'I've got plenty more. Keep it. That way, you've got something to hand should the urge strike.'

'Then thank you.' Making no further attempt to hand it back, she tucked it under her arm. They paid and left the tearoom and set out to stroll along Outertown Road which had a good view across Hoy Sound. Mary slipped her free hand into the crook of Joe's elbow. Just to stop herself from slipping, of course. As they walked, their feet crunching in the fresh snow, the fingers of her other hand kept drifting to the sketchbook, caressing the pages. Despite being unable to imagine wanting to draw again, there was something irresistible about the feel of the paper, its weight and texture. She could almost imagine running a pencil across one of the pages, seeing how the line brought out the dimpled surface of the sheet. Perhaps Joe was right – it was good to know she had paper to hand should she ever want to draw again.

Chapter Thirteen

Three days later, Mary and Sally were in Stromness between watches, searching the shops for items they could give to Elspeth, who was making up a next-of-kin parcel to send to her son. They had made enquiries on Elspeth's behalf and found that relatives could write to family members in prisoner-of-war camps whenever they wanted, subject to strict rules, and send four parcels a year. Elspeth had immediately sat down and dashed off a letter, taking care to write no more than the regulation two sides of notepaper. These letters, however, could not include any enclosures, not even a drawing. With Christmas coming, Elspeth had also wanted to send a parcel right away, and Mary, Iris and Sally hadn't had the heart to say that it was probably too late for it to reach Don in time. They had pored over the *Prisoner of War* magazine from the Red Cross and learned that each parcel had to be processed in London before being sent on. With the numbers of families wanting to send parcels to loved ones in prisoner-of-war camps across Europe, Mary was sure the processing centre must be full to bursting with packages all needing to be checked and rewrapped. Even if the volunteers did process them quickly, they then needed to be transported across Europe and censored by the Germans before finally being sent on to the correct camp. Personally, Mary thought they would be lucky to get a parcel to Don before the spring. Nevertheless, it would be a boost to Elspeth and Archie's spirits to know there was one on the way, and the girls had promised to look out for suitable items when they were off duty.

'Do you think he would like a novel?' Sally paused outside a bookshop. 'I know I would if I was stuck in a camp with nothing to do.' She fingered the St Christopher's medallion around her neck.

'We ought to focus on the basic necessities.'

'Books *are* necessities.'

Mary rolled her eyes. 'If you were stranded on a desert island, what's the first thing you would look for – food, water and shelter or a book?'

'I wouldn't say no to a book on how to survive on a desert island.'

Mary was unable to fight back a smile. 'But supposing there wasn't one lying conveniently close to where you wash ashore?'

'Anyway, Don's not on a desert island. He's in a camp.'

'I know, but remember he would have had nothing but his uniform when he was captured, and who knows what state that was in after his ship was torpedoed. He's dependent on the Germans and the Red Cross for everything, and they're hardly likely to be generous. The magazine mentioned things like soap, razors, pyjamas and towels.'

Sally looked horrified. 'Goodness, I'd never really thought…' She looked down at the pendant. 'It must have been the same for Aldo.' She was speaking of the Italian prisoner of war she'd met while in hospital earlier that year. 'Imagine having nothing but the clothes you're standing in. I can't begin to think what that must be like.' Sally's voice had sunk to a murmur, giving Mary the impression she had forgotten her presence and was talking to herself. 'He had nothing… he even had to hide his St Christopher so it wouldn't be taken from him. Yet he gave it to me.'

By this time she was attracting curious stares from passers-by. A bitterly cold December day was a day for marching from shop to shop in the shortest time possible, hat pulled down and collar turned up against the wind. However, Sally seemed heedless of discomfort and stood, lost in thought, her eyes focused on some distant scene. Mary shot several glances into the warm, welcoming interior of the bookshop until she could bear it no longer. She seized Sally's arm and pulled her through the door. 'Come on. My fingers are going to drop off if we hang outside any longer. If you insist on a book, we'll choose an adventure story for Don, then we'll see if we can get some soap and razors.'

Sally gave no resistance and followed Mary to examine the selection of novels.

'Do you think he'd like a John Buchan?' Sally asked.

'That's Joe's favourite author.' As soon as the words were out of her mouth, Mary wished she could take them back. She had teased Iris about always mentioning Rob in conversations and now she was doing it with Joe.

Thankfully, Sally didn't seem to have noticed. Still holding her St Christopher, she raised her chin and faced Mary with the air of someone who has reached a momentous decision. 'I'm going to send him a parcel, too.'

'Who?' Surely she couldn't mean Joe.

'Aldo, you idiot. Who else?'

'What – why?' Mary frowned. 'You're not getting sweet on him, are you?' Mary hadn't approved of Sally's friendship with the prisoner of war. Not because she had anything against Aldo – although she had only met him a couple of times, he seemed like a kind man who was making the best of a bad situation, even if he tried to push the boundaries of what was permissible for a prisoner. No, it was just that a relationship with an enemy could only be doomed to failure. Mary felt protective of Sally. Superstitious, romantic Sally seemed to lack the layers of protection against the world that others seemed to develop naturally. There was a freshness and innocence to Sally's spirit that Mary would hate her to lose. She had come through her father's death and the serious injury of her beloved uncle with that innocence untarnished. If a man was the cause of Sally losing faith in love and the general goodness of people, she vowed she would make that man sorry he had been born.

'Don't be silly. You know I'm in love with Adam. Which reminds me' – Sally pulled an envelope from her pocket – 'I mustn't forget to post his Christmas card. He hasn't replied to the letter I sent when I heard about his posting to Orkney, so I think it must have gone astray.'

Mary's misgivings over Adam increased, but she held her tongue. After all, it was quite possible Sally's letter *had* gone astray. 'I look forward to meeting him,' she said, silently adding that she would withhold her judgement on Adam until then, and woe betide him if she thought he was toying with Sally's affections.

'I'm sure he'll be in touch soon. I know you'll like him. Anyway,' she said, replacing the envelope in her pocket, 'Aldo was kind to me, so I'd like to do something for him in return.' Sally's face clouded. 'It must be awful to be away from his family at Christmas, in a place he finds cold and dark, not knowing when he'll be able to return home and see his family. At least we're able to go home on leave. It could be years and years before he sees them again.'

'Put like that, I suppose it would be a nice thing to do. I don't mind chipping in.' She didn't have much to spare, but knowing that Aldo had far less made her want to help.

'Really? That's wonderful.' Sally's eyes shone. 'You're the best friend ever.'

Which only made Mary feel worse about disliking Adam.

–

'What a wonderful idea. You've got a kind heart, Sally.' Elspeth, who had been folding a pair of pyjamas for the parcel to Don, bestowed a beaming smile upon Sally, who had just informed Elspeth of her plan to send a parcel to Aldo.

'Do you really think so?' Sally paused in the act of arranging the driftwood by length. 'I was worried you might not approve, considering what happened to Don.'

'Nonsense. Your Italian lad's got a mother at home who's probably worried sick about him, as I am for my poor Don. I'd like to think there are generous women looking out for our boys who are POWs in Germany. At times like this, when the world is filled with hate and suspicion, I think we women need to set an example and remind people about the power of compassion.'

It was three days after Mary and Sally had shopped for Don's parcel. Mary, Sally and Iris all had the afternoon off duty and had taken the now cleaned and dried driftwood to Curlew Croft to make the Christmas tree. The *Kelpie* was anchored off Hoy for a few days, needing repairs, so both Joe and Rob had been granted leave and were staying at Curlew Croft. Although Elspeth had protested that they needed rest and should use the time to relax, both of them had helped with some of the heavy work that needed doing around the farm. There were more pails of water by the door and beside the sink, and a good supply of the dried peats were stacked beside the fireplace. When she had arrived, Mary had noticed that several cracked roof tiles had been replaced. Now it was dark, they sat in the large kitchen by lamplight, examining the driftwood and trying to decide upon the best way to build a Christmas tree.

'I won't be able to afford much, but I'll try and put together some basics like soap and razors. I've got some chocolate coupons saved up, so I'll see if I can get hold of a slab of chocolate for him as well.' Sally, looking gratified with Elspeth's approval, arranged the largest pieces of driftwood on the floor in a circle.

'You don't have to do it all by yourself,' Elspeth said. 'I'll put in a pair of socks and a spare face flannel.'

'That's ever so kind, but you don't have to. I don't want to take anything that you'd intended for Don.'

'Nonsense. I want to. There's still plenty for Don.'

'I'll send something too,' Iris said. 'I bought a pair of woollen gloves for Don, only Elspeth had already got some, so Aldo's welcome to them. I've got more than enough of the brushed cotton I used to make a pair of pyjamas for Don.' She pointed at the folded blue striped pyjamas set aside for inclusion in Don's parcel. 'I could make a pair for Aldo if someone gives me a hand with the hems.'

'I will,' Mary said. Listening to the others' approval of Sally's scheme made her feel ashamed of her initial disapproval. Sally was right – Aldo had seemed a kind, friendly lad who, after all, could not be to blame for where he was born. Having paid for some shaving soap for Don's parcel, and having already bought or made gifts for her parents and her friends here on Orkney, she'd only had enough money to enclose a few cigarettes. The others' generosity made her want to contribute more. 'I can't sew anywhere near as neatly as you, though.'

'That doesn't matter. I'll use the same pattern as I used for Don's pyjamas and do all the cutting and placing of seams.' Iris was already fishing the pattern from the sewing box. 'I've got a free day tomorrow, so that should be plenty of time to put the pieces together, and I can sew the seams at quiet moments on watch. It would save a lot of time if you could sew the hems and add the buttons.'

'I can do that,' Mary said, glad she could help. 'By the time Sally has found out how to send a parcel to the POW camp, we'll have them ready.'

'You're all so kind. Thank you. I'll be able to enjoy Christmas more knowing we've helped make it a little easier for Aldo.' Sally looked at the pile of driftwood. 'Now, where shall we put the tree?'

Elspeth suggested the parlour, where it was less likely to get knocked over by people working in the kitchen. 'We'll eat our Christmas dinner in the kitchen, but we'll all be more comfortable in the parlour for most of the day.'

Seeing Elspeth absorbed in the Christmas preparations reassured Mary they had been right to arrange Christmas at Curlew Croft. It was giving Elspeth and Archie something to occupy the long hours of darkness when they were forced to sit inside. Mary remembered only too well how, after the dreadful loss suffered by her own family, the cheerless midwinter evenings had seemed to stretch out to eternity. She wouldn't wish them on anyone else.

The group moved through to the parlour. Mary hadn't often been there, as life in Curlew Croft tended to revolve around the large kitchen. In the parlour, comfortable chairs were ranged around the fireplace. Lamps were dotted around the room, casting their golden glow on photographs, vases of dried flowers and china figurines. There was also a large bookcase. The first time Mary had been in the room she had consulted it eagerly only to discover it was full mostly of almanacs dating back to the eighteen hundreds, manuals on care of various animals and books on the flora and fauna of Orkney.

There was a round table under the window holding a few newspapers and a book called *Food Facts for the Kitchen Front*; Sally made a beeline for it. 'Why don't we build the tree here?' she said with a glance at Elspeth.

Elspeth nodded. 'It would certainly brighten up this side of the room. We keep the blackout blinds closed all day at this time of year – it's not worth the fuss of opening them when we don't use the room during daylight hours. It does make the room rather gloomy, though. Having the tree here would be perfect.'

They set to work. Archie supplied a lump of wood that was heavy enough to make a stable base, and Rob, claiming his engineering skills made him best qualified, took everything out to Archie's workshop in an outhouse at the back of the cottage. When he returned, there was a neat hole drilled into the base and a hole the same size through the middle of each piece of driftwood. He had also collected a long, narrow steel rod about five feet in length, which he stuck into the drilled hole in the base. Now they could thread the sticks onto the rod, which acted as the trunk of the tree. With the longest sticks at the base, the 'tree' tapered to a point formed by the shortest sticks – little more than twigs – at the top. Once they were all attached to the rod, they arranged the sticks at different angles, giving the whole thing a pleasing, Christmas-tree shape.

They stood back to admire their creation when it was complete.

'That looks even better than I'd expected,' Sally said, walking around the table to view the tree from all angles. 'With the driftwood being nearly white, it looks like a snow-covered tree. I like it.'

Iris went to collect all the string snowflakes they had crocheted, and those, with several green and red ribbons tied in bows, made the tree look very festive.

'The only thing missing is the smell,' Iris said. 'Nothing says Christmas quite like the scent of a real Christmas tree. And oranges. But seeing as we can't have either, this makes a good substitute.'

'We would never put our decorations up before Christmas Eve at home,' Sally said. 'It feels strange to put them up so early. In a good way, though.' She turned slowly, taking in the whole room, her lips pursed. 'It still feels like something is missing, but I don't know what.'

'I think it all looks perfect,' Iris said. 'It's been fun decorating. It's always up to my dad and me to get the tree, but my mother refuses to let anyone else decorate it. It has to look just right for all the parties we have.' Iris bit her lip and looked down, blinking. 'Had,' she corrected herself.

There was an awkward silence. It was clear that for a brief moment, Iris had thought herself back to happier days before her father had been lost with his ship. Mary knew that feeling well. Sometimes when she heard some-thing she knew would have interested Owen, she would still catch herself looking forward to sharing it with him. Then the weight of memory would crush her heart when reality hit and she remembered she would never see him again. It happened less often now. For Iris, though, this was her first Christmas without her father, and the pain must still be sharp, and all the more difficult because she was estranged from her mother.

Mary took a step towards Iris, unsure what to say but wanting to offer comfort. Rob got there first and put his arm around her, drawing her to his side. Iris gave him a weak smile. 'I suppose I ought to try writing to Mother again. She's going to find Christmas very hard this year. Maybe this time she won't send the letter back unopened.'

Rob gave her a squeeze. 'Keep trying. She'll come round before long, I'm sure.'

Elspeth glanced at the clock on the mantelpiece and clapped her hands with a gasp. 'Oh goodness. Did you say you were on watch at six, Sally? We need to eat. We can't send you off to that cold signal station without some hot food inside you.'

And they hurried off to the kitchen to eat Elspeth's delicious root vegetable soup, accompanied by generous chunks of buttered bere bannock.

After tea, Sally had to leave for the signal station while Iris and Mary, who were on first watch the next morning, said they ought to get an early night and would walk with Sally to Kyeness. Although Joe and Rob were staying at Curlew Croft that night, they both announced they would walk the girls to the Wrennery.

'It'll be like old times, walking up and down that path in the dark,' Joe said. 'Although it'll make a change having pretty girls for company.'

Once they'd parted company with Sally at the signal station, the group seemed to split naturally into two couples, each sharing a torch which cast a dim circle on the ground, just bright enough to reveal the path and any lumps of rock that might trip them up. Iris and Rob lagged behind, and Mary guessed Iris was still upset.

'Poor Iris,' she said, slipping her hand onto Joe's elbow. 'Family celebrations like Christmas and birthdays are so difficult at first.'

'She'll be all right,' Joe said. 'Rob'll make sure of that.'

Mary gave a soft laugh. 'I know.'

They walked a few steps in silence, listening to the crunch of their stout shoes upon the stony path and the distant roar of the sea. Then Joe said, 'Birthdays!'

'What?' Mary risked taking her eyes from the path to shoot Joe a puzzled glance. It was too dark to see anything more than his profile in silhouette.

'Birthdays,' Joe repeated. 'I've known you for nearly a year, and I don't know when your birthday is. Admittedly, you spent most of that year letting me know how annoying you find me, but I feel we know each other well enough by now to celebrate each other's birthday. Mine's in April. When's yours?'

'Oh, I don't really celebrate my birthday.'

'Nonsense. Everyone should celebrate their birthday. It's the one day in the year where you get all the attention to yourself.'

'Not me.' Mary blurted the words before she could snatch them back.

'Why? Do you share your birthday with someone else? That's tough. A birthday should be your own special day.'

'Oh, it was special. Until…' Mary sighed. Seeing the quizzical look Joe directed at her, she hesitated. Explaining herself meant revealing the grief that had overshadowed her life from childhood. Then, recalling her resolve to be more open with her friends, she decided it was high time to start. After all, she felt she could trust Joe, and didn't want to hide the truth about herself any longer, especially when the time it weighed most heavily upon her heart was fast approaching. 'I suppose I should tell you. I'm a twin, you see.'

'Wow – why have you never mentioned that before? Where is your twin now? You must really miss her.'

'I do. All the time. She died the day before our ninth birthday.'

Joe looked horrified. 'Oh no. I'm so sorry, Mary. How awful. And there was me yammering on about how special birthdays are.'

'You weren't to know.' Mary drew a deep breath. 'I loved having a twin. We were identical, so alike only our parents could tell us apart, and we even managed to fool them sometimes. We did everything together.'

'What was her name?'

'Martha.' She snorted. 'What can I say? My parents are strict, chapel-going people.'

'Good thing they didn't call you Hephzibah, then.'
Mary giggled.

'Don't tell me, you were the wild, independent one and Martha was the dutiful daughter who always helped around the house and never complained.'

'I see I'm not the only one who went to Sunday school. No, if anything, Martha was the one who egged me on to more mischief. She was the one who wanted to climb the cliffs or go paddling while we were in our Sunday best. I followed her everywhere. As I said, we did everything together.'

Perhaps it was the dark that hid Joe's expression, but it felt easier to talk about Martha than she'd expected. It had become a habit not to speak of Martha because her mother had got so upset whenever her name was mentioned. Mary and her father had stopped talking about her, not wishing to give her mother any more grief. 'We did everything together, including getting diphtheria.' Mary swallowed, as fragments of those dreadful days came back to her and she could almost feel the smothering thickness in her throat.

She jumped as Joe's gloved hand covered hers and gave it a squeeze. 'I'm so sorry. Is that how she died?'

Mary nodded then remembered Joe couldn't see her. 'The awful thing is, everyone thought I was going to die, and Martha didn't seem to have it so badly. I don't remember an awful lot about being ill, but I do recall that the family scraped the money together to pay for a doctor to visit. I remember my mother sitting by the bed, promising to buy me some ice cream as soon as I was well enough. Then when I was on the mend, Martha just… faded away. Some complication with her heart.'

–

Joe heard Mary's story out in growing horror. What could you say to something like that? He opened his mouth then closed it when no adequate words came to mind. Instead, he gave Mary's hand a squeeze.

Mary gave a shaky laugh. 'Goodness, what a gloomy end to the evening. I thought we were supposed to be getting into the Christmas spirit. I don't even remember how the subject came up.'

'My fault. I asked you when your birthday was.'

'Ah. Well, in return for hearing me out so patiently, I'll tell you. It's actually on the tenth of December.'

'The tenth? Wait, today's the seventh, isn't it? But that means it's on Thursday.'

'Please don't think you have to do anything.'

'I want to. Aren't you doing something special with Iris and Sally?'

'I haven't told them.'

'But you're friends.' Why did they have to have this conversation when it was too dark to see Mary's face? He could only see her as a dim shape against the black sky. There weren't even any stars out to cast their pale light. He couldn't understand why she would keep her birthday a secret.

'I told you, I don't celebrate my birthday any more. Because it's not just my birthday, it's Martha's, too.'

There was a pause while they navigated a rocky section of the path. In the dim circle of torchlight, it was all too easy to lose one's footing. Once they were back on a more level surface, Mary said, 'Martha died the day before our birthday. Obviously, no one was in a state to even remember our birthday, let alone celebrate, when I turned nine. Then the next year, the first anniversary of her death was horrible, and no one wanted to celebrate my birthday the day after. It was too painful a reminder that I was growing up and Martha never would.'

Joe could see it made sense, although it seemed a shame that the one day of the year when Mary should have been treated like a queen, her family seemed set on forgetting the date. 'I think we should do something. The *Kelpie* will still be in the anchorage so I'm sure I'll be able to get leave.'

'Oh, no. Like I said, I've got out of the habit of celebrating.'

'I think it's a habit you should relearn. How did you mark the day when Martha was alive?'

'I can hardly remember.' There was another pause, then: 'We were excused from helping around the house. I remember that. On our eighth birthday, we were allowed to invite a friend each for tea, and we had my mam's oggies and cake.' Mary's voice had lightened, and even though he couldn't see her face, he knew she was smiling.

'Sounds like you had a good day.'

'We did.' And she sounded surprised. 'I've always tried not to think of our birthdays – it's always been too sad a reminder. But we had fun that day.'

'Wouldn't you like to celebrate your birthday again? When are you off duty on Thursday?'

'I'm on night watch Wednesday night, so I've got the day off after I finish.'

'Very well, why don't you have a sleep in the morning, and I'll take you out to lunch? Bring Sally and Iris if they're free.'

He braced himself for a rejection. To his surprise, however, she replied, 'I'd like that.'

'So,' Mary said once they had reached the end of the path and were groping for the section of wire fence that could be lifted aside to give access to the lane. 'Your birthday is in April? Let me guess – April the first.'

'Right first time.'

'Seriously?'

'Scout's honour.'

'Well, that's a birthday I won't forget. You must have been teased about it as a child.'

'Tell me about it. Every year I'd get the same old jokes – I was born a fool.'

And he couldn't help wondering if he wasn't being the world's biggest fool, for he had an idea for a surprise gift that could backfire horribly. Yet the idea refused to go away, and he knew he had to do it.

Chapter Fourteen

With the *Kelpie* stuck in the anchorage, Joe had plenty of time to work out what to do for Mary's birthday. He managed to catch Sally in Stromness the next day and discovered that Iris also had the day off after sharing the night watch with Mary, and Sally was free in the afternoon. When she heard what he had to say about his planned surprise for Mary, Sally said she'd be delighted to help and she was sure Iris would want to join in, too. After they parted ways, he made the trip to Curlew Croft at a time when he knew Mary would be on watch, meaning there was no chance of bumping into her there.

Elspeth was only too pleased to oblige when Joe told her what he wanted. 'The poor lass,' she said. 'What a terrible tragedy. To think she lost her twin so young. No wonder she doesn't like to celebrate her birthday.' She listened to Joe's idea and nodded. 'It's a risk, I'll grant you, but I think she'll like it. Now, I won't hear of you taking us all out for a meal. We'll have it here. I can make the pasties, although they'll have to be vegetable ones. They'll go well with mash. And I can whip us up a carrot cake. How does that sound?'

'It sounds wonderful, but I don't want to put you to any more trouble. You've done so much for us already.'

'Nonsense. It's the least I can do. You bring everyone here and we'll treat Mary to the birthday she deserves.'

'I can't believe it's your birthday tomorrow,' Sally said as she and Mary strolled down Victoria Street in Stromness. 'Why didn't you tell us?'

Mary's duties had kept her apart from Iris and Sally the day after she had told Joe about her birthday, so she hadn't had the chance to mention it to them until the evening. By that time, they had heard from Joe and were full of the arrangements he had made with Elspeth to celebrate at Curlew Croft. She had been tired and hadn't felt up to the emotional upheaval of talking about Martha, so when challenged on why she had kept her birthday secret, she had mumbled something about not knowing them well enough last year, which was perfectly true. Now it was the day before her birthday and she still hadn't told her friends the whole story.

An army car rattled up the street towards them, and Mary stepped to the side of the street to let it past, pulling Sally with her. The pause gave her time to consider her reply. The subject was still painful, and she didn't want to tell Sally now, only to have to repeat herself for Iris's benefit. She was also not looking forward to their pity, yet they were her friends, and it felt dishonest somehow not to tell them about such a significant part of her life.

'It's… a bit complicated,' she said finally, once the car had disappeared around a bend in the road.

Sally gave her a startled look. 'What's so complicated about the date you were born?'

'It just is. Look, I'll tell you, I promise. I'd rather tell you and Iris together, so I don't have to repeat myself.'

'Fair enough.' Sally walked on in silence for a few steps. Then she flashed Mary a mischievous smile. 'I bet you told Joe, though.'

'I... well, yes.'

Sally clapped her hands. 'I knew it! I told you he was perfect for you. Admit it – if you can tell him things you haven't even told me and Iris, then he's the one for you.'

'I'll admit no such thing. He put me on the spot, that's all.' She couldn't deny that telling Joe about Martha had felt right, though, and she was looking forward to her first birthday celebration for fourteen years. She had Joe to thank for that.

'Protest all you like. I know I'm right.'

Thankfully, Mary didn't have to answer, for they had reached their destination – the little chemist where Sally wanted to get some balm for her chapped lips. Deciding not to go inside the cramped shop, Mary waited for her outside. After a while, she crossed the street to look in a window, and her attention was arrested by a beautiful carved wooden picture frame. The unusual design was formed of strange creatures with horses' heads and long, sinuous, fish-like bodies. Each side of the frame was composed of two of these beasts, their heads at each corner and their tails winding into an intricate knot at the centre.

'Oh, that's lovely.' Sally had emerged from the chemist without Mary noticing and now stood at Mary's elbow, gazing at the same picture frame. 'Are you thinking of getting it for Joe?'

'Why Joe?'

'Because of the kelpies.'

'Is that what they are? I thought they were just a flight of the artist's fancy.'

'There's a picture of one in that folklore book Iris gave me for my birthday.'

Mary studied the wooden kelpies on the frame, marvelling that she'd been friends with someone from a ship called the *Kelpie* without wondering what a kelpie actually was. 'It would be the ideal gift for him.' She had been knitting him a hat and scarf for Christmas, but she could always send them to her father instead. Then she saw the price, pencilled upon a discreet label in the lower left corner. 'Blast. It's twelve shillings.' She turned her back on the window with a tug of regret. 'Take me away from here, Sally. It might be perfect but I can't afford it. Joe will have to put up with that wonky hat and scarf instead.' She sighed. 'I wish I could knit as well as you and Iris.'

'He'll love it because you made it for him,' Sally said, taking Mary by the arm and leading her in the direction of the Wrennery.

Mary refused to rise to the bait.

–

They were just approaching the point where Victoria Street merged with Dundas Street when a tall man in naval uniform dashed out from a side street, nearly colliding with them.

'Excuse me,' he said and seemed to be on the point of hurrying off when he stopped and stared at Sally. 'Sally Hartley? That's never you, is it?'

Even if Mary hadn't picked up on the young man's slight Yorkshire accent, she could have worked out his identity solely from the scarlet flush glowing upon Sally's cheeks.

'Adam,' Sally said, sounding a little breathless. 'How lovely to see you! I was wondering when I would meet you.'

So this was the Adam Sally had told them all about. Mary studied him with interest. To her surprise, instead of the devastatingly handsome heartbreaker that Mary had pictured, Adam appeared to be quite ordinary-looking. He had light brown hair, neatly cropped and combed beneath his cap and twinkling blue eyes. His face was pleasant – attractive but nothing special, with a friendly, open expression.

'I'm glad I bumped into you,' he said. 'Sorry I've not been in touch much since I got here. It's been a busy time.'

His apology sounded sincere, and he came across as genuinely sorry not to have met Sally before. It made Mary question her judgement and wonder if she hadn't been unfair to him. She had, after all, never met him until today, and she was only disposed to dislike him because she feared he was leading Sally on. What if she was wrong, and Adam genuinely liked Sally but simply hadn't had the opportunity to ask her out? Or just wanted to be friends, and Sally had misinterpreted his intentions? Mary could quite believe it possible that romantic, tender-hearted Sally could construct a love affair out of very flimsy evidence. After all, she was convinced Mary and Joe were meant for each other.

'Well, you're here now, and that's the main thing,' Sally said. Her blush had faded to a paler shade of rose, giving her an attractive glow. 'Where are you based?'

Adam certainly didn't seem immune to her charms, for he smiled and took her arm. 'HMS *Proserpine*,' he said, naming the base at Lyness on Hoy. 'Is there somewhere we can go for a drink and catch up on old times? You and...' He eyed Mary enquiringly.

'Oh, this is my friend, Mary Griffiths.'

'Lovely to meet you, Mary.' Adam held out his hand.

Mary shook it, and that's when Adam turned the full force of his smile upon her. It was the kind of smile it must take film stars years to perfect, practising for hours a day in front of a mirror. A proper Dazzler with a capital 'D'. It was designed to make the recipient feel like the most beautiful, fascinating woman he had ever laid eyes upon. It took Mary a moment to recover. 'Pleased to meet you,' she managed when she had regained her breath.

Her suspicions returned in full force. She could no longer blame Sally for falling for this man, not if he had ever directed that smile at her. Mary doubted she would have been immune herself, had she not been able to compare him to Owen. *And Joe*, a tiny voice in the back of her mind prompted her. She ignored it.

Adam, however, seemed oblivious to the effect he'd had on her, making Mary wonder again if she was jumping to conclusions. He turned back to Sally. 'What do you say? Have you got time for some tea?'

'Oh, I'd love to.' Sally still sounded flustered, and Mary wondered if Adam had just treated her to the Dazzler. 'We've got time, haven't we, Mary?' She didn't wait for Mary's reply but went on, 'There's a lovely little cafe up a side street, just along there.' Sally pointed it out.

'Sounds perfect,' Adam said. He turned in the direction Sally had indicated, then glanced at his watch and slapped his forehead. 'I don't believe it. I completely forgot I've arranged to meet a friend. Can we arrange another time?'

Sally's face fell. 'Of course. I quite understand.'

'I'll let you know when I'm free.' And then he was off, dashing back down Victoria Street.

'What a shame,' Sally said, resuming her walk to the Wrennery. Then she brightened. 'Isn't it wonderful we bumped into him like that, though? Just think, if we hadn't stopped to admire that picture frame, we would have missed him. I can't help thinking it was meant to be.'

Mary didn't know what made her do it, but as she followed Sally, she glanced back after Adam's retreating form. She was just in time to see him stop beside a pretty young woman in ATS uniform. He offered her his arm, and together they strolled up the street.

Mary bit her lip. Should she tell Sally? But when she turned, it was to see Sally already looking at the couple. 'I'm sorry, Sally,' she said.

'He said he was meeting a friend.' Sally's expression defied argument. 'There's nothing wrong with him being friends with a girl. You keep telling me you and Joe are just friends.'

Mary couldn't argue with that, so held her tongue.

'Isn't he lovely?' Sally asked as they walked on, seeming genuinely untroubled at the sight of him with another woman. 'I'm so glad you've met him. What do you think of him?'

Mary had only an instant to reach a decision. 'He's nice,' she said. Who knew? Sally could be right, and the ATS girl could be no more than a friend. Sally knew him better than she did, after all. If Sally believed the best of him, then Mary owed it to her to trust her judgement.

'Oh, I knew you would like him,' Sally said. 'It's wonderful he's at Lyness. Maybe we'll be able to visit him. I've always wanted to go to Hoy.'

Thankfully, Mary didn't need to say much, for Sally continued to sing his praises all the way back to the Wren-nery. Mary made up her mind to observe Adam carefully and give him the benefit of the doubt in the meantime. However if it turned out he was merely flirting with Sally and leading her on, Mary would see to it he suffered.

Thoughts of Adam couldn't occupy her mind for long, though. Not with her birthday approaching. It was years since she had looked forward to a birthday, and she couldn't wait to find out how Joe planned to make it special.

Chapter Fifteen

'Happy birthday!' Sally was waiting for Mary in the entrance hall of the Wrennery when she and Iris returned from their night watch. It was already the best birthday she'd had since her long-ago eighth birthday, with Iris producing a bottle of lemonade and insisting on toasting her at the stroke of midnight. Iris had then offered to stand watch alone so that Mary would be fresh the next day. Mary, always an early riser, had insisted upon relieving Iris at five. Even now, after the walk from Kyeness, she felt full of energy and eager for what the day had in store.

After shedding their outer wear, they headed straight for breakfast. 'I asked the cook to put aside a plate of bacon and eggs for you,' Sally said.

'You angel.' Anyone returning from night watch at Kyeness arrived only about fifteen minutes before the kitchen stopped serving breakfast. This usually meant finding nothing left to eat but the last lumpy scrapings of the porridge pot or just enough cornflakes to feed a mouse.

Iris eyed the congealed dollop in her bowl with disfavour then cast a longing look at Mary's plate of scrambled eggs, two whole rashers of streaky bacon and mushrooms. 'You couldn't have pretended it was my birthday too?'

'No. It's Mary's special day. Shut up and eat your porridge.'

Mary hastily swallowed her first mouthful to stop herself from choking. 'Honestly, Iris, I'm happy to share. I dread to think what Sally bribed the cook with to get me all this.'

'No. Iris is perfectly fine with porridge. Aren't you, Iris.' It wasn't a question. Sally shot Iris a glare that promised dire retribution should Iris pinch so much as the tiniest, most shrivelled mushroom from Mary's plate.

Iris threw up her hands in a gesture of surrender. 'Your breakfast is safe from me, although I appreciate the offer.'

To do her justice, Iris finished her porridge without complaint and went to fetch Mary a cup of tea. Mary couldn't fail to notice that although Iris liked her tea with milk, she was drinking it black, whereas Mary's tea was white. Mary could only conclude that Iris had given her the last of the milk. Maybe having a birthday wasn't so bad after all.

After breakfast, they went up to their cabin. Once Mary and Iris had changed, Iris pulled a parcel from the wardrobe and handed it to Mary. 'Happy birthday. It's not much, I'm afraid, but I've spent most of my spare cash on Christmas.'

Mary felt the present. It was wrapped in newspaper and tied in a red ribbon, from the same length of ribbon they had used to decorate the tree. It was a thin package and squashy to the touch. If Iris had had more warning of her birthday, Mary would have guessed it was a garment she had made, but two days wasn't enough time for even Iris to make something new, considering she had spent the majority of that time on duty. 'You really didn't have to get me anything. What is it?'

'Open it!' You'd have thought from Sally's shining eyes that she was the birthday girl.

Mary unwound the ribbon and opened the parcel. Inside were two pairs of black nylons. 'Thank you, they're exactly what I needed. Where on earth did you find them?' Mary was down to her last pair of nylons and she'd had to mend several runs. She'd searched for new ones each time she'd been to the shops in the past month, but they had become impossible to find. Other Wrens wrote home with lists of essential items they were running low on, but Mary couldn't bring herself to ask her parents for anything when she knew how badly the shortages were affecting them.

'My Aunt Sybil sent them from York.'

For some reason, Iris had rolled up the nylons before wrapping them. When Mary unrolled them, a hard, cylindrical object fell out and dropped to the floor. She picked it up and saw it was an Elizabeth Arden lipstick in a gorgeous shade of vermilion.

'Oh, Iris, you shouldn't have! I love it.' Looking in the mirror, Mary applied it. Although she would never have dared to buy such a dramatic shade for herself, she had to admit it suited her even better than the Gala lipstick she had bought from the NAAFI.

'I wanted to. You deserve it. Sally's right, this is your special day and we want to spoil you. And look.' Iris took the lipstick from her and dabbed a little on the back of her hand and blended it with a little cold cream. Before Mary realised what she was about to do, Iris dabbed it upon her cheeks and smoothed it in it with deft fingers. 'See – you can double it up as rouge. It's a lovely shade on you.'

Glancing back at her reflection, Mary saw that Iris had subtly emphasised the line of her cheekbones. She had to admit, she had never looked so sophisticated in her life.

'Thank you,' she said, turning her head this way and that to admire her reflection.

'My turn!' Sally bounded up to Mary and kissed her on the cheek. 'Happy birthday.' She pressed yet another newspaper-and-ribbon-wrapped parcel. It felt hard and lumpy; Mary couldn't begin to guess what was inside.

Unwrapping it revealed three pencils, already sharpened, and an india rubber. Closer inspection revealed the pencils were B, 2B and 4B pencils – soft pencils for drawing. Four years ago she would have been overjoyed to get such a gift. 'Thank you, Sally. That's really kind.' She didn't want to sound ungrateful, but she had told the girls she had no desire to draw again, and here was Sally spending money she probably needed for other things on items Mary would never use. Then she thought of Joe. Once Sally had forgotten about them – after Christmas, perhaps – she would give the pencils to him. He would put them to good use.

Her lack of enthusiasm must have shown, for Sally said, 'I know you said you didn't draw any more but… well, your drawings were so beautiful, I can't bear to think of you never drawing again. Don't feel you have to use them, but they're here in case you need them. I sharpened them for you.'

Mary swallowed. 'Thanks, Sally. That's a lovely thought.' And although she doubted she would use them, she knew she could never give them away. Because she couldn't bear to disappoint Sally, she put the 2B pencil and scrap of paper in her coat pocket. 'There. If I ever get the urge to draw, I'll have a pencil to hand, thanks to you.'

Sally's expression brightened. 'I'm so glad. You'll get it back one day, I'm sure you will. You can't have all that talent for nothing.'

After tidying their cabin, Mary's long night on watch was finally catching up with her, so she settled down for a nap so she would be fresh later on, and Iris decided to do the same. Sally went to run some errands before having to leave for the afternoon watch. Mary woke at twelve and went for a quick bath before dressing in a woollen skirt and thick jumper. She had a moment's regret as she looked at her reflection. Why couldn't she have had a summer birthday? Then she could be off to meet Joe in a light summer frock instead of these ungainly clothes.

Wait. Why did she care what she looked like? She and Joe weren't sweethearts. Still, she took extra care with her hair, deciding to leave it loose, placing hair grips above each ear to tame it a little and keep it from falling into her eyes. A glance at her watch showed her it was nearly time to meet Joe. She collected her coat, hat, gloves and scarf and was about to leave when she hesitated, glancing at the new lipstick on top of the chest of drawers. It was her birthday, after all, and Iris had chosen the dramatic colour well. She dropped the coat upon her bed and applied the lipstick.

The door opened and Sally flew in. 'Oh, good. I didn't want to miss you. Have a wonderful afternoon, and save me some cake.'

'There's cake?' Suddenly Mary experienced a thrill over her birthday that she hadn't had since she was eight. 'What are we doing?'

'It's a surprise. Anyway, I'll walk down with you. Joe's waiting outside. You look lovely, by the way. Your hair suits you like that.'

Mary put a hand to her hair, feeling suddenly unsure. She usually pinned her hair into a tight roll in the nape of her neck and it felt strange to feel the curls upon her shoulders. Perhaps she would feel more comfortable if she put it up. She took a step towards the mirror.

Sally caught her arm. 'Don't look so worried. You look fine. Come on.' Then she addressed the lump under the blankets that was Iris. 'And you need to get a move on.'

Iris responded with a groan and stuck her tousled head from under the covers. 'All right. I'm moving.' She squinted at Mary. 'Sally's right – you look amazing. Now go and enjoy yourself, and I'll see you later.'

-

As Sally had said, Joe was waiting for Mary in the lane outside the Wrennery. Sally, who had come out with her oppo, waved them off and promised to meet them as soon as she got off duty.

Mary turned to Joe. 'What have you got planned? Sally's being very mysterious.'

'All in good time. First of all – happy birthday.' Joe kissed Mary on the cheek. 'Many happy returns.' He stepped back and looked at her, and there was a look in his eyes that reminded Mary that Joe had initially wanted to walk out with her. 'Being twenty-two obviously suits you.'

'How did you know my age? Did Sally tell you?' Her indignation helped her resist the impulse to touch the place on her cheek where his lips had been.

'Why – was it supposed to be a secret?'

'I suppose not. But it's only fair if you tell me your age in return.'

'Twenty-five.' He offered Mary his arm. 'Now we've got that out of the way, we can begin the celebrations. We're due at Curlew Croft for two, so that gives us about an hour before we have to leave. What would you like to do now – a stroll? A look around the shops? You've picked a nice day for a birthday.'

Mary had scarcely noticed the weather until now, apart from noting the icy bite to the wind. Joe was right – the sun was out, and it was the kind of crystal clear day that you only got in winter. The snow that had fallen at the start of December had all melted, and she felt as though she could see every blade of grass on the hills that rose up behind the town.

'Why are we going to Curlew Croft?'

'It's where we're having lunch.'

'I hope Elspeth hasn't gone to too much trouble.'

'It was her idea, although Iris, Sally and I have all helped out. In fact, Iris should be haring over there now to help out with the last minute preparations.'

'Poor Iris. I wondered why Sally made her get up so early. I bet she's regretting taking most of the watch last night.'

'So now that's settled, what would you like to do?'

'Actually, I'd love a cup of tea. I haven't drunk anything since breakfast.'

'Your wish is my command. We'll go to the Beehive.'

Once they were in the little cafe, with a pot of tea between them on the table, Joe said, 'I suppose now is the best time to give you this.' He reached into his coat pocket, which hung on the coat stand beside him, and pulled out a large envelope. Mary's name was written on the front. Now he had got it out, however, he held onto it, looking uncertain. 'I drew something for you.'

'That's lovely. Can I see?'

Still Joe hesitated. Mary gave a half laugh, puzzled. 'Well, can I see it or not?' What was the matter with him? He had never been bashful before.

'I had to draw it, but now I think it might have been a bad idea.'

That only increased Mary's curiosity. 'This is ridiculous. Hand it over.'

Before Joe could stop her, she snatched the envelope and opened it. Inside was a sheet of paper sandwiched between two rectangles of card. Joe winced as though it might contain explosives.

'Honestly, I don't know what the problem is,' Mary said, lifting the top piece of card to see what was on the paper. 'I love your—oh.' Her vision tunnelled until she could see nothing but Joe's drawing. It was a portrait of her, but not only her. It showed her on the balcony at Kyeness Signal Station, peering through an Aldis lamp, clearly signalling to a ship. Mary supposed that as Joe had once worked at Kyeness, he had no difficulty remembering its exact appearance and the view of the coastline. It wasn't this that had caused her exclamation of surprise, however. There was another figure in the drawing. Another her, standing behind, peering over the Wren Mary's shoulder to see the sketch, her face glowing with an expression of what could be mingled pride and love. This other Mary's hand hovered a little way above the signaller's shoulder, not quite touching.

Once the initial surprise wore off, she looked more closely and noticed there were slight differences in features between the two. The figure standing behind the signaller had a slightly rounder face; her brows not as arched as Mary's. She couldn't be sure if it was deliberate or just down to the difficulty of drawing two identical faces. 'It's not me,' she said. 'Is this Martha?'

'That was partly the idea. I wanted to show you that she'll always be with you, because she's here in your heart.' Joe still looked anxious. 'I hope you don't mind. I thought it would be a way of including her in your birthday.'

'I love it.' Mary brushed Martha's face with her finger-tips, careful not to smudge the soft pencil. 'I like the thought of her watching over me.' Then she saw that the hand hovering near the signaller's shoulder had a ring on the fourth finger, and that there was a pencil tucked behind her ear. 'Why the ring and the pencil?'

'Ah.' Joe looked, if anything, even more awkward. 'As I was drawing, the Martha figure became two things at once. It's hard to explain. While she's definitely Martha, she also became another you.'

Mary frowned at him. 'How much rum had you drunk before you drew it?'

'None. This drawing was fuelled by nothing more than tea from the petty officer's mess.' Joe pulled a face. 'Although I swear they mix it with engine oil.'

'Then what do you mean?'

'I suppose drawing Martha made me think of all you've lost, and the life you might have had if you hadn't lost first Martha then your fiancé. So while the second figure is Martha, she's also the person you might have been. I wanted you to see that she's still here, that you're still essentially the same person you used to be, and I think if the woman you might have been could see you now, she'd be just as proud of you as Martha would.'

Mary blinked, the picture blurring from the tears welling in her eyes. She hastily pulled out her handkerchief and dabbed her eyes, not wanting to spoil the drawing with tear blots.

She was so choked up she hardly knew how to respond. All she could do was give Joe a weak smile and assure him she thought it was beautiful. Joe seemed to understand that she needed time, so moved the conversation onto other topics. Mary slipped the portrait back into the envelope and put it away carefully in her bag. Although she did her best to listen to Joe's opinion of the articles in the latest edition of the *Orkney Blast* – a newspaper for the men and women serving in the forces on Orkney – her attention kept drifting back to the picture.

'Oh my goodness.' Joe's voice cut through her thoughts. He was looking at his watch. 'Time to go. We don't want to be late for your birthday lunch.' He paid their bill and then they set off for Curlew Croft.

While they were still in Stromness, walking down Victoria Street, they heard the sound of running footsteps behind them and a voice called their names. They turned to see Rob hurrying to catch up.

'Are you on your way to Curlew Croft?' he asked, once he had wished Mary a happy birthday. 'Good. I thought I was going to be the last one there. Iris would have killed me.' He fell into step with them.

Mary was only too pleased to have Rob join them. She let their conversation about the *Kelpie's* repairs drift over her while she pondered the drawing. It was a beautiful gesture that must have taken up most of Joe's spare time, and it was clear he had poured a great deal of thought and care into it. Was that the act of a friend or did it mean he hadn't given up on them becoming sweethearts? She found she didn't have an answer. Another question she couldn't answer was whether she had changed her mind and would welcome their friendship becoming something more. She couldn't wait to show the portrait to Iris and Sally to hear their opinions.

Chapter Sixteen

The moment she entered the kitchen of Curlew Croft, she was enveloped in the delicious aroma of cooking only seconds before being enveloped in an enthusiastic hug from Elspeth. 'Happy birthday, lass. Now, once you've put away your coat and washed your hands, we'll sit down to the meal right away. I've had a hard time fighting Archie off the pasties.'

Mary didn't mind at all; the walk had sharpened her appetite and the delicious smells rising from the dish on the table made her stomach rumble. 'I hope you haven't gone to too much trouble, Elspeth.'

'Not at all. It was a pleasure.'

'But this close to Christmas, and with all your worry over Don…'

'There, now. To tell you the truth, it does me good to have you young ones in the house. You've brightened up the place, that's for sure, and it's lovely to have more than just the two of us sat at the table.'

When Mary went to sit in her usual seat, Elspeth stopped her. 'Not today. You get the seat of honour at the top of the table.'

'And you have to wear this.' Iris handed her a paper crown, made from a sheet from the *Orkney Herald*. 'Sally made it and said I had to make sure you put it on.'

'Probably give me five years bad luck if I don't.' Feeling very embarrassed, Mary placed it on her head and took her seat at the head of the table. There were more surprises to come when Elspeth took a tray out of the oven piled with golden brown pasties.

'Joe told us about the oggies that were your favourite dish from home, so I've made you these as a treat. No meat, I'm afraid, as I've been saving the coupons for Christmas.'

Mary looked at the food in wonder. 'I can't believe you've done all this. How did you know I liked oggies?'

'You mentioned it to me once,' Joe said.

Mary was aware of Iris and Rob exchanging knowing glances, and she braced herself for an inquisition later on. 'Well, thank you.' She made an effort to keep her tone light and not meet Iris's gaze. Her stomach rumbled, and she laughed, feeling the tension break. 'My stomach thanks you, too. Let's tuck in.'

It was the happiest birthday she'd had in many years. Simply sitting around the table with her friends and sharing the food lovingly prepared by Elspeth was a joy Mary hadn't expected. It didn't matter that the food was simple. What mattered was the proof that she had friends who cared about her enough to go to all this trouble when everyone was busy and had their own worries. Although she felt a little silly wearing the hat from Sally, she refused to take it off, knowing it was a way Sally could join in with the meal despite being on watch. Throughout the meal, however, part of her thoughts were constantly on the drawing that still resided in her bag, and the feelings of the artist who had drawn it. Although she was half-dreading the questions from Iris and Sally that she knew would come, Mary also longed to talk it all over with them, and ask them what they thought about Joe.

Her opportunity came later in the evening. Sally breezed in from the signal station and tucked into the food that had been put by on the range to keep warm for her. The others were in the parlour by this time, admiring the way the Christmas tree looked by the light of the candles that Elspeth had arranged around it. Mary and Iris sat with Sally in the kitchen while she ate, and Mary plucked up the courage to show them the portrait. After checking the door was closed between the kitchen and the narrow stone-tiled passage that led to the parlour, she pulled the envelope from her bag and showed the portrait to her friends.

'It's an amazing likeness,' Sally said, not taking her eyes from the picture.

'I can't believe he drew this from memory,' Iris said. 'When I tried drawing a portrait at school, I had to concentrate really hard on the person's face. I could never have drawn her from memory. Admittedly, art was my worst subject. Why did he draw you twice, though?'

'It's because Joe's in love with Mary and drawing her once wasn't enough.' Sally had the same dreamy look she always had when talking of romance.

Usually Mary would roll her eyes at this kind of pronouncement, but now she was all too aware that her friends didn't know about Martha. The last thing she wanted was for them to find out from Joe. Iris and Sally had both taken her into their confidence about things close to their hearts, and she owed it to them to be the one to tell them about Martha. 'Listen,' she said, ignoring Sally's jibe, 'there's something I need to tell you.' And she explained about Martha, just as she had told Joe.

Iris and Sally were so sympathetic, she couldn't understand why she had found it impossible to tell them about her twin before.

'What a tragedy,' Sally said, her eyes suspiciously bright. 'I wondered why you'd kept quiet about your birthday until now. How sad, that your birthday is a reminder of your loss.' She flung down her fork and pulled Mary into a hug, flooding Mary's senses with the scent of Pears soap. 'I'm glad you felt able to tell us about Martha. I expect you found it difficult to talk to your parents about her, knowing how upset it would make them.'

Mary could only nod, her throat too tight for speech, overcome at Sally's understanding.

'I feel the same way when I want to talk to my mother about my father. I can see how painful she finds it, so I've never been able to learn much about him.'

'It does feel like a weight off my chest now I've told you,' Mary said eventually, pulling away and dabbing her eyes. Iris patted her shoulder and handed her a handkerchief. Something about her awkward expression made Mary giggle, breaking the tension.

'What did I do?' Iris asked.

'Nothing. Just being your usual upper-class self, and I wouldn't have you any other way.' She wiped her eyes and picked up the portrait, pointing at the figure of her twin. 'This is how Joe imagines Martha would be had she grown up.' She told them about Joe's idea for the portrait then went on, 'I can't tell you how special this gift is to me. I tried to draw Martha a few years ago, imagining what she would look like had she survived. It just looked like me, though.'

Sally stuck up her hand, looking like a pupil trying to catch her teacher's attention. 'The picture in your diary!'

she said. 'I thought it was odd, when your other drawings were of the scenery or buildings.'

Mary nodded. 'I started it on my eighteenth birthday. Owen had just joined up and I was wishing she was still around to cheer me up. I spent hours in front of the mirror.' She gestured at Joe's picture. 'Joe's done a much better job, giving her slightly different features.'

'It's a beautiful drawing,' Iris agreed, 'but don't think you can distract us from what Sally said before. She thinks Joe must be in love with you, and for once I have to agree with her.'

'For once?' Sally shot Iris an indignant look.

'Well, you're always quick to accuse people of being in love with each other.'

'Like you and Rob? I was right then, wasn't I?'

Iris had the grace to blush. 'All right. But we're getting off the subject again.' Iris looked at Mary. 'It's clear he wants more than friendship, no matter what he says. What do you want?'

'I… I'm not sure.'

'Then work it out because if there's no way you can return his feelings, you need to make that clear. He might have told you he's happy to be just friends, but I don't think he's given up on you.'

'I know. You're right.' Mary sighed. 'I'm confused. When I first met Joe, and he came on so strong, I thought I couldn't love again after Owen.'

'And now?' Iris gave Mary a look she must have picked up from one of her schoolmistresses, with arched brows, holding her gaze and forcing Mary to think.

'I genuinely don't know. But I think if I could love anyone again it would be Joe.'

'I knew it!' Sally clapped her hands. 'I think you two would be perfect together.'

'Keep your voice down! He's in the next room and I don't want him to overhear. I said I don't know how I feel. I know I need to work it out, though.' Mary looked back at the picture, studying the image of the adult Martha. 'You know, when I first met Joe I thought he was a bit brash, the way he tried to ask me out right away. I avoided him for ages after that. But I'm glad I gave him another chance. Now I think his brashness is just a front for someone much more sensitive and imaginative than he likes to let on. He understands me so well.' She pointed at the drawing of Martha. 'He said that as well as being Martha, she also became another me; that he hadn't intended it when he started drawing but the idea came to him as he was working. She's supposed to be the me who I might have become had Owen not died.'

'She looks softer. Happier,' Sally said.

Mary nodded. 'The thing is… if Owen hadn't died, I might be married to him by now. I might never have joined the Wrens or met you. Or Joe.' She hesitated, then went on in a rush. 'I don't think I can bear to think of not knowing you all.'

'That doesn't mean you're happy Owen died,' Sally said gently. 'It's what my mum always says to me. We have to make the best of the hand we're dealt. However bad things get, there's always a silver lining if we look hard enough.'

The trouble was, Mary didn't have to look too hard for her silver lining, and it was hard not to feel guilty. She had loved Owen and would never have regretted being his wife. However, now she had experienced the satisfaction of making a contribution to the war effort, and made friends she would never have known had she not joined the Wrens, she found she couldn't wish herself back to her former life, no matter how much she mourned Owen. It wasn't a comfortable thought.

Then it hit her. 'That's why the other person in the drawing is me as well as Martha.' She blurted it out before she was able to think it through fully, and groped for her next words while Iris and Sally looked at her with eyes wide in expectation. 'The person I would have been never happened. In a way, she's dead, and a new me was born.'

Sally was nodding. 'I never looked at it quite that way before. Who knows what I would be doing now if my uncle hadn't had his accident? I wouldn't have moved to Whitby and met Adam, for a start. I suppose that's my silver lining.'

In Mary's opinion, Sally eating her heart out over a man who would probably never love her in return didn't sound like much of a silver lining, but she wasn't going to argue. 'Remember when we were talking about the stars and magic?' she asked her. 'I said I couldn't see how distant balls of gas could affect my life. Well, even though I haven't changed my mind, there is a wish I'd like to make now. I wish for us all to make the most of the opportunities we've been given right here and now, and for us all to have the best possible Christmas.'

She glanced at the portrait again and added in a lower voice, 'Because we'll never know when the good things we have will be taken from us.'

She noticed the pencil stuck behind Martha's ear. She knew she had to say goodbye to that version of Mary – she had died with Owen. It was a shame that her talent for drawing seemed to have died with him too, though.

–

'Have you found out how to get your parcel to Aldo?' Mary asked Sally as they walked down the track to Stromness. It was two days after Mary's birthday and she still hadn't fully worked out how she felt about Joe's portrait. Oh, she loved it and thought it the most wonderful gift she had ever received, but it was the thousand thoughts that tumbled into her head whenever she studied the picture of Martha/lost Mary that had sent her into a spin. She found she wanted to talk over her thoughts with Joe. Unfortunately he had been unable to get any further leave, and *Kelpie* had resumed her duties along with her sister ships. She hadn't even had the comfort of signalling him, for her watches hadn't coincided with the times the minesweepers passed Kyeness. She hoped he didn't think she was upset with him; she had been so overwhelmed by her confusion that she hadn't been able to say much to him apart from how lovely she thought the drawing was, and even then she had been so choked she hadn't sounded convincing.

Now, at the end of a busy morning watch, she was tired of her own thoughts and realised she had neglected other matters. Like how to get a parcel to an Italian prisoner of war on an island on the other side of Scapa Flow. It was important to Sally so, however strange Mary thought the idea, she wanted to support her.

Sally sighed. 'There hasn't been time. I've asked around but no one seems to know. And everyone thinks I'm mad to be sending gifts to a prisoner.' They walked on in silence for a while. It was another cold, clear day, and Mary gazed out across the sparkling aquamarine waters, hardly admitting even to herself that she was looking for the *Kelpie*.

'Actually,' Sally resumed eventually, sounding thoughtful, 'it would almost be as easy to take a bus out to St Mary's.'

'St Mary's?' With half her mind on the *Kelpie*, Mary couldn't immediately remember where St Mary's was.

'I'm pretty sure the buses go there,' Sally said. 'You know – it's the nearest village on Mainland to where they're building the causeways. Aldo's camp is on Lamb Holm, which is just across the water from St Mary's so if I could get there, maybe I could find a way to deliver his parcel.'

Now Mary understood. St Mary's was the village closest to the construction site on the south-eastern end of the island, where a vast operation was underway to build a series of causeways linking Mainland with Lamb Holm, Burray and South Ronaldsay. The Italian prisoners of war were providing much of the labour for the project.

'Are you mad? You'd probably end up getting arrested. You can't just walk up to a bunch of prisoners and expect to be allowed to talk to them.'

'I wasn't going to. I was going to ask one of the guards. There must be guards. Or maybe I could ask one of the civilian engineers.'

Mary shook her head. 'You'd never be allowed anywhere near the works.'

'Have you been there? Do you know how it's set up?'

'No, but it stands to reason it will be fenced off.' Mary laughed. 'Although if you persuaded Iris to go with you, I bet she could talk her way in. She might only be an ordinary Wren, but with her accent she could persuade anyone she was an officer. She—' Mary broke off, seeing the glint in Sally's eyes. Her heart sank with a thud. 'Oh no. I wasn't serious.'

But she was too late. 'Brilliant idea,' Sally said. 'We've all got the day off the day after tomorrow. We'll go then.'

Mary groaned. One of the Wren signallers had gone down with a bug, meaning many of the other Wrens, Iris, Mary and Sally included, had been taking extra watches for the past couple of days. In return, their CO had managed to organise their watches so they got extra time off once the Wren was back on duty, which was due to happen tomorrow. 'I was looking forward to planning the rest of our Christmas celebrations.'

'We can do that on the bus.'

Mary could see there was no getting out of it. Anyway, she knew she would have to go along to stop Sally doing anything that might get her into trouble. 'All right then. I'll leave you to find out about the buses.' So much for a peaceful day off.

They had reached the highest point of the path by this time, and by unspoken consent they both paused to take in the view. Now they were well into December, the days were so short that most of their walks to and from Kyeness were done in the dark. Mary was prepared to face the biting wind for a few minutes longer if it gave her this rare chance to enjoy the scenery.

Sally drew a deep breath, and Mary knew that she was also savouring the crisp, clean air. 'I don't think I'll ever take this sight for granted. On a day like today when you can see right across Scapa Flow to South Ronaldsay, you could almost forget there was a war on.'

'Apart from all the warships – not to mention the gun placements and barrage balloons,' Mary said with a smile. But she knew what Sally meant. When faced with such beauty, it was hard to believe that life-and-death struggles were happening elsewhere in the world. Even though there was evidence of the war in just about any direction they looked, at the same time Orkney felt like a protected haven, rather like being inside the glass dome of a snow globe.

'I would love to have seen it before all the military installations were built,' Sally said. 'It must have been so peaceful.'

'Me too. Maybe we'll see it like that one day.'

Without warning, Mary felt what she could only describe as a faint tingle in her fingertips. She thrust her hands into her pockets, and yelped in pain when something sharp stabbed her thumb through her glove.

'What's wrong?' Sally asked.

Mary pulled off her glove and scowled at the bead of blood welling on the tip of her thumb. 'Your blasted pencil. What possessed you to sharpen it to such a lethal point?' She stuck her thumb in her mouth and gradually the throbbing pain eased.

Sally winced in sympathy. 'There'll be some sticking plaster back in the Wrennery.' She took one final look at the view then stepped back onto the path.

Mary made to follow her then stopped dead. It suddenly hit her what the tingling in her fingers had meant. She put her hand back into her pocket and curled her fingers around the pencil, careful to avoid the dagger-sharp lead this time. Funny how right it felt in her hand. She hadn't felt like this in a very long time.

'You go on,' she said to Sally. 'I think I want to stay up here for a while.' She didn't say why. If the sudden urge to draw vanished, she didn't want to make too much of it.

Sally paused and looked back. 'Is everything all right?'

'Trust me, I'm better than I've been in a long time.'

'I don't mind staying if you want company.'

'I'm fine, honest. There's something I need to do.' There was a flat rock a little way off the path that would make a good seat; Mary sat there once Sally set off down the hill. As soon as she was sure Sally wouldn't turn back, she pulled the pencil and paper from her pocket. Although it was too cold to sit here for long, Mary knew she had to try and draw something. She had the strange feeling that she would lose the urge and never regain it if she didn't use it right away.

She looked out across Hoy Sound then rejected it as a subject. Although she would love to draw it, she didn't have time to do it justice now. There was also the issue of security. Photographs of the area were strictly forbidden, and even though she wouldn't include military structures in any picture, she didn't want to risk trouble. No, she needed to start with something small.

Growing in a crack in a rock on the verge were a few shoots of grass and a single fragile thrift flower. The flower was long dead, desiccated and bleached from exposure to the elements. Mary fancied she could hear a faint papery rattle as the flower trembled in the light breeze. This was what she wanted to draw.

Resting the paper on her gas mask case, she gazed at the flower for a few minutes, studying the spindly stem. Before drawing anything she had always done this – examined the object minutely until she felt she knew every nook and cranny in perfect detail, and could almost feel the textures of all its surfaces. It was an act almost like meditation, and until now she hadn't realised how much she had missed this part of drawing. Finally, when she could still picture the flower with closed eyes, she put pencil to paper and began to draw.

Half an hour later, she held the drawing at arm's length and studied it, her head tilted to one side. It wasn't the best thing she'd ever drawn – she hadn't got the texture and shading of the stalk quite right, and she wasn't happy with the perspective of the flower head. Nevertheless, it was clearly thrift, and she was pleased with how she had managed to capture the way the rock it grew in had weathered, revealing the various strata. It was a start and an encouraging one at that. She couldn't wait to tell Joe.

She rolled up the paper and put it in her pocket with the pencil then pulled her gloves back on and set out down the path with a spring in her step.

It was only when she reached the bottom of the track that it hit her. Her first thought had been for Joe and his reaction when he knew she had started drawing. Of course she was looking forward to telling Sally and Iris as well, but it was Joe who had first come to mind. Joe who had encouraged her without pressuring her. Joe who seemed to understand her better than any other. Joe who, she could no longer deny, Mary was in great danger of falling in love with. If she was honest with herself, she had known it for weeks. It had taken Joe's portrait to enable her to realise that it was no betrayal of Owen or her earlier self to admit she had feelings for another. She was simply allowing herself to accept the silver lining.

–

That evening, as Joe stood on the signal deck and deciphered the standard challenge signalled from Kyeness, he recognised Mary's signalling. He made the proper response, then added: 'Recovered from birthday?'

A moment later the reply came. 'Drawing again. Can't wait 2 show u.'

Chapter Seventeen

'Here you are, girls. You'd better hop out here. They won't let you into the site.'

'Where are we?' Sally asked the private they had managed to hitch a lift with.

'St Mary's.'

Mary gasped with relief as she scrambled down from her perch on a wooden crate. The private was an erratic driver, and her knuckles were white from gripping the crate beside her to prevent herself being thrown against the side of the truck each time they rounded a corner. Praying her legs would support her, she hopped out of the truck then steadied Sally and Iris when they jumped down. After a cheery wave from the driver, the truck sped off, spraying them with dust and gravel.

Iris brushed down her skirt and said, her voice dripping with sarcasm, 'I can't tell you how glad I am that you persuaded me to accompany you on this jaunt.'

'I'm sorry. This was a stupid idea. We should go.' Sally clutched a shoebox to her chest. It contained the gifts they had put together for Aldo. For once she had lost her cheerful optimism, and Mary couldn't blame her.

They hadn't been able to see out from the truck but now they were in the village of St Mary's, she had to admit they couldn't have picked a bleaker spot to visit on their day off. There was no dramatic scenery similar to the high cliffs on the western side of Mainland, where they were based. Instead, flat fields stretched out on one side, with the grey waters of Scapa Flow lapping on the other. In between, low cottages huddled on the shoreline. More trucks sped past, depositing yet more dust on their clothes and the air resonated with the drone of heavy machinery accompanied by occasional booms. The sight that made Mary catch her breath, however, was the construction going on across the water separating Mainland from a tiny island a short distance away. Huge steel towers stood on either side of the Sound, with cables stretched between them. Baskets swung precariously from these cables. This was evidently the system used to transport rubble which was then lowered into the water.

It was clear that, as the private said, they wouldn't be allowed into the construction area. She could see gangs of men loading up the baskets and others heaving them into place. It was well organised and necessarily so – one wrong move and men could be crushed beneath tons of stone or swept away in the fast-moving currents swirling through the partially constructed causeway. Outsiders who didn't know what they were doing would not be allowed anywhere near the workers.

Sally gazed across at Lamb Holm. 'He's living *there*?'

Mary followed her gaze. A more dismal sight she couldn't imagine. It was so flat it was barely more than a greyish-green line hovering above the water. It was utterly without shelter; she could imagine the wind must howl across the island with no respite. A far cry from the warmth of Italy. Not that she'd ever been to Italy, but the name summoned up images of sun-warmed villages perched on green hilltops, vineyards and olive groves and clear blue skies. The Italian prisoners might be enemies, but Mary found room in her heart to pity them. It must have been a cruel shock to be transported here.

The thought galvanised her. Squaring her shoulders, she said, 'Come on. We can't give up now we've come this far.'

'Quite right,' Iris said. 'I caught the back of my leg on a crate, and I don't want to have sacrificed a precious pair of nylons for nothing.'

They set out for the works, although what they were going to do when they got there, Mary had no idea. They were just approaching what looked like a vast mess tent, thinking someone in there might be able to help, when a car passed them and parked on the verge.

'Isn't that Stewart Irvine's car?' Iris asked.

'Dr Irvine?' Sally asked.

'He'd be plain Mr Irvine now, if I had my way,' Iris said, directing a scowl at the man's back.

Any answer was made irrelevant when Stewart climbed out and surveyed the works.

Iris quickened her step. 'What are you doing here?'

Stewart gave a little start and span around. His shoulders relaxed when his gaze fell on the girls. 'Oh, it's you. I could ask you the same question.'

'We asked first.'

Mary couldn't blame Iris for her antagonistic attitude. Mary wasn't exactly a fan of his either, after his careless driving and subsequent failure to diagnose a concussion had left her and Iris stranded in Kyeness Signal Station in the middle of a storm with no means of sending a vital message.

Stewart shrugged. 'Not that it's any concern of yours, but I'm here to meet a friend – one of the officers running Camp Sixty.'

'Camp Sixty?' Sally stepped forward, looking eager. 'That's the POW camp on Lamb Holm, isn't it?' When Stewart replied that it was, she asked, 'I don't suppose you could ask him to deliver this parcel to one of the prisoners? It's not wrapped, so you can see there's nothing inside that shouldn't be.'

'Ask him yourself.' Stewart indicated an army officer approaching at a brisk pace from the tents. 'Philip,' he said when the officer reached them, 'let me introduce these lovely young ladies.' He named each of the three friends in turn, then introduced the officer as Lieutenant Philip Crow. 'I believe they have something to ask you.'

Sally showed the lieutenant the box. 'We were hoping you would deliver this to one of your prisoners of war, Aldo Vanni. He was kind to me when I met him in the hospital earlier this year, and I wanted to return the favour.'

The officer took the box and examined the contents, then gave a tiny shrug. 'I don't see any harm in it. On one condition.'

'What?' Sally looked apprehensive.

'Stewart and I are about to dine in Kirkwall, and we'd welcome some female company.'

Mary exchanged glances with her friends. She could see from their expressions that they were thinking the same thing. While they had nothing against Lieutenant Philip Crow, none of them felt like renewing their acquaintance with Stewart. Iris, whom Stewart had pursued, must feel especially reluctant. Then Iris glanced at the dreary island of Lamb Holm and gave a tiny nod. 'As long as you promise to deliver the parcel to Aldo, we've got time to eat.'

Mary gave a mental shrug and allowed Stewart to usher her towards his car. They could probably have got Aldo's parcel to him via the Red Cross but it might have taken weeks to go through the system even though, being in Stromness, they were under thirty miles from Aldo's camp. It seemed important for Aldo to get his gift in time for Christmas. Even Mary could see that. The lieutenant was doing them a huge favour by delivering the parcel, so the least they could do was spend some time with him in return. Her only regret was that they would be away from Stromness for longer than planned. She had hoped to spend the remainder of her day off drawing, to see if the sketch she'd done of the thrift was a one-off or if her artistic talents were reawakening.

Stewart didn't look impressed at having to dine with the girls. This didn't surprise Mary, considering they had been involved in the incident which led to his suspension. However, he held the car door open for them without voicing any complaint.

As Mary slid across the spacious back seat to make room for the others, her hand fell on a piece of paper. 'Here,' she said, holding it out to Stewart, 'I think this must be yours.'

She hadn't so much as glanced at the paper at this point. Yet Stewart's reaction made her wonder what it was. His face flushed crimson, and he snatched the paper from her hand so fast it gave her index finger a stinging paper cut. He stuffed it in his pocket saying, 'Thanks. Just… something I was working on.' Before it disappeared, she caught a glimpse of columns of scrawled writing and numbers, although it flashed before her eyes too fast for her to make out any of the words. Something about the layout struck a chord in her memory, but she couldn't place it. As she sucked her finger, she tried to work out what it was about the writing that prodded the back of her mind, but the memory proved elusive, and she gave up the struggle. If it was important, she was sure she would remember in due course; struggling to bring it to the surface only seemed to force it deeper.

After a much smoother drive than the one that had brought them to St Mary's, the girls clambered from the car in Kirkwall, and accompanied the two men through winding streets and into a smart-looking restaurant. They sat at a table near the fire, much to Mary's relief. The journey in the back of the truck had been bitterly cold, and she still hadn't warmed through. There was a brief silence whilst they studied the menu. Once they'd given their orders, Stewart still didn't seem inclined to talk. Mary couldn't help an inward smile, thinking that she, Iris and Sally would be the last people Stewart would want to dine with. Thankfully Philip didn't seem to notice the tension and seemed willing to carry the conversation himself.

'I'm interested to know how a Wren based in Stromness could befriend one of the POWs,' he said to Sally. 'How did it happen?'

'Oh, I met him in the spring when I was in hospital. Aldo was there at the same time, recovering from an appendectomy.'

At this, a spark of recollection lit Philip's eyes. 'Ah, now I know the prisoner you mean. I remember him falling ill.' He nudged Stewart. 'Not your finest hour, old boy!'

Stewart muttered something about an atypical presentation. Mary didn't understand quite what he meant although guessed it was an excuse for him missing acute appendicitis when he'd examined Aldo. From what Sally had said at the time, Aldo had nearly died because of

Stewart's misdiagnosis, and Sally had never warmed to Stewart as a result.

Philip clapped Stewart on the shoulder. 'I'm only teasing. And I'm sure this current misunderstanding will soon be cleared up, and you'll be back on your rounds before long.'

Stewart looked mollified, and the conversation moved on. At the end of the meal, which Mary thoroughly enjoyed, Philip paid the bill, waving away the others' offers of payment. 'Wouldn't dream of it. Can't think when I last had such an enjoyable afternoon. Well, I must be getting back.' He addressed the girls. 'Are you ladies going to be able to get back to Stromness? I dare say I could hitch a lift to St Mary's if you're going to have a problem and let Stewart drive you back.'

Iris glanced at her watch. 'There's no need. There's a bus leaving in an hour, and I've got some errands to run in Kirkwall. I'm sure the others agree.'

There was an edge to her voice that defied the others to request a lift with Stewart, although Mary didn't need any prompting. She had no desire to spend another half an hour or so in Stewart's company, and was confident Sally felt the same way.

'Definitely,' Sally said. 'I need to see about getting some new shirt collars. I couldn't get the right size in Stromness.'

'Well, it was lovely meeting you,' Philip said when they were outside and about to go their separate ways. 'I'll make sure Vanni gets his parcel.' Then he frowned. 'I say, I'm not aiding a budding romance? I couldn't condone—'

'Oh no,' Sally assured him. 'He was kind to me, and I wanted to do something nice for him in return. But there's nothing going on between us, you have my word.'

'That's all right then. Well, cheerio.'

'Gosh, I'm sorry, girls,' she said once Philip and Stewart had driven away. 'I never intended us to spend the day with Dr Irvine. Who'd have thought we'd bump into him in St Mary's of all places?'

'I seem to remember him mentioning he had a friend there,' Iris said. 'That was why he was on hand to look at Aldo when he fell ill. Don't worry about it, Sally, you couldn't have known. At least we know Aldo's going to get his gifts.' Then Iris frowned. 'Sally — is something wrong?' For Sally had put her hands to her temples as though suffering from a sudden headache.

'No, I'm fine. I just got a sudden feeling.' Sally continued to massage her temples. 'Something about Stewart,' she explained eventually. 'I think it's to do with my accident but I can't remember.' Finally she dropped her hands and shook her head. 'Probably nothing important. The doctor told me my memories of that day would probably be confused.'

For some reason, though, Mary couldn't shake off a suspicion that there was something odd going on with Stewart. Taken together with his reaction to the paper she had found in his car, there seemed to be too many questions about his behaviour. Why had he chosen to stay in Orkney despite his disgrace? Why did they keep seeing him on the cliffs for no apparent reason? Mary wouldn't rest easy until she had a satisfactory answer.

Chapter Eighteen

The following day, after finishing the morning watch and grabbing a bite to eat, Mary dashed up to her cabin to fetch the sketchbook Joe had given her and the pencils that had been a gift from Sally.

'Don't tell me you're going out in this?' Iris said, for although the sun shone it was bitterly cold.

'I have to. You know why.' When she had returned to the Wrennery after drawing the thrift she had shown the sketch to Iris and Sally, full of hope that she had at last unlocked her ability to draw. Fear had soon crept in, though, and when she had confessed her anxiety that it was just a one-off drawing, the others had encouraged her to try drawing something else as soon as possible. Having sacrificed her day off to deliver Aldo's parcel, she was keen to spend time drawing today.

However, when she was perched on a slab of rock opposite the tumbledown stone barn she wanted to sketch, she had to agree with Iris. 'Why couldn't you have come back in the summer?' she muttered, as though her desire to draw was a friend who had returned after a long time away. She removed her gloves, cursing the impossibility of controlling a pencil while wearing them. 'We had some lovely warm spells this summer, ideal for drawing in the open air. But oh no – you have to reappear when it's so cold I think my fingers will drop off if I take off my gloves for more than five minutes.'

Still, the light was good. The low slanting rays touched the stone blocks of the barn with gold and cast strong shadows, clearly defining the texture of the uneven walls. Mary started to draw, hesitantly at first then with more confident lines as the barn took shape on the page.

'Mind if I join you?'

Mary dropped her pencil at the sound of Joe's voice directly behind her. It hit her stone perch with a clatter and rolled into a clump of dead weeds. 'Bugger! The lead better not be broken – Sally gave it to me for my birthday.' Then she felt her face burn and imagined the scolding she'd get from her mam if she caught her talking like that. 'Sorry. You weren't supposed to hear that. What are you doing here?'

Joe retrieved the pencil and handed it back. 'I managed to wangle some time off. Had to after the last signal you sent. I met Sally and Iris in Stromness and they told me where you were.' He held his hand out for her sketchbook. 'Mind if I take a look?'

Ever since she had finished the drawing of the thrift, she had wanted Joe to see it. Now, as she leafed through the pages, she hesitated. What if he didn't think it was any good? His own drawings were so wonderful, she knew her sketches must seem rudimentary in comparison. After all, she was self-taught yet he had hoped to do an art degree. He'd had proper lessons. However, there was no avoiding it now. She found the drawing where she had tucked it for safekeeping and handed it to him. 'It's not very good,' she said. 'I didn't have long and my fingers were numb. It's not finished but I—'

'Stop apologising. This is beautiful.'

Mary examined his expression for any sign that he was just flattering her, but he looked genuinely impressed. 'You really think so?'

'Yes. If you want my advice, don't try adding to it. You've captured it perfectly. I love how you made the flower look so dry and fragile. I feel as though I could pluck it from the page.'

Mary felt her face heat again although for altogether different reasons than before.

'Can I see what you're drawing now?' When she nodded he sat beside her on the rock and craned his neck to see the picture of the barn.

Mary drew a sharp breath. When Joe had sat down, his knee pressed against hers, and her face grew even hotter. What was happening to her? He rested a casual hand on her shoulder so he could see her work, and she had to resist the impulse to unknot the scarf from around her throat and fan her face.

'You've got real talent,' Joe said. He went on to describe what he enjoyed about the picture of the barn, but Mary couldn't concentrate. All she was aware of was the heat of his hand upon her shoulder even through the many layers she was wearing, and she couldn't focus on his words. She heard something about light and texture but couldn't piece it together in her mind to make sense of it.

Get a grip on yourself! She told herself while she nodded and smiled at something Joe had said.

'And what would really finish it off perfectly would be a clown holding a dead seagull. What do you think?'

'Yes, lovely.' Mary frowned as Joe's last words filtered through her consciousness. 'Sorry, what?'

Joe was doubled over, laughing. 'Your face! But I get the message. I'm distracting you from your work. Don't let me stop you. I'm sure you want to carry on. I'll keep you company if you don't mind.' He pulled paper and pencil from his pocket. When Mary said she would enjoy the company, he moved to a rock a few paces away. To give them both space to work, he said.

Mary appreciated his consideration. She bent over her drawing, trying to give the appearance of concentration while really she was trying to arrange her thoughts into some kind of order. Apart from the brief moment in the Beehive when she had held Joe's hand, she had never been so aware of his physical presence. While she enjoyed his company, she had never felt any attraction towards him. Now, while she tried to get the lines of the stone door lintel right, she kept shooting surreptitious glances at Joe and found herself fascinated by his hands. She shivered suddenly, imagining how it would feel to entwine those long, dextrous fingers with hers.

Stop it! You're supposed to be drawing. She forced herself to focus on her work, turning away slightly so Joe wasn't a constant presence in the corner of her eye. It wouldn't look good if, after half an hour, Joe asked to see her sketch only to see she had added nothing to it. Something strange was happening to her. Why was she only noticing Joe now? It felt as though part of her, something buried in her inmost being, had been encased in ice for years and now was gradually thawing.

She shied away from what that might mean. She was used to who she was now and change frightened her. She lowered her head, narrowing her focus to the lines on the page. Even so, every now and again, she couldn't resist shooting a sideways glance at Joe when she thought he wouldn't notice. Sometimes she got the impression he had been watching her a split second earlier.

Concentrate! See how the weight of the roof tiles are making the roof ridge bow slightly. She sketched the curve, arranging the composition so the apex of each gable end lined up with the hills rising in the background.

She glanced at Joe again. She wasn't even aware she was doing it until he turned and their gazes met and locked. It felt as though a fist had been driven into her stomach, knocking the air from her lungs. Some power held her, paralysed, unable to tear her gaze away until she thought she might drown in the twin dark pools of his eyes. She shivered.

Immediately his face creased with concern. 'You must be frozen. I forgot you've been out here longer than me. Do you want to go back?'

She both did and didn't. The Mary emerging from frozen sleep wished she could stay out here for ever in Joe's company. The Mary who was frightened of what these new feelings might mean won out. She nodded. 'My hands are about to drop off.'

'Here.' Joe sat beside her again and took her icy hands between his and massaged them. A magnetic force seemed to twist her head so she was looking into his eyes again. Seriously, what was wrong with her? No matter how many gulps of air she drew, her lungs still felt starved of oxygen.

He smiled, his eyes crinkling in an attractive fashion. 'Is that better?'

'What? Oh.' She dropped her gaze to her hands, sandwiched between his. 'Yes, they're much warmer. Thanks.'

She pulled on her gloves then tucked her pencils away in her pocket. When she went to close the sketchbook, Joe stopped her. 'Can I see?'

'I haven't added much since you last looked.' Still, she turned the book so it was the right way up for him.

'And you were afraid you had lost your ability to draw! This is really good.'

'Thanks.' Mary had to admit she was pleased with her attempt. It might be nowhere near finished, yet she liked what she had done.

'If this is what you can do after a long break from drawing, I can't wait to see what you do when you've got back into the swing of it.' A pause, then, 'This is a real cheek, but I'd love to have this when you've finished it.'

'Really?'

'I wouldn't ask if I didn't mean it. This barn is a perfect picture of Orkney, and you've managed to convey something about the Orkney resilience; the way it's been battered by all weathers, yet is still standing.'

'If you like it you're welcome to it once it's finished.' Warmth blossomed in her chest. 'No one's asked for one of my drawings before.'

Joe rose and brushed down his clothes. 'Even better. In years to come I can boast of having an early Griffiths, drawn before the artist became famous.'

'Not as famous as you, surely?'

Joe shook his head, laughing. 'Whoever heard of a famous accountant?'

'Come on, if we're going to indulge in daydreams of me being a famous artist, I want you to be one too. Speaking of which, since you've seen my drawing, the least you can do is show me yours.' *I'll show you mine if you show me yours.* Good grief. Now she was reverting to being a giggling schoolgirl.

Joe shrugged, looking a little self-conscious. Then he pulled the paper from his pocket and handed it over. Mary took it, puzzled at his apparent embarrassment. He hadn't been bothered about showing her his work before.

Then she unfolded it and understood. She'd assumed that he, too, had been drawing the barn, and had been interested to compare their work. Yet his subject hadn't been the barn. It had been her. She supposed she shouldn't be surprised; he had shown a great talent for drawing people, after all. Hadn't he drawn her from memory for her birthday present? Like her drawing, it was unfinished. However, with only a few sparse lines he had managed to capture Mary's figure and make it recognisably her. She was bowed over her page, a pencil poised above the paper, and even though her face was only seen in profile and drawn with minimal lines, he had managed to convey a sense of concentration. Mary felt her face burn, knowing that what she had been concentrating on was not her work but Joe. There was even a hint of her breath misting in the air, bringing home to her just how cold the day was. She hadn't been aware of it at all whilst she had been drawing. Or thinking about Joe.

Her heart seemed to stutter when a thought struck. This picture explained why she had felt his gaze upon her while she had been drawing – it wasn't because he was unable to take his eyes off her; it was because she had been his subject. She tried to ignore the swoop of disappointment.

She gave a laugh and worked at keeping her tone light. 'You make me look so studious.'

'It's how you appeared to me. You seemed to be totally absorbed.'

Good thing he didn't know what had seized her attention.

Joe's gaze shifted and fixed on a point over her shoulder. 'Anyway, we'd better make a move. I don't like the look of those clouds.'

Mary twisted round to look and saw slate-blue clouds rolling in. She shuddered and gathered up her sketchbook and pencils. 'I'll be really fed up if my drawing gets soaked now I can actually draw again.'

But Joe shook his head. 'It looks more like snow to me. Let's get back.'

—

The first flakes started to fall just after Mary had packed away her sketchbook, tucking it inside her coat to keep it dry. She tilted her face to the sky and laughed as the feathery flakes fell on her cheeks and clung to her long dark lashes. Joe wanted to do nothing more than pull Mary close and taste the snow on her lips. It was only the prospect of her scathing indignation that helped him control his wayward impulses.

Having said that, he had detected a change in her today. He had sensed her looking at him several times while they were drawing, although he had only managed to catch her looking that one time. He had thought she seemed more self-conscious than usual; she had always been natural and easy in his company before, whereas this time she had seemed embarrassed to be caught watching. Were her feelings for him changing or was it just wishful thinking on his part?

'Mary, do you—?' Idiot! He strangled the words just in time.

She looked at him, eyebrows raised, the ghost of her smile lingering in her expression. 'What?'

Do you have feelings for me? Do you want to be mine? Do you love me? He wasn't entirely sure what he had been about to blurt out. Whatever it was, it would have been a mistake. She'd been in love with her fiancé, a hero from the *Royal Oak*. She wasn't going to give her heart to an accountant who was now a mere signalman. 'Are you on watch tomorrow?' He could only hope she didn't notice the hesitation and hasty change of words. 'I think we're due to sail out past Kyeness tomorrow. I'll be sure to send you a signal if you're there.'

A tiny crease formed between Mary's brows. However, she only said, 'I'll look out for you. I'm on the afternoon and night watches.'

And the moment passed. Joe released a breath then said, 'We've got a new minesweeper in our group so keep an eye out for her – the *Swallowtail*. There are a lot of youngsters on the crew.'

'I hope the U-boats stay away then. Have there been any more sightings? Well, I suppose sighting is the wrong word, but you know what I mean.'

Joe had clean forgotten about their last sweep of the area around Kyeness. 'Actually we did detect some unidentified signals on our Asdic sweep yesterday. They disappeared fairly quickly though so it was probably a false alarm.'

The look Mary gave him made him instantly regret telling her. There was real fear in her eyes, reminding him all over again that her fiancé's fate was never far from her mind. 'I don't understand. How are they getting past the loop undetected?'

'It was probably nothing. A large shoal of fish or something.'

'Are you telling me a load of fish torpedoed the *Snow Queen*?'

'Of course not. But Asdic picks up signals from a lot of underwater objects, not just submarines. Anyway, I don't think the U-boat that got the *Snow Queen* will try again. It didn't get far before it was detected.'

Mary didn't reply, and they walked in silence for a few paces. Joe hoped he had sounded more convinced than he felt, because he didn't want her to worry. Personally he was concerned that a U-boat had made it as far as Orkney without being stopped, let alone past the loop and into what should have been secure waters.

When Mary spoke again it was with a forced lightness that told Joe that she, too, didn't want to dwell on dangers outside her control. 'If the snow gets much heavier, it's going to make the walk back to Kyeness difficult this evening.' She wrinkled her nose. 'It might be Christmassy, but slogging through deep snow in the dark isn't going to be much fun.'

Hardly were the words out of her mouth when she slipped and would have fallen had not Joe steadied her by flinging his arm around her shoulder.

'Thanks,' she said, grinning up at him.

Her face, flushed from the cold, was so luminously beautiful it made Joe's breath catch in his throat. Instead of pulling away as he'd expected, Mary lingered a moment in his hold and continued to gaze at him, her eyes widening. Their faces were so close, Joe only had to stoop a little more and he would be kissing her.

An instant later, a large snowflake landed on Mary's eyelashes, making her blink and step back. The tension melted away as quickly as the fragile snowflake, and Joe released a shaky breath. That had been close. Kissing her could have been a terrible mistake, costing him their friendship. She had already made it clear she wasn't attracted to him, and he needed to accept that.

When she was ready to continue, he took a shred of comfort in the easy way she leaned on his arm. Their companionship was precious to him, and he would do nothing to spoil it.

Nevertheless, when he recalled the way she had looked at him just now, he couldn't completely silence the chime of hope that rang in his heart.

Chapter Nineteen

The snow continued to fall most of the night, and Mary was proved right in her prediction – the path to Kyeness had become treacherous. The Wrens who arrived at 2300 to relieve her and Iris from the evening watch warned them to go slowly, as the snow was so deep it hid the line of the path. 'Your best bet is to follow our trail if it's still visible,' one of the new Wrens said. 'Although we lost the path a few times.'

Her warning was needed. While the Wrens' footprints were clearly visible near Kyeness, they quickly disappeared; several times Mary or Iris strayed off the route and found springy heather underfoot. They were forced to feel their way, painfully aware that a sprained ankle could have serious consequences in these conditions. Thankfully they made it back to the Wrennery without any accidents.

'First thing tomorrow,' Iris said as they trudged up the stairs to their attic cabin, 'we're going to see if we can buy a walking stick each. They'll make it easier to feel the path.'

They awoke the next morning to a transformed world. The snow had stopped falling and the sun was shining. The streets of Stromness gleamed blue-white, the buildings changed overnight from grey stone to sparkling ice. Spirals of smoke rose from the chimneys. The children walking to school threw snowballs, their shouts and laughter sounding oddly muffled.

Mary wanted to do nothing more than return to bed after breakfast and huddle under her blankets. True to her word, however, Iris dragged her and Sally out to the shops to look for walking sticks. 'You'll thank me later when you have to walk back to Kyeness. This snow doesn't look like it's going to melt any time soon.'

Sally, predictably, was in raptures over the weather. 'Won't it be marvellous if it lasts until Christmas?' she said, turning in a circle once they were outside, gazing at the snow-covered scenery. 'It's like a fairy tale.'

'You'll change your tune once you have to walk to Kyeness in the dark. It took us twice as long.'

'You'll get used to it. I used to live up on the North York Moors, remember. This is nothing compared to the snow we had there. Anyway, the walking sticks are a good idea.' Sally grimaced. 'Shame about the expense, though. Money's pretty tight, what with all our Christmas plans and getting things for Don Heddle and Aldo.'

'I've still got a bit of money tucked away from my allowance,' Iris said. 'I took care not to spend it all when my mother cut me off. We can use that if you're short.'

'Thank you, Iris. We'll pay you back,' Sally said, and Mary nodded in agreement.

'It would be a great help,' Mary said. 'Thanks, Iris.' Like Sally, she had been wondering how she was going to make her pay last. 'Have you heard from your mother?'

Iris's face clouded. 'Not yet. I keep writing, but so far she hasn't replied.'

'That's awful,' Sally said. 'I couldn't imagine being at odds with my mother.'

Iris looked glum. 'Our relationship was difficult at the best of times. I always got on better with Daddy.' She broke off, her voice quavering.

It wrenched Mary's heart to see Iris upset. Christmas was a time for family, so it must be a painful reminder not only of her father's death but her estrangement from her mother. Mary patted Iris's arm. 'She'll come round,' she said. 'Keep trying. I'm sure she'll want to make things right with you once the initial grief fades.'

Iris raised her chin fractionally. 'I hope you're right. That reminds me, though. I bought her a lovely scarf for Christmas. I must get it to the post.' She bit her lip. 'I'll send another letter, too, although I doubt she'll reply. She still blames me for Daddy being in that convoy.'

'That's ridiculous,' Sally said. 'It's not as if you organise the convoys.'

Iris sighed. 'I can't help asking myself; what if things had been different? He requested a posting near me because he was against me getting involved with Rob. If I hadn't, he might still be alive.'

'You can't blame yourself for that.'

'I try not to. Rob's done his best to make me see I'm not responsible.' Despite her sorrow, Iris's face glowed at the mention of Rob as though there was a lamp shining out from behind her eyes. It occurred to Mary to wonder if she would ever look like that if she fell in love, and for some reason Joe's face flitted across her mind's eye.

'Do you think your mother blames herself?' Sally asked. 'I mean, didn't she insist your father put a stop to you seeing Rob? Maybe she feels guilty and that's why she can't bring herself to make it up with you.'

Iris stopped and stared at Sally. 'I hadn't looked at it that way before. You could be right.' Then the tiny flare of hope that had dawned in her expression disappeared. 'Although she was so cruel. I don't know how we can ever get past that.'

'Bereavement makes you do funny things,' Mary said, remembering her own behaviour in the early days of her grief. 'Everyone reacts differently.'

'That's right,' Sally said. 'Take my mum. I don't think she's ever recovered from my dad's death, not really. He was the love of her life, and she says she's never wanted to marry again even though more than one man has asked. Yet one of our neighbours in Whitby was widowed two years ago. They were a lovely couple – there's no doubt she was deeply in love with her husband – but six months after the funeral she was married to a widower from Robin Hood's Bay, and they're very happy together.'

That gave Mary pause for thought. When Owen had died, she had thought she would never find love again, had never so much as found another man attractive. Until now. She thought again of the intense awareness she'd had of Joe the day before when he had caught her. She'd felt as though time had stood still, and she'd forgotten all about the snow and the cold, only aware of Joe's deep brown eyes boring into hers. She hadn't felt like that since… since Owen.

She found herself lagging behind Iris and Sally as she sought to come to terms with a looming suspicion: was she falling in love with Joe? She had been wandering her own personal maze of grief for so long that she thought she had lost her way. Now, though, it was possible that her serpentine wanderings had brought her to a new place. A place where she had room in her heart for another without denying the love she would always hold for Owen.

Iris turned and paused. 'What are you doing back there – trying to imitate a statue? You'll freeze!'

It was only then that Mary realised she had stopped walking. Giving herself a mental shake, she broke into a trot and caught up with her friends. She reached them just in time to hear Sally say to Iris, 'All I'm saying is, give your mother time. She'll come to her senses, and when she does, she'll know she won't want to lose her daughter.'

'You're right. Thanks, Sally,' Iris said. 'All the more reason to get that scarf and letter in the post.' She started walking again, the snow crunching beneath her shoes. 'Anyway, we've got walking sticks to buy.'

And while they went about the business of choosing walking sticks that would hopefully prevent accidents in the snow, Mary tried to rid her mind of unsettling thoughts of love.

–

Armed with their new walking sticks, Mary and Iris made lighter work of the trail to Kyeness when they returned that afternoon. Mary quickly found that Iris's theory had been correct – using the sticks they could feel their way ahead and determine if they were still on the rocky path or about to put a foot into a hole or stray into the heather.

'Have you decided what to get Elspeth and Archie for Christmas?' Iris asked her when they paused for breath at the top of the hill. Even with the walking sticks, each step used more energy when their feet sank into the snow.

'I thought about it a bit more yesterday,' Mary said. 'I'd like to do a drawing for them but I don't know if I'm good enough.'

'Of course you are. That's a wonderful idea.'

'I don't know what to do in the time, though. There's only a bit over a week to go, and we're going to be busy.'

'Why not give them the picture of the barn? They'd love that.'

'Oh. I... well, I promised it to Joe.'

'Really?' Iris shot her an amused look; that one word loaded with insinuation. 'You've been seeing a lot of Joe lately. Are you sure there's nothing more than friendship between you?'

Mary opened her mouth to deny it, then changed her mind. Iris had gone through a lot of soul searching before finally admitting she was in love with Rob. Teasing aside, Mary knew she could trust Iris to give her honest opinion and help her work out her feelings for Joe. 'I don't know,' she admitted. 'I don't know how I feel.'

Iris rubbed her gloved hands together, giving Mary a thoughtful look. 'That's new. What's happened to change your mind?'

'I wish I knew. I was fine before when we were just friends. I mean, at first Joe made it clear he...' Mary groped for the right words, not wanting to sound big-headed.

'Fancied you rotten?' Iris finished for her with a grin.

'Well... yes.' Mary ducked her head, unable to return Iris's knowing look.

'And now you feel differently. What's the problem? Joe will be thrilled.'

'I might feel differently but I don't know if I have genuine feelings for him or if it's just a passing crush. I like him too much to mess him around.'

'But you feel something?'

'Yes, but it's so confusing. I've never felt awkward with him before and now I hardly know how to act.

Nothing feels right.' Mary gave an exasperated huff. 'I don't even know how to stand or move my arms. It's like I've forgotten how my joints work. And I can't concentrate when he's around.'

'It sounds like you've got it bad.'

'But is it love?'

'Mary, you're putting too much pressure on yourself. There's no way of knowing if it's love if you've only started feeling this way recently. This is why we go on dates with the people we're attracted to. It gives us the time to work out how we feel. You must have done that with Owen.'

Mary shook her head. 'We were always friends. After Martha died, we did everything together. I never woke up one day and decided I was in love with him. We gradually changed from friends to sweethearts. I can hardly remember a time when he wasn't one of the most important people in my life.'

'Look, don't worry too much about it. You just need to let Joe know you wouldn't be averse to going on a few dates with him. Then see how it goes from there.'

'But how do I let him know?'

Iris leaned on her walking stick and regarded Mary with a frown. 'You've never had any difficulty speaking your mind before. Why the problem now?'

Because she badly wanted it to work out. The answer sounded in her mind, so clear she was surprised Iris didn't hear. Iris was right, though. She'd never had a problem speaking her mind before. She needed to stop fretting and let Joe know... what? She wasn't sure how she felt. Iris had already given her the answer, though. *This is why we go on dates.* She would ask Joe on a date. Oh, she knew it was the done thing for the woman to wait for the man to ask her out. That wouldn't work in this case, though, because he had already asked her out and she had told him in no uncertain terms that she would only go out with him as friends. He wouldn't ask again, so she had to do the asking.

But how? For the first time she appreciated how difficult it must be for some men to ask women out. Although she might have a reputation as a plain speaker, she cringed at the prospect of looking Joe in the eye and confessing that if he still felt the same way, she would like to go on a date with him.

'Have you ever asked out a man?' she asked, in the hope that Iris could give her some pointers.

'Me? No fear. It's not at all the done thing.' Then Iris caught her eye and had the grace to blush. 'Fine. Granted, it was hypocritical of me to tell you to ask Joe out, but what choice do you have?'

None. Not if she wanted things to change. 'Maybe Sally can suggest how to do it.'

She and Iris exchanged glances and said, 'No,' at the same time. Sally had been eating her heart out over Adam for years. If she thought it was acceptable to ask out a man, she would have done it ages ago and saved herself years of heartache.

Mary was still mulling over what to do when they arrived at the signal station. She forgot her worries for a while when faced with the view from the signal room. Kyeness in the snow was breathtaking. Across the shimmering waters, the hills of Hoy rose in shades of icy blue and white instead of their usual green, gold and brown. Snow clung to the cliffs, glittering like diamond dust, so bright Mary had to squint to prevent her eyes from being dazzled. There were only a few places where the pristine white carpet was scuffed with footprints – the trail the Wrens used to get to and from Kyeness from the

Wrennery and along the path around the cliffs, leading to the geo where Archie kept his boat.

'Funny,' she said to Iris who had climbed up to the signal room behind her, 'I didn't think Archie would be going out in his boat in this weather.'

'I'm sure he wouldn't. Why?' When Mary pointed out the footprints, Iris shrugged and said, 'Perhaps he went down to make repairs.'

'I didn't think of that. You're probably right.' Mary concentrated on the water, familiarising herself with the vessels sailing around Hoy Sound. Along with a few smaller boats – mostly fishing boats – there were four minesweepers doing their regular sweep of Hoy Sound. It was a sobering thought that the fourth vessel must be HMS *Swallowtail*, added to the group to replace the destroyed *Snow Queen*. Even so, her heart lifted at the sight of the *Kelpie* at the head of the flotilla.

'There she is,' Iris said, coming to Mary's side. Like Mary, her gaze was fixed on the *Kelpie*, although her thoughts would be fixed on Rob rather than Joe. 'Does Joe know you're on watch now? What's the betting he signals you before five minutes are out?'

Sure enough, only a couple of minutes later, a light flashed from *Kelpie*'s signal deck. First of all, it transmitted a standard identification – totally unnecessarily, considering the minesweeper was close enough for Mary to identify the ship through the telescope. Not that she needed to – the *Kelpie*'s unique layout of masts and funnels was engraved on her memory.

Iris grinned. 'I'll leave you to signal, shall I? I think that was for your benefit.' She went to make an entry in the log book, leaving Mary to pick up the Aldis lamp and signal back that the message had been received.

A moment later another signal flashed, eradicating all doubt that it was Joe on watch. Just one word: 'Mary?'

Mary grinned and sent back, 'Who else has the patience 4 ur luna c?'

'Luna c?' A pause, then: 'Lunacy. V clever.' This was followed by the string of dots that was shorthand for laughter.

And then she knew how she could ask him out. She would do it using the signal lamp. That way she wouldn't blush, stammer or get tongue-tied. True, anyone else on the ship who could recognise Morse would be able to read the message, but when Mary had spoken to Joe before about sending personal messages, he had always assured her that no one else in view of the signals had the time to stop and spell out the messages. Iris would be able to follow the message by listening to the clatter of the shutter though. She thought for a moment.

'You couldn't make us some tea, could you?' she called to Iris. 'I'm parched after that walk.'

'Course.'

Mary didn't need to turn to see Iris leave; she could hear her descend the steel ladder through the hatch in the floor. As soon as the metallic clang of feet on the rungs died away, Mary drew a shaky breath. 'This is your chance, Griffiths,' she said under her breath. 'Don't mess it up.'

She raised the Aldis lamp again and sighted the *Kelpie*. Doing her best to control the sudden shake in her hands, she sent: 'R u free 2nite 4 a d8?' The minesweepers were heading for their anchorage, so she hoped Joe would be able to come ashore that evening. However, no sooner had she sent the dash-dot-dot for the 'd' at the start of 'd8' when the *Kelpie* pitched into a deep trough between two unusually large waves. She had a horrible feeling that the vital part of the message, the bit about it being a date, hadn't got through. She held her breath, waiting for Joe to send back that he'd received the word.

'T sounds gr8. C u 1900 in NAAFI.'

T? Mary stared at the *Kelpie*, which was now rounding the headland, in bemusement. Then it hit her. Joe must have only received the first dash of the letter 'd' and not seen the following two dots, let alone that she'd followed it up with an '8' at all. He'd interpreted it as 'T' for 'Tea' and thought she'd invited him for a drink. As friends. So much for trying to be clever. Still, she would see him this evening. Somehow she would make him understand she'd wanted a date.

Chapter Twenty

Mary trudged to the NAAFI after her watch, still bewailing the mischance that had made Joe misinterpret her message. It was common for a ship on the sea to pitch, making the signaller lose sight of the signal before a word could be completed. However, it was usually obvious to the signaller that he had missed the end of the word and would ask the signaller at the signal station to repeat. If they hadn't developed this game of attempting an increasingly obscure shorthand, Joe would have known the message was incomplete.

When she entered the NAAFI, she cursed her fate even more. The NAAFI was noisy, crowded and so smoky it made her eyes and throat sting. While it was a fun place for a group of friends to meet and have a shouted conversation about anything other than the war over a drink and a game of cards, it was not exactly the place for a romantic rendezvous. If she were Sally, she would take it as a sign that she and Joe were meant to be nothing more than friends.

She squared her shoulders as she looked around the crowded room. She wasn't Sally; now she was resolved to work out her true feelings for Joe, she would see it through.

Her heart gave an odd thump when she caught sight of him sitting in the corner, waving at her. She weaved her way through the throng and sat down opposite him.

'What would you like to drink?' Joe asked, rising.

Mary shook her head. 'Nothing. I'm fine.'

A bump in the back of her chair jolted her forward, banging her ribs against the edge of the table. 'Sorry, love,' said a man in army uniform, who Mary vaguely recognised as one of the men stationed at the Ness Battery. He sat at the table next to them and proceeded to enter into a conversation with his fellows, roundly abusing his sergeant, officers and everything on Orkney. He was so close and spoke in a carrying voice, which meant Mary couldn't help overhearing every word he spoke. No matter how she tried to block the nasal voice and the string of obscenities, it kept invading.

'How was your day?' she asked Joe, desperately trying to focus on him and work out how to bring the conversation round to the subject of their relationship.

'All the better for your signals this afternoon,' Joe said with a half-smile that set her insides aflutter.

This was the perfect opening. She drew breath, still not entirely certain exactly what she was going to say.

'And as for the bleeding weather, don't get me started,' said the voice from the next table, as easy to ignore as a foghorn. Contrary to his words, the private then went on to rail against the cold, the wet and the fog without needing any prompting at all.

It was no good. The NAAFI was about as romantic as a compost heap, and certainly not the place for a conversation about the state of their relationship. And if she could hear every word said on the next table, surely they would be able to hear her.

'Why don't we go for a walk?' she asked Joe, raising her voice to block out a complaint about the ceaseless wind.

'But it's dark.'

'I know. I could really use some fresh air, though.'

'Because you don't get nearly enough of that up at Kyeness,' Joe replied with a grin. Nevertheless, he rose and pulled on his coat.

Once they were outside, Mary let out a breath of relief. 'I'm sorry, but I was going to go mad if I had to listen another word from that private.'

'He was a bit much, I agree. Ah well, it's a beautiful night.' Joe offered her his arm. Mary took it gratefully, for the snow had been reduced to slush beneath hundreds of tramping feet, and now the slush had frozen, making the way treacherous.

Joe was right, though; it was a beautiful night. The sky was clear, and the blackout meant that even in the middle of the town, the stars were bright. The Milky Way arced above them like a snowy road through the sky. A crescent moon provided enough light to show them any obstacles. If Mary had been able to order the perfect night for a romantic conversation, she couldn't have thought of a better one. Her heart sped up. This was it. She had to say something now or she might not get another opportunity.

She drew a shaky breath, wishing her throat didn't feel so tight. 'Joe, do you—?'

Her words ended in a squeal as her right foot slipped on the ice, and it was only the fact that she was holding Joe's arm that stopped her from falling flat on her back.

'Careful!' Joe hauled her upright and held her steady.

'Thanks.'

They walked a few more steps, Mary taking more care to place her feet where there was still a layer of snow to give her shoes more grip.

'You were about to say something,' Joe prompted after a moment.

'Oh, yes. I… do you think…' It was no good. 'Do you think the Heddles would like a drawing for Christmas?'

'I'm sure they would love one.'

Joe went on to praise her talent, but Mary only half listened. She never normally had any trouble speaking her mind, so why couldn't she get the words out now? *Joe, do you still have feelings for me?* Eight words, that was all. Eight words to put an end to her doubt once and for all. For the first time, she felt sympathy with Sally rather than exasperation that she had drifted into a friendship with a young man and not been able to express her feelings. After falling into the habit of friendship, it was harder and harder to change the course of a relationship. Although Mary and Owen had started out as friends, they had been only children when they had first known one another. Their relationship had evolved naturally from friendship to love as they had matured. With Joe it was different. If Mary had been able to return Joe's feelings when he had first expressed an interest, she would have had nothing to lose. Now she stood to lose Joe's friendship if he no longer felt the same way about her. She was fast coming to realise how much his friendship meant to her, and she didn't want to risk it.

'Have you decided what to draw?' Joe's voice jolted her from her introspection.

'No. I would have drawn Curlew Croft, but you've already done that.'

They walked in silence for a few steps. Then Joe said, 'How about the Ring of Brodgar? Have you been there? I'm sure I've heard Elspeth say that's where Archie proposed.'

'That sounds just the place. They're not using it for military manoeuvres, are they? Iris, Sally and I planned to go there on one of our days off, but the army were driving tanks through there and wouldn't let us near.'

'I don't think so. I'll check. When's your next day off? I can take you if you like.'

'Yes please. I'm free tomorrow. Is that too soon? I'm on night watch tonight.'

'Tomorrow would be ideal. We're staying in harbour tomorrow so I should be able to get leave.'

A whole day with Joe. Surely then she would be able to work out how to move their relationship from friendship to something more.

She shivered and moved closer to Joe. Much as being close to him affected her, the shiver was purely from cold. Even through her gloves, her fingers were turning numb. The clear night, stunning as it was, also meant the cold was about as intense as she had ever experienced.

'Ready to go back inside?' Joe asked. 'I suppose the NAAFI is the only option.'

'I think so. The Fourpenny Bash will be over, and we'll have missed the start of whatever film they're showing at the Garrison theatre.' The Fourpenny Bash was a lavish spread of baps, cakes and tea put on in the church hall each afternoon by the Women's Voluntary Society for the servicemen and women.

Mary put up no argument when Joe turned to retrace their steps to the NAAFI. She didn't want to say goodbye to him yet, and it was too cold to stay out any longer.

Considering she had to walk back to Kyeness for her night watch later, it was a bad idea to get cold now.

The foghorn-voiced private was still holding forth to the poor unfortunates sitting with him. This time, however, Mary spotted free seats on the other side of the room, where it was quieter. They both bought cups of cocoa, and Mary sat with both hands wrapped around her mug to warm them. Now she didn't have to battle to be heard, could she explain to Joe about him not fully receiving her signal?

'Fancy a game of backgammon?' Joe asked.

Mary accepted, grateful for something to do while she tried to work out what to say.

In the event, she got so absorbed by the game that the whole problem of Joe slipped from her mind. In fact she lost all track of time and it was only when she won the deciding third game that she glanced at her watch.

'Oh my gosh,' she cried, springing to her feet, 'I have to go or I'll be late.'

'I'll walk you to the Wrennery,' Joe said, pulling on his coat.

It was only when they reached the Wrennery door that she remembered that Iris was having supper with Elspeth and Archie and would be going straight to the signal station from there. 'Bother. I forgot I'd have to walk to Kyeness alone.'

'I'll walk you there,' Joe said. 'You shouldn't do that walk alone in the dark.'

'Don't be silly. You'd miss the liberty boat. I've done the walk alone before, and now, thanks to Iris, I've got my walking stick.'

'There's plenty of time. Trust me.'

In all honesty, Mary didn't need much persuasion. Maybe a secluded walk to Kyeness under the stars would be what she needed to inject some romance into the evening. She hurried into the Wrennery to collect her torch and walking stick then returned to Joe, glad it was dark so he couldn't see how flustered she was. A lot was riding on the walk. If she couldn't bring up the subject of her relationship on a cosy walk on a crisp, clear night then she doubted she would ever find the opportunity.

Yet again, though, it seemed impossible to move away from the comfortable friendship they had fallen into. As they walked up the lane all she could think to talk about was their planned drawing expedition to the Ring of Brodgar. They spoke of the different views she might choose, from one taking in the whole ring to a detail of a single stone, and how long they might expect to have good light to draw by. All the while she only paid half her attention to the conversation. The other half of her mind was occupied in wondering if the only way she could change the subject would be if she were blessed with some of that Christmas magic Sally kept talking about.

Finally when they reached the highest point of the walk, she paused to catch her breath after the long climb through the snow. She didn't want to release Joe's arm at all. If she had worked out one thing during the walk, it was that she wanted to be more than friends with him. Although they had spent the evening doing nothing more exciting that walking and playing backgammon, she wished all of her evenings could be spent that way, in the company of this kind man who made her laugh and understood her better than any other man alive.

She gazed up at the stars. Sally would probably tell her to make a wish. Mary didn't believe in any superstitious nonsense such as wishing on stars. No amount of wishing would give Joe a change of heart. He either loved her or he didn't. A point of light in the sky could have no effect on Joe's feelings.

She frowned when she looked at the northern horizon. 'That's odd. It looks like a fire out to sea or some kind of reflection.' She pointed out the smudge of violet light. As she watched, it seemed to flare and rise up in the sky, turning from violet to red to green. 'What is that?' she breathed.

Joe stood still, his face turned to the sky. Then suddenly he laughed. 'It's the Northern Lights,' he said. 'I've been so attuned to war – bombs and fires – it took a moment to work out what was happening.'

Mary watched the lights, entranced. Scarcely realising what she was doing, her hand groped for Joe's and gripped it hard, while she blinked tears from her eyes at the beauty of the sight. 'I've longed to see the Northern Lights. It feels like a dream.'

'A good one, I hope.' Joe squeezed her hand.

Mary gave a little laugh. 'Sally would probably say something about making a wish.'

'What would you wish for?' There was an unusual intensity to Joe's voice that made Mary's breath catch in her throat. This was it – the perfect romantic moment. She couldn't have hoped for a more auspicious occasion. Now was the time to tell Joe how she felt.

He was waiting for her to speak, and she had no idea what to say. 'What I wish… I don't know if it's possible…'

'Anything's possible on a night like tonight.'

Joe moved closer until all she could see was his face, crowned with the glow of the aurora. She only had to stand on tiptoe and their lips would meet. She lifted her hand to his shoulder and caught a glimpse of her watch as she did so, the dial dimly illuminated by the aurora. 'Oh my gosh,' she said, 'I didn't realise it was so late. You'll miss the boat if you don't hurry.'

Joe stooped until his breath caressed her cheek. 'I don't care. I'll take any punishment for your sake.'

'What?' She placed the flat of her hand on his chest to stop him moving any closer. It was as though every doubt she had ever had about her feelings for Joe coalesced into a cold, hard lump in her chest. 'Don't say that.'

'Why not? I love you, Mary, and I thought you had feelings for me. Let's enjoy the moment and forget about tomorrow.'

But the magic had dispersed, leaving Mary cold, although she couldn't adequately explain why. She only knew she couldn't allow Joe to be punished for her sake. She had to make him leave. 'I'm sorry,' she said. 'But this' – she pointed at the dancing ribbons of light – 'maybe it's all too perfect. It's too much like a dream or a romantic film. It's not like real life. What happens tomorrow and the day after, when the magic has gone, and it's just cold daylight? I don't want to spoil what we have – our friend- ship.'

'Friendship.' His voice fell flat. 'Of course, if that's what you want.'

Of course it wasn't. She wanted to declare her love. But something was stopping her. She wished she could explain the inner workings of her mind to him, but she couldn't make sense of it herself, let alone explain to him. All she knew was that something felt wrong and it strangled the declaration of love she'd been prepared to make only moments earlier. 'Please go,' she said. 'I couldn't bear for you to be punished for helping me.' She hesitated then, because she couldn't bear to lose their friendship altogether, added, 'I'll still see you tomorrow, won't I?'

–

She still wanted to meet him tomorrow? Joe couldn't work her out at all. Heartsore and confused as he was from her rejection, he couldn't bear to lose her friendship altogether. 'I hope so. Assuming I catch the boat.' Although he doubted he would get there on time and, being honest with himself, he could do with a few days to think over what had just happened. When she had held his hand and gazed up at him, he had been so sure he had seen love and longing in her eyes. But maybe it had been no more than reflected radiance from the aurora.

Mary sighed. 'I'd have never let you walk me to Kyeness if I'd known you would get into trouble.'

'Like I said, I wanted to be with you, even if it's just as friends.' He did his best to keep his voice even and not let any trace of pleading into his tone, much though he was tempted to beg her to reconsider. He shouldn't be surprised that Mary saw him as nothing more than a friend. A young woman as witty and beautiful as her could have her pick of the men who must be lining up for her attention. What would make her choose a dull signalman and former accountant? He would be grateful for her friendship and not embarrass her or himself by trying to change her mind.

'I'm sorry. I thought—' Mary's voice sank to a murmur, and Joe couldn't be sure if she was still speaking to him or merely thinking aloud. 'But I don't suppose I'll ever be ready.' Was that a note of regret in her voice? Joe tried not to let himself hope. Better for his peace of mind if he accepted she would never be his sweetheart.

Then Mary squared her shoulders and looked Joe in the eye. 'Anyway, I've got to get to Kyeness and you might still make it to the boat if you run.'

'I can't let you go alone.'

'Yes you can. I do this walk alone often enough, and I've got my walking stick if I'm savaged by a marauding seagull.' She gave him a little push then marched towards the signal station without looking back.

Even so, Joe waited. Mindful of a recent rule banning servicewomen from leaving the bounds of Stromness alone at night – apparently introduced for their safety during the long blackout hours – he couldn't just abandon her. The lights in the sky illuminated the hillside enough for him to watch her until she was safely inside the signal station. Only then did he turn his back on her and hurry to Stromness as fast as the icy conditions would allow. Above him the glow faded to a red smudge on the horizon then disappeared altogether.

He knew it was futile even before he set out, but seeing as Mary had been so upset by his misleading her, he knew he had to try to catch the boat for her sake. He took a crumb of comfort in the knowledge that she had still been disappointed at the prospect of not seeing him again that week. He couldn't understand why she was so annoyed with him, though. He thought women wanted men to make big romantic gestures to win their hearts. What could be more romantic than wanting so badly to be with her that he was prepared to face punishment for doing so? Not that he'd needed to make any kind of gesture after the aurora had obliged so wonderfully. His mistake had been in getting so carried away with the romance of the moment that he had misread Mary's body language. She had held his hand, leaned against his shoulder. He had been so sure that meant she felt the same way as him. Well, he realised his blunder now. Maybe it would be better for them both if he stopped seeing her; he didn't think he could pretend to want nothing more than friendship any longer.

When he reached the pier, skidding on a patch of ice, there was no one but a rating from the *Kelpie* who had also missed the boat. He was gazing across the water, taking drags from a cigarette which he had smoked down to a stub. When he saw Joe, he dropped the dog-end and ground it under his heel.

'Boat's long gone, mate,' he said. 'Bleedin' 'ell. Who'd have thought it – the golden boy himself getting into bother. Come on, I know where we can doss down for the night. Can't wait to see the look on the skipper's face when he realises his precious yeoman of signals missed the boat.'

As he'd expected, when he finally managed to get to the *Kelpie* the next morning, he was obliged to appear at Petty Sessions as a defaulter where he received a tongue-lashing from the skipper. As punishment he was sent below to the galley to scrub potatoes when not standing watch and confined to the ship for a week. He had a twinge of regret when the liberty boat left without him in it. It was for the best, though. He'd had a night to think it over and had decided that he needed a break from Mary so he could work out whether he could endure the pain of being just friends now he knew he would never earn her love.

Three hours later, his hands red and raw, he was released from the galley to go on watch. As he made his way through the ship, he was surprised to find his shipmates standing in huddles in the narrow corridors, deep in conversation. Not feeling in the mood to talk, he pushed past and was about to climb the ladder leading to the main deck when he overheard a young stoker say, 'Ten bob says we're going to the Med.'

Joe froze, his hand on the ladder. 'The Med? What's happened? Are we leaving?'

'Where've you been all morning? Haven't you heard – orders arrived this morning. We're heading down to Harwich on Boxing Day for ten days' embarkation leave, then it's off to who knows where. My money's on the Med.'

'It'll be the Arctic convoys,' said another stoker gloomily.

Joe didn't wait to hear more but hastened up the ladders to the signal deck, his head in a whirl. He'd been based in Orkney for so long, he'd taken it for granted he would stay for the duration of the war. He couldn't take any interest in where the *Kelpie* was being sent. All he knew was that he wouldn't be near Mary. Now, more than ever, he regretted missing the liberty boat. So much for having time to reflect on their relationship. Being confined to the ship until Christmas, he had only one day left to spend in her company.

At least the bombshell had made one thing quite clear – he was not going to leave Orkney until he had done all in his power to win her heart.

Chapter Twenty-One

'Excuse me, Miss Tredwick, Miss Griffiths!' A man's voice hailed them from a distance as Mary and Iris picked their way cautiously over the icy paving stones. They were returning to the Wrennery after their night watch.

Iris paused and glanced over her shoulder. 'Isn't that the lieutenant who took us to lunch with Dr Irvine?'

Mary looked back. 'I think so. I wonder what he can want.' She grinned at Iris. 'Perhaps you've made a conquest and he's come all the way from the other side of the island to track you down.'

Iris quelled her with a look. 'You can stop that right now unless you want a lump of ice down the back of your neck.'

They waited for the lieutenant to catch them up. When he got closer she could see it was definitely the man they had met at St Mary's. She groped for his name. Philip Crow; that was it. He held a box under one arm that looked like a shoebox, the lid secured with string.

When he caught them up he greeted them, and after exchanging pleasantries, he said, 'It's a bit of luck seeing you here.' He tapped the box. 'I was looking for your Wrennery to drop this off for your friend, Miss Hartley. You've saved me a trip.'

'For Sally?' Mary took the box and saw it did, indeed, have Sally's name written on it. 'What is it?'

'A gift from Aldo Vanni. A thank you for the Christmas gifts.'

'Oh my goodness. You won't get into trouble, delivering a parcel from a prisoner?'

'Don't worry. It's all been inspected. Nothing to cause trouble for anyone.'

Once Philip had taken his leave, Mary gave the box an experimental shake and heard a rattle inside. 'I wonder what's inside.'

'Only one way to find out. Come on.'

They raced back to the Wrennery and took the stairs two at a time. They found Sally in their cabin, sitting cross-legged on her freshly made bed, darning a hole in her seaman's jersey.

'Present for you,' Mary said, handing her the box.

Sally listened, wide-eyed as Mary explained where it was from. 'I hope he didn't go to too much trouble. I never expected anything in return.'

'Hurry up and open it.' Iris hovered by Sally's shoulder, tutting with impatience when Sally picked at the knot fastening the parcel, getting nowhere. In the end, she marched to the chest of drawers and rummaged in her drawer for a few seconds before pulling something out and slamming the drawer closed. 'Here,' she said, pressing a penknife with a mother-of-pearl handle into Sally's hand. 'For goodness' sake, cut the string before I explode.'

'I can't do that. It's so wasteful.'

For once, Mary agreed with Iris. She was burning with curiosity to learn what a prisoner of war could possibly send to a Wren. She had to resist the urge to snatch the box from Sally and slice the string herself. It was only by dint of clasping her hands behind her back that she managed to control herself while Sally picked at the knot.

At last the string unravelled, and Sally lifted off the lid. Inside were several pieces of carved wood – driftwood, Mary guessed – and on the top was a postcard.

'What does it say?' Iris asked.

Sally picked up the card. 'Thank you to my English angel. Merry Christmas. Aldo Vanni.'

'Is that all?' Iris sounded disappointed.

'There's not room on the card for much more.'

'Let's have a look at the carvings.'

Sally lifted one from the box. 'They're animals.' She held up the carving she was holding for Mary and Iris to see. It was a lamb, beautifully carved. It was small, nestling in Sally's palm, yet tiny details like the eyes, nose and mouth and the lamb's curly fleece were clear to see.

'Strange thing to send,' Iris said.

'I told him how much I missed my uncle's farm. Perhaps that gave him the idea. We kept sheep.'

'I don't think all the carvings are sheep,' Mary said, looking in the box. 'Let's see the rest.'

There were three more lambs, a cow and donkey. There were other carvings, though, that weren't animals at all. Sally lifted out a carved man wearing robes with a crown on his head. 'It's a crib scene,' she said, her face glowing with delight. 'How wonderful. Look, here are the three kings, and these must be shepherds. Yes, look, they're holding crooks.'

Mary looked and saw the three shepherd figures did, indeed, have crooks with their distinctive curved heads etched into the wood.

Sally rummaged in the box again. 'This must be Mary and Joseph. Oh, and look, there's even a tiny manger with the baby Jesus.' The baby was little more than an oval lump in the manger, but the minute lines carved into the driftwood made for a convincing representation of straw. 'This is just perfect. I said the decorations at Curlew Croft weren't complete, didn't I? This is what was missing – a crib scene. It's just the thing for their mantelpiece. I can't wait to show Elspeth.'

Each piece was passed round and the girls exclaimed in delight over each new detail they saw. However, when Sally carefully packed them back in the box, ready to take to Curlew Croft, Iris said, 'But Aldo only got your gifts a few days ago. How could he have done all this in such a short time?'

'I didn't think of that,' Sally said, biting her lip. 'He must have been working on it for weeks, and it wasn't meant for me originally. I wish I could ask him about it.' Then she shook her head and retied the string around the lid. 'I don't suppose I'll ever know. I'll just have to accept it as another wonder that's happened this Christmas.'

At the mention of Christmas wonders, Mary was engulfed in cold shame. While on watch, she had managed to lock away the memory of her, Joe and the Northern Lights in the tiniest compartment of her mind. Now it was as though the lid had burst open, flooding her head with the images and sensations of the previous night. She closed her eyes in an attempt to ward away the picture of Joe's pained, confused face, but there was no escaping it. She had hurt Joe and didn't even understand why. When Iris had asked her about her evening, she had given a noncommittal answer, too ashamed to reveal what had happened. At some point she would have to confess, although she was glad of the distraction provided by Aldo's gift. Hopefully it would give her time to work out what to tell her friends, as she dreaded their reaction.

'What are we going to do today?' Iris asked. 'You do realise it's Christmas Day a week tomorrow and this is our last free day all together before then?'

'Why don't we take a trip somewhere?' Sally said. 'We've got everything ready for Christmas, haven't we? Your choice, though, after I dragged you all the way to St Mary's the other day.'

The mention of a trip plunged Mary into deeper gloom, reminding her as it did of the plans she'd formed with Joe. Plans he wouldn't now be able to keep. 'Actually, there's still one gift I haven't organised, and I'll need a trip out to do it. You know I was planning to do a drawing for Elspeth and Archie?' The others nodded. 'Well, Joe suggested the Ring of Brodgar, because it's where Archie proposed to Elspeth.' Mary's voice wobbled a little but she recovered herself. 'Joe was supposed to take me today, but he missed the liberty boat.'

'Why?' Iris nudged her playfully. 'What did you do to make him lose track of time?'

'Nothing! Mind your own business, Iris.' Seeing Iris's shocked face, Mary drew a deep breath. 'I'm sorry. I didn't mean to snap.' Aware that her hands were balled into tight fists, she drew another breath and forced her hands to relax. 'I'm tired, but that's no excuse for biting your head off. Forgive me?'

Iris's face softened. 'Of course.'

'Anyway,' Mary hurried on, 'Why don't we go to the Ring of Brodgar later?'

'I think that's a wonderful idea. I've always wanted to go there,' Iris said. 'Come on, Mary. Let's grab some breakfast before they stop serving, then put our heads down for a quick nap. There's no point in going anywhere before the sun rises.'

Mary followed Iris downstairs, knowing she would have to tell her friends about Joe soon, before the strain of keeping it secret made her lash out again. It was the anticipation of their disbelief and disappointment that held her back. If only she could work out why she had shied from Joe at the last moment, it would be easier to make the confession.

–

'Here you are, girls. This is where I have to drop you.'

Mary scrambled from the back of the truck they had hitched a ride in and thanked the driver – a Wren taking supplies to the Royal Navy Air Station at HMS Tern. With crunching gears, the truck sped away, leaving Mary, Iris and Sally alone on the deserted roadside. On one side of the road, a loch lapped at the snowy shore, and a low hill rose on the other side, crowned with many stones, stark grey against the snow. Mary was relieved to see the stone circle was deserted and not, as she had feared, overrun with tanks.

'It's huge,' Sally breathed, gazing at the ring in awe. 'Just looking at it makes the back of my neck go all tingly.'

For once, Mary didn't make a caustic remark about Sally's over-fanciful imagination. She, too, could feel the weight of history pressing upon her shoulders. No doubt about it, this place had held deep significance to countless generations; the air was charged, making her nerves sing. If she strained her ears, she could swear she would be able to hear layer upon layer of prayers and incantations, stretching back to the unimaginable past. Her fingers itched to capture the scene. She could only hope to convey some of the atmosphere as well.

'Let's go up. I want to see the stones up close before I decide upon the composition.' So saying, she picked her way through the snow and walked up the slope.

'Good thing we brought our walking sticks,' Iris said, then promptly slipped backwards with a squeal and collapsed into a concealed hollow in an inelegant heap.

Mary could hardly stand upright from laughing. 'Yes, it means I can do this.' She held her walking stick for Iris to grab and use to haul herself back to her feet. 'I think you must have fallen into a rut made by the tanks. Joe said the army's been all over here.'

Taking more care this time, they made it to the stone circle without further incident. Now Mary could see the stone circle was surrounded by a deep ditch. Thankfully, once they'd made their way around the ditch for a short distance, looking for an easy route across, they found a causeway that enabled them to reach the stones without having to scramble through goodness knew what obstacles might been hidden in the ditch beneath the deep layer of snow.

'Are you really going to sit here in the snow and draw?' Iris asked, rubbing her hands together. Each word was accompanied by puffs of vapour hanging in the air.

'I don't have much choice if I'm going to get this drawing done for Christmas,' Mary replied. 'Why don't you two go for a walk to keep warm whilst I'm working?'

They didn't need much persuading and wandered around the circumference of the huge stone circle, leaving Mary to select the view she wanted to draw. She soon found it. One of the stones was split down its length which, together with the layer of snow clinging to its north face, gave it an interesting shape. Mary decided to place this stone in the foreground of the composition. She could then fit a further seven or eight stones, which would be enough to hint at the circular shape of their layout. With distant snowy hills forming the background, and the long shadows cast by the stones across the snow, Mary couldn't wait to see the picture take shape on the page. She made a seat from their bags, rested her sketchbook on her knees and started to sketch the outlines.

Some time later, the sound of approaching laughter drew her attention away from her drawing. She looked up to see Iris and Sally striding towards her.

'Don't tell me you're still at work,' Sally said. 'We've walked all the way to the Stones of Stenness and had a stroll beside the loch. You must be frozen. We've been gone over two hours.'

Until that moment, Mary hadn't been aware of the cold. Now, however, she was aware of the pinch in her fingertips. 'I suppose I did lose track of time.'

Sally bounded up beside her and peered at the sketch. 'That's beautiful. I've come over all goose-pimply just looking at it.'

'Are you sure that's not due to the cold?' Mary asked with a grin.

'No, Sally's right.' Iris had joined them and now looked over her other shoulder. 'This is amazing. Very mysterious and dramatic. Elspeth and Archie are going to love it.'

Warmed by her friends' praise, Mary held the sketch-book at arm's length and eyed it critically, comparing it with the actual view. She had to admit she was pleased with the result.

'It's not quite finished – I need to work on getting the contrast right between the layers of stone.' On seeing her friends' pained expressions, she hastened to add, 'Don't worry, I'll do it when we get back.' She stood, wincing at how stiff and cold she had become. 'Good grief, it's perishing! I could do with a walk myself to warm up.'

'Let's walk to the Stones of Stenness, then,' Iris said. 'You shouldn't miss those, and we'll be more likely to hitch a ride back to Stromness if we walk on to the main road at Stenness.'

Stamping her feet to restore the circulation, Mary packed away her drawing materials. Then they set off at a brisk walk to the other side of the stone circle, crossing the ditch on a causeway on the opposite side to the one they had used to cross into the stone circle and then down the hill towards the road.

'It's a shame Joe couldn't be here, seeing as drawing the Ring of Brodgar was his idea,' Sally said.

'Why did he miss the boat last night?' Iris asked.

She was definitely going to tell them; she just needed a bit more time, that was all. 'Oh, he lost track of time. Anyway,' she hurried on, thinking fast, 'what about you, Sally? Did I see you had a letter from Adam? Has he finally noticed how wonderful you are?'

That did the trick. Sally's expression softened. 'It was from Adam, yes. Just general chat. I really think it shows he has feelings for me. I mean, he didn't say anything in the letter, but he probably felt embarrassed, knowing the letter would be censored. He's quite shy, really.'

'Maybe you should tell him about Aldo's gift. That might spur him to a declaration.'

'Do you think that would work?' The hope in Sally's voice made Mary regret her flippant suggestion.

'You never know,' was the only encouragement she could give in all good conscience.

'On the subject of letters, I got a letter from Aunt Sybil yesterday,' Iris said.

'How is she?' Sally asked.

'She's fine. Full of encouragement for my work in the Wrens and wishing me a happy Christmas. She sent a parcel but I'm saving that for Christmas. I don't suppose I'll get anything from my mother.'

'Give her time,' Mary said. 'She'll come round eventually, I'm sure of it.'

Iris gave a wistful smile. 'I hope you're right.' Then she made a gesture with her hand as though signalling the end of that line of conversation and addressed Mary. 'Anyway, don't think you can get away without telling us all about your date. We want to hear all the details.'

'Yes, tell us.' Sally bounced on her toes. 'Where did you go? Did he kiss you? I bet he did.'

Mary had to stop this now before Sally started organising the wedding dress. 'It wasn't like that. There was… a moment.'

She paused, searching for the right words. Sally pounced before Mary could continue. 'I knew it! He kissed you, didn't he? Don't deny it.'

'No, listen.' Mary stamped her foot in frustration as she tried to order her thoughts. Iris and Sally stared at her in surprise, the laughter fading from their faces. Finally having a pause, Mary drew a steadying breath before resuming. 'I've been wanting to say something all day but I didn't know how. We went for a walk, and it was so romantic.' She told them about the Northern Lights before concluding, 'It was perfect. And then he went to kiss me, and I just couldn't.'

'What do you mean?' Iris asked. 'Don't you fancy him then?'

'I don't know.' Her words ended in a wail. After bottling up her emotions all day, it was suddenly a relief to talk. 'I thought I wanted him to kiss me, but when he tried, I pushed him away. Then I could see he was confused but I couldn't explain why I couldn't kiss him. I still can't.'

Sally patted her arm. 'Slow down. Think back. Did he do or say anything that you didn't like?'

Mary shook her head. 'No. We were looking at the Northern Lights. It was a beautiful moment.' She gave a little laugh. 'I even said that if you'd been there, you would have told us all to make a wish.'

There it was again – the twist of panic. 'That's odd,' she said. 'It's reminded me of something but I can't quite recall what.'

Iris slipped her hand through Mary's other arm and gave a tug to resume their walk. 'It'll come. Probably when you're least expecting it. And I'm sure everything will work out. Like Sally, I'm convinced the two of you belong together. My advice is, don't avoid him – that would only make things worse in the long run. Talk to him.'

'Good advice, except we won't see each other until Christmas Day. He missed the boat, remember?' She explained how it had happened.

'That's a shame, but don't you think it's romantic?' Sally said. 'I mean, he must have known he would miss the boat if he walked you to Kyeness. He willingly did something he knew he would get punished for just so he could be with you.'

'I knew you would say that,' Mary said. 'Maybe you're right. Only it makes me feel…' She struggled to put her thoughts into words. 'Like I owe him,' she finished. 'I don't like being in debt to anyone.'

'I'm sure Joe doesn't look at it that way,' Iris said. 'He thought it was a price worth paying. He won't want anything in return.'

Mary didn't reply. Together with the elusive memory, the notion that she owed Joe was an itch in the back of her mind. She didn't understand why it bothered her yet she couldn't shake the feeling. She worried over it until they crossed the narrow causeway separating the Loch of Stenness from Loch Harray and the Stones of Stenness loomed into view. She made a conscious effort to enjoy the view and leave the worrying sense of debt for another time. She was probably making up problems where they didn't exist, too used to tragedy and loss. She could only hope that Iris was right, and when she saw Joe again, they would be able to work through the problem.

Chapter Twenty-Two

When a brisk walk around the Stones of Stenness failed to warm them up, the girls decided to head for the main road and hitch a ride back to Stromness.

'What I wouldn't give for a steaming cup of tea and a bowl of soup right now,' Iris said, stamping her feet and wrapping her arms around her body as they stood by the roadside, on the lookout for a passing car or truck.

As luck would have it, only a couple of minutes later, an army truck rattled towards them and pulled to a halt. The driver stuck his head out of the window. 'Where are you going, girls?'

'Stromness.'

'It's your lucky day. Hop in.'

A few minutes later, the truck dropped them on Cairston Road before trundling to the depot. This still left the girls a bit of a walk into town, so they set off at a brisk pace.

'Oh no, that's Stewart,' Iris said in an undertone when they reached the harbour. 'I hope he doesn't spot us.'

Mary looked and saw it was indeed Stewart, talking to a man she vaguely recognised but couldn't place. 'Who's that man he's with?' she asked, also keeping her voice low. Quite why they felt the need to lower their voices she didn't know, as the air rang with the shouts of the men loading and unloading goods from the boats, and the only way Stewart would be able to overhear them was if she and Iris were yelling to each other through megaphones.

'I don't know, but he looks familiar.'

At Sally's suggestion, they turned up a side road and left the harbour behind. 'I know who that man is,' Sally said after a while. 'Malcolm Pence – he's the skipper of the *Puffin*.'

'I wonder what Stewart could want from him?'

Mary shrugged. 'He seems to know people from all over Orkney. Through his work, I suppose.'

'You're probably right. Anyway, forget him. I'm frozen. Let's grab a bite to eat at the Beehive,' Iris suggested.

Knowing the Wrennery would be perishing cold at this time of day, the others agreed and soon they were tucking into hearty portions of vegetable pie in the deliciously warm cafe, talking about the sights they had seen that day. However, Mary couldn't help noticing that although she would have expected Sally to be full of talk about the mysterious stone circles, she only seemed to have half her mind on the conversation. For most of the meal, she sat with her eyes downcast and her mind seemed elsewhere.

Presently Iris sat back with a sigh, her plate scraped clean. 'If it hadn't been for having to dodge Stewart just now, this would have been a perfect day,' she said. 'A glorious walk, beautiful scenery and now a filling meal.'

'And I've made a good start on Elspeth and Archie's present,' Mary reminded them. There was a lull in the conversation while the waitress cleared their plates and they ordered fatty cutties – soft curranty biscuits that Mary had developed a taste for, as they reminded her a little of Welsh cakes. 'What about you, Sally? You've been quiet. What's your favourite part of the day?'

'Not seeing Stewart, that's for sure.'

Iris shook her head. 'You're never going to forgive him for misdiagnosing Aldo, are you? I mean, I feel awkward around him because I was stupid enough to go out with him a few times, but I would have thought you'd have got past your dislike by now.'

Sally bit her lip. 'It's not only that. I don't know why, I just feel uncomfortable around him. I wish he'd moved away after getting suspended.'

'Maybe he doesn't have anywhere else to go,' Mary said. 'I do think it strange he keeps skulking around the cliffs in this weather, though.'

Sally's head snapped up as though she'd just thought of something. 'The cliffs. What does that remind me of?' After a moment she shook her head. 'It's no good. It felt like something was on the tip of my tongue, but it's gone. The more I try to remember, the further away it gets.'

'It'll come back when you stop trying,' Iris told her. 'Probably wake you up at two in the morning. That's what happens with me.'

The bell on the door jangled, accompanied by a blast of cold air as it opened. Mary, who was facing the door, glanced up. 'Speak of the devil,' she murmured. 'No, don't look,' she said quickly, to stop Iris and Sally craning their necks. 'Stewart's just walked in.'

Sally shrank into the shadows. 'I hope he doesn't see us.'

Mary, too, was reluctant to talk to him. While she didn't share Sally's mistrust or Iris's embarrassment, she didn't feel particularly comfortable around Stewart. She studied her teacup, determined not to catch his eye, and was relieved when he took a seat on the opposite side of the room, near the door, without appearing to notice them.

'I think we're safe,' she said to the others. 'We'll have to pass his table when we leave, but I don't think he'll see us here.'

'Shame we ordered fatty cutties; we could have slipped out while he was ordering,' Iris said.

There was nothing they could do, however, as the waitress was already approaching their table bearing their order. The girls kept their voices low as they spoke so as not to attract Stewart's attention, and Mary glanced his way every now and then to make sure he wasn't looking.

Much to her relief, he appeared to be concentrating on scribbling some notes in a little book. She didn't think too much of this at first until she recalled the page she had found in his car, and her memories clicked into place. 'Oh my gosh, I'd completely forgotten,' she muttered to Iris and Sally. 'Remember that bit of paper I found on his car seat when he gave us a lift that day?'

'What of it?' Sally asked, brushing crumbs from her jersey.

'I'd forgotten all about it, but now I remember seeing it covered in numbers. Times, I think. He snatched it back before I had a chance to look properly. The thing is' – Mary shot another glance at Stewart to be certain he wasn't looking their way – 'when we were going to collect driftwood for the Christmas tree, I remember now that I saw a scrap of paper blow past. And I thought that had numbers on it. I was sure I'd seen someone moving up on the cliffs, too.'

Iris heard Mary out with her head tilted to the side, eyes narrowed. 'And we've seen Stewart up on the cliffs several times.'

'So you don't think it's a coincidence?' Mary had been braced to defend her suspicion and was taken aback to find Iris jumping to the same conclusion as her. 'You think Stewart's been noting down times of…' but here inspiration ran out. 'What would he need to note down, do you think?'

'No idea,' Iris said, and Sally looked equally blank.

'I'd love to see what he's writing,' Mary said, dabbing up the last crumbs on her plate with her finger. Once she was satisfied there was nothing left of her fatty cutty, she pulled out her purse and handed Iris enough change to cover her meal. 'You pay the bill, I'm going to try and take a look at what he's writing. See you outside.'

She pulled on her outer gear then made for the door. She hadn't taken more than three steps when she saw that merely passing his table on the way to the door wouldn't allow her to see what he was writing. His right arm was curled around his notebook, making him look like a schoolboy taking a test. She toyed with the idea of greeting Stewart as she drew level with him to give her an excuse to get close enough to see past his shielding arm. No, that wouldn't work. Remembering how he had snatched the paper from her in the car convinced her that he would slam the book shut the moment he knew anyone was close enough to read what he was writing.

Looking past Stewart, Mary noticed two Wrens occupying the table next to his. One she knew well, as she was also a visual signaller based at Kyeness. The other she recognised by sight as a recent arrival whose work involved maintaining the anti-submarine nets in Hoy Sound. Changing course, Mary weaved past two other tables to reach the Wrens. Much to her relief, Stewart remained too absorbed in his work to notice her.

'No Christmas for me this year,' the Wren Mary didn't know so well was saying. 'They've decided it's the best day to mend a section of the net.'

Mary hastened to interrupt their conversation, privately deciding to take the Wren aside for a stern lecture next time she saw her at the Wrennery. Hadn't she seen any of the posters warning against careless talk? She placed a hand on the foolish Wren's shoulder and greeted them both then addressed her next remark to the visual signaller. 'Evelyn, I saw you had a parcel yesterday and was burning to know what it was. A gift from your fiancé?'

That did the trick. Evelyn was newly engaged to a Fleet Air Arm pilot and was only too keen to talk about him. She plunged into a breathless description of the almost-impossible-to-find scented soaps he had sent. While she was talking, Mary angled herself so she could peer over Stewart's left shoulder.

She had just got a glimpse of the page when her foot caught the leg of Stewart's chair. He twisted round to glare at her, covering the notebook with the flat of his hand as he did so.

'I'm so sorry, how clumsy of me,' Mary said. Then she affected a start, as though she had only now registered Stewart's identity. 'Oh, Dr Irvine. How lovely to see you.'

Stewart was forced to smile and murmur a greeting.

'Actually, I'm glad I bumped into you,' Mary told him. 'I wanted to thank you again for the lovely meal the other day and for introducing us to Lieutenant Crow. I don't think we could have got our parcel to that POW without your help.'

'No problem at all,' Stewart said, 'I was happy to help.' He smiled, although it looked forced.

While he was speaking Mary darted a glance at the book and made a mental note of the few jottings that his hand wasn't covering. She drew a breath. In for a penny, in for a pound. 'Oh, I see I've interrupted you at work.' She pointed at the notebook.

'Yes, I... writing my next article.'

'Can I see?' Mary reached for the book.

'No!' Stewart slammed his hand over it. His features froze in an expression of pure panic for an instant before he schooled them into a polite smile. 'Forgive me. I don't like people reading my work until it's finished. I hope you understand.'

'Of course.' Holding this false smile was starting to make her face ache. It was clear she had seen all she could so she looked for an escape. 'Ah, I see Iris and Sally are waiting for me. I must dash.' With a cheery wave she sped out, allowing her smile to slip the moment she was outside.

'Well?' Iris said, gripping Mary's arm. 'What did you see?'

'Hang on.' Mary led the way down the steps and didn't speak again until they were on the busy main street. 'I wanted to be sure Stewart didn't come out of the cafe and overhear us.' She filled the others in on what she had done.

'But did you see anything before he covered it?' Iris asked.

'Yes. And I'm sure it was the same kind of list I saw in the back of his car and on the paper I saw on the cliffs.'

'What did it say?'

'I got a better look this time, although it was still only for a couple of seconds. I think I can remember a few lines, though. I need to jot it down before I forget.'

Seeing that they were passing one of the side streets that led to the piers, Mary turned into it and, after brushing the snow from a low wall, perched on it. She took off her gloves and handed them to Sally saying, 'Hold these for me, will you?' Then she pulled out a piece of paper and pencil from her pocket, mentally thanking Sally for her gift. Aware of Iris and Sally leaning over her on either side, their eyes fixed on the page, she wrote down all she could remember, pressing the paper firmly to her lap to prevent it from being whipped away in the breeze. The page had been divided into four columns, and she had glimpsed the last four lines. 'This is how the page was set out,' she said, drawing three lines to divide the page into four columns. 'The first column was definitely dates, and the dates I saw were yesterday's date and the day before.' She wrote: *15 Dec, 16 Dec, 16 Dec, 16 Dec*, one below the other in the first column.

'The next column had letters,' she said, chewing the end of her pencil as she visualised Stewart's book. Blessing her sketching experience which had given her a good visual memory, allowing her to recall details after only a fleeting glance, she wrote: *P, M, ?, P*, in the column next to the dates. 'I can't remember the letter for the second row,' she said to explain the question mark. 'I can't remember all of the next two columns, but I think this is what I saw.' In the line for the fifteenth of December, she wrote: *11.15 o* in the third column and: *13.30 i* in the fourth column. 'All of the numbers had an i or o after them, I'm certain of that. But I can't remember any other numbers apart from the last row, which had "13.30 i" in the fourth column. Oh, and it had "25-12" next to it. I particularly remember that because it was circled.' She wrote it in and put question marks in the remaining entries. Then she drew a circle around the final entry exactly as it had been in the original and stared at the strange numbers and letters, willing them to make some kind of sense. However, apart from the dates, she couldn't work out what it all meant.

'I can't make head nor tail of it,' Sally said, shaking her head. 'What does P and M mean?'

'I wish I could remember the letter in the second row,' Mary said. 'It might have given us a clue.'

'The numbers might be times,' Iris said.

'I suppose,' said Sally, 'but what do the letters next to them mean?'

'Could they be numbers too? Zero and one?'

'Zero what, though?' Mary asked, frustrated. The paper fluttered in the brisk breeze, and she held it tighter. 'I mean, it could be anything.'

'Place names?' Iris suggested. 'Orphir and…' She frowned, and Mary knew she was racking her brains for an Orkney place beginning with I. Mary, too, was trying and failing to think of one. Finally, Iris's eyes lit up. 'Isbister.'

Mary started to laugh. 'This is ridiculous. There's no way we can make any meaning from a set of random numbers and letters. For all we know, it could be a list of his meals.' She pointed at the top line. 'The day before yesterday he had porridge at fifteen minutes past eleven with…'

'Oysters,' put in Iris.

'Or onions,' Sally said.

'And at 1330 precisely he had indigestion,' Mary finished.

Iris pulled a face. 'Don't blame him, poor chap, if he's reduced to eating oysters with porridge. Everyone knows you should have oysters with lemon.'

They all looked at one another then simultaneously burst into gales of laughter, earning disapproving looks from a pair of elderly women who happened to be walking by.

Mary stuffed the paper into her pocket. 'Come on. Let's go back to the Wrennery. I'm chilled to the bone, and there should be a fire in the common room by now.'

Spurred on by the thought of a warm room and possibly even a mug of cocoa, Mary rose and strode out, only to be stopped after a few steps by Iris grabbing her arm.

The laughter had died from Iris's face, and she looked from Mary to Sally with an expression of apprehension. 'It has to mean something, though, doesn't it?' She frowned as though measuring her next words. 'What I'm trying to say is, why are we trying to work out what Stewart's notes mean? Do we think it's something suspicious? Because if so, we should report it.'

'You're right. I hadn't thought of it that way.' Mary slipped her hand in her pocket, feeling the paper. Did it hold the key to some nefarious scheme? But it seemed so outlandish. 'I suppose I was just curious, having seen his lists a few times over the past weeks.' She shook her head. 'No. I mean, I don't particularly like Stewart, and he was an awful doctor, but this is most likely wholly innocent. He writes articles for the papers, doesn't he? This is probably some way of keeping track of his submissions – you know, subjects, dates submitted, time handed in and time he got a response from the editor back out.'

'In, out, in, out, shake it all about,' Sally chanted, and they all laughed again and set off back to the Wrennery.

Despite feeling easier in her mind, however, Mary couldn't help feeling curious. She would keep the notes for now. Maybe show them to Joe. She would keep her eyes and ears open to see if she could work out their meaning.

–

The warmth of the common room, a steaming mug of Ovaltine and a boisterous game of rummy soon drove thought of Stewart's mysterious notes from Mary's mind. She was dealing out the cards for their fifth round when another Wren marched in. 'Post,' she announced, flourishing a bundle of letters. All the Wrens in the room crowded around her as she sorted the mail into pigeon holes.

'Tredwick,' she said, holding out three letters.

Iris pounced on them with a cry of delight. Seeing the handwriting on the first envelope, she ripped it open, shoving the others in her pocket without a glance. 'It's from Rob,' she said.

Leaving Iris to retire to her armchair with the letter, Mary hovered with Sally in the group awaiting their letters. Although her common sense told her not to expect anything, each time the Wren glanced at a new letter, Mary found herself holding her breath, only to release it in disappointment when it turned out to be for someone else. Not a note to her from Joe. It was a ridiculous hope when he must be stinging from her rejection. Nevertheless she didn't turn away until the Wren reached the last letter and seemed to be about to place it in a pigeon hole.

'No, wait. This is for you, Griffiths. I didn't see you there.'

The flare of hope died as soon as Mary took the envelope and recognised the cramped handwriting of Owen's mother.

Sally, looking disappointed to be left out, swept the half-dealt cards into a pile and set about shuffling them. Seeing Iris was absorbed in Rob's letter, Mary opened her own, although with less eagerness than Iris. Inside was a Christmas card printed on paper so flimsy Mary thought she'd have trouble getting it to stand up.

'Who's it from?' Sally asked.

'Owen's parents.' The picture on the front showed a robin perched upon a snowy holly branch. Most of the message inside the card was taken up with a bold, printed message wishing the recipient a 'Merry Christmas and a Happy New Year.' Mary snorted and read it to Sally. 'Not likely, considering we're at war with no sign of an end. You'd think the card makers would think up something more appropriate.' It seemed especially cruel for Owen's parents to be forced to send cards bearing cheery greetings when they had never got over the loss of their only child.

There was a handwritten message from Owen's mother at the bottom of the card. Mary winced and read it to Sally. 'We both think of you all the time and are so proud you joined the WRNS in Owen's memory.'

Sally placed the cards in a neat pile on the table. 'How lovely of them to think of you. It can't be easy, though, feeling you always have to live your life in Owen's memory.'

Mary stared at her. Was that what Sally really thought? She glanced at Iris, expecting her to chime in with her opinion. It was only then that she noticed that Iris was gazing white-faced at Rob's letter, blinking as though trying to hold back tears.

'Iris? What's the matter?'

Iris turned tragic eyes upon her friends. 'Rob's being transferred.'

Mary felt awful for her, knowing only too well the stress of living from letter to letter, never knowing if a loved one was safe and well at any given moment. 'Oh no. I'm so sorry. Does he say which ship he's moving to? Maybe he won't be far away.'

Iris shook her head. 'He's not changing ship. It's the *Kelpie*. The whole ship is being sent elsewhere.'

A lead weight dropped into the pit of Mary's stomach. 'What, the whole crew?' Was Joe leaving? That's what she wanted to ask but she dreaded the answer too much to be able to form the question.

Iris nodded.

'Where?'

'I don't know. He wouldn't be able to say in a letter, anyway. I only know the *Kelpie*'s leaving because we'd worked out a code. They're not going until after Christmas, though. There's that to be thankful for at least.'

Mary dropped into her chair. 'I suppose so.'

Iris reached over and clasped Mary's hand. 'I'm sorry. I was so caught up thinking of Rob I forgot Joe will be leaving too.'

The old Mary would have shrugged her off and retreated into her own dark thoughts. The temptation was there, but she knew it would help to share her fears. She was also aware that doing so would support Iris by letting her know she wasn't alone. 'We still have Christmas,' she said. 'We'll just have to make the most of the time we have left.' Maybe by then she would have sorted out her feelings. Whatever she decided, she knew she couldn't let Joe leave without letting him know how she honestly felt.

Chapter Twenty-Three

Mary soon got confirmation of her suspicion that she wouldn't see Joe until Christmas. The next day she received a forlorn signal from the *Kelpie*: 'No leave b4 xmas. Peeling spuds.' After a pause when Mary didn't respond apart from sending the signal to show the last word had been received, Joe sent: 'Miss u.'

This last message gave Mary reason for hope, taking it to mean that Joe was willing to forgive her for the way she had treated him. Glad Joe seemed to be dwelling on his faults rather than hers, she sent back: 'Your fault 4 missing boat.'

His signal came back: 'I know.'

Mary felt a pang of remorse. She had meant her message to be taken as good-natured teasing, but it looked like Joe had taken it as an admonition. That was hardly fair considering she was the one who owed an apology for her behaviour that evening. As she pondered what to send back, she glanced over her shoulder to make sure her oppo wasn't in a position to read or overhear her message. If she had been with Iris or Sally, she wouldn't have minded, but her oppo that day was a stickler for protocol; Mary didn't want to end up on report this close to Christmas. Thankfully she was still in the galley on the lower floor, so Mary relented and sent back: 'Miss u 2.'

Thankfully it was a quiet watch, and once the *Kelpie* and the other minesweepers were out of sight, there was little to do besides updating the log. Once Mary had done that, carefully omitting the more personal messages, she opened her sketchbook to add the finishing touches to the drawing of the Ring of Brodgar. All it needed was a little work to emphasise the many strata of the standing stones, and it would be complete. Mary couldn't wait to see Elspeth and Archie's faces when she presented it to them.

Thinking of presents sent her thoughts scampering back to Joe. She'd knitted him a hat and scarf but now she felt she wanted to give him something more. She owed it to him, somehow, considering he was not only being so understanding but had also willingly accepted punishment in exchange for walking her to Kyeness. She knew what she wanted to get him – the frame she had seen in Stromness. It would be the perfect size for the sketch of the barn that she had promised him, and what better design than one made of kelpies? There was no way she could afford it, though – twelve shillings was more than a week's pay. December had already been an expensive month, and Mary had very little money left, not to mention that she owed Iris for her walking stick. The frame was simply too expensive and she couldn't bear to ask for a loan from her friends. Not that either Sally or Iris would have much to spare. Today being Friday, she would be able to collect her pay at the end of her watch. However, once she had paid half of the money she owed Iris, sent a postal order to her parents and added two shillings to the Christmas kitty, she would be left with the grand total of two shillings and sixpence to last her for the rest of the week. Nowhere near enough to get the frame.

Unfortunately, now she had thought of it, there was nothing else she wanted to get him. Not that two and six would get much, and she didn't have time to make anything else. She sighed as she gazed out to sea. She would have another look around the shops this afternoon and pray she could find something perfect for practically nothing.

–

'It's no good,' Mary said to Sally the next day as they trudged through the snow for the afternoon watch. More snow had fallen in the night, blotting out the trail the Wrens had forged through the older snow, meaning they were taking great care not to lose the path, feeling their way with their sticks. 'I can't find a present for Joe that I like half as much as that frame.'

'Mary, you've already made him a hat and scarf. He'll love them. Why do you need to give him anything else?'

'I just want to get something nice for him to make up for having to spend all his free time in the galley this week.'

'But he knows you're strapped for cash at the moment. He won't mind.'

'*I'll* mind. He deserves more.'

Sally gave her a long look. 'You're not trying to make up for giving him the brush-off are you? Because I'm sure he'd much rather have an honest conversation.'

Mary squirmed. 'I know. I will talk to him, I promise. I still want to get him the frame, though.' Mary didn't know how to explain it. She hardly knew herself. She had never liked to feel beholden to anyone else, and she felt beholden to Joe at the moment. Although there was more to it than that, she shied from examining her motives too closely.

All she knew for sure was that giving him a lovely present felt the right thing to do.

'Very well,' Sally said, 'why don't you try this? Tell him you've got a plan for a present but it will take a few weeks. Then after Christmas you can save up for the frame. Don't buy something just for the sake of it. If the frame is the perfect gift, I'm sure he won't mind it being a little late.'

That was a good idea, and Mary told her so. 'It'll mean no days out or cinema trips until I've bought it, mind,' she added.

'I'm stony broke too,' Sally said. 'Nothing but the Fourpenny Bash for me on my days off until at least February.'

Having settled on Joe's present, Mary carried on to Kyeness with a lighter heart. That left her more space in her thoughts for the mystery of Stewart's notes. It was so frustrating not to have an idea what they meant yet have a sinking suspicion they had great significance. She couldn't report a bad feeling to her superiors or the police, though. She needed more.

They hadn't been on watch long when Mary spotted a familiar fishing boat. 'There goes the *Puffin*. Looks like she'll cross the loop in a few minutes so we might as well call Lower Skaill.'

'Mrs Spence will have her alarm clock set to make sure she has dinner ready when he arrives home just after 1330,' Sally said.

'1330?'

'You know – Mr Spence always seems to return at the same time.'

1330. Why did that ring a bell? Annoyingly, as was so often the case, the thought eluded her the more she tried to grasp it. While she grappled with the memory, Sally picked up the telephone and reported the inbound *Puffin*.

Inbound… outbound… Lights were switching on inside Mary's head.

'Oh my goodness. I think I've got it. Hold on.' Mary bolted from the signal room, her feet scarcely touching the rungs of the ladder in her hurry. As soon as her feet hit the ground floor, she lunged for her coat which hung on a hook beside the door and rummaged in her pockets. For a horrible moment she thought the paper must have fallen out, then her fingers closed over it. She pulled it out and raced back up the ladder.

Thrusting the page under Sally's nose, she said, 'Look – "P" is for *Puffin*. "1330" is the time it passes this point.'

'What about the i and o?'

'Inbound and outbound. It was when I heard you on the phone, reporting the *Puffin* outbound that it all slotted into place.'

Sally took the paper from Mary and studied it. 'It certainly fits,' she said. 'What about the "M"?'

'I suppose it must be another boat. I think Stewart's been making lists of boats going in and out of Scapa Flow, with dates and times. I bet you anything, if I'd seen more of the list, there would be initials matching other boats.'

'But why?' Sally pointed at the circled '25-12'. 'And what does this mean?'

'No idea. I've got a bad feeling about it, though.'

Sally looked at the paper again. 'If he was making notes about naval vessels, I'd be more worried. But what harm can there be in noting times of civilian boats?'

Mary shrugged, feeling helpless. 'It's not something we can take to the authorities, is it? I mean, didn't Stewart say he was writing an article about Orkney's fishing industry?

This could just be observations he's made for the article, although I can't think what use a list of times would be for it.' She couldn't think what use it would be for anything; that was the problem. She simply had the feeling it was important, and if she didn't work out why soon, something awful was going to happen.

–

Christmas Eve arrived and the girls went down to an early breakfast, discussing plans. They only had one watch that day – Sally in the morning and Mary and Iris in the afternoon. From six that evening they would all be on leave for three whole days.

'Don't you love Christmas Eve?' Sally said, stirring her porridge. 'I always think the day feels full of possibility, as if things could happen on this day that are impossible on ordinary days.'

'Maybe you'll be able to think up another parlour game for tomorrow, then,' said Mary, who had been jotting ideas on the back of an envelope while she waited for her tea to cool. 'I've got charades and consequences, but that's all I can come up with.'

Iris took the list from her. 'Leave it with me. That's my area of expertise. We used to play loads of parlour games each Christmas. It was my favourite part of the day.' Her eyes became unfocused and her face was lit with a soft smile, obviously looking back to happier Christmases. Mary saw the moment that the memory of her father's death hit her with fresh force, for she suddenly looked away, blinking, her lips pressed together. Mary knew that feeling all too well.

She squeezed Iris's arm then, sensing that sympathy would fracture her fragile control, said, 'But how will you manage without your butler to organise the games this year?'

Iris chuckled and punched Mary's arm. 'Idiot.' She dabbed her eyes then picked up Mary's pencil. 'Let's see,' she said in a brisk business-like voice, 'There's The Minister's Cat, Squeak Piggy Squeak, Forfeits…'

Iris scribbled her ideas down as she spoke, and by the time the girls had finished breakfast they had enough parlour games planned to last them until Easter. After Sally had dashed off in the dark with her oppo, Mary and Iris returned to their cabin to finish the cleaning they had left undone in their hurry to get to breakfast. Once everything was in order, they set about packing everything they would need for their stay at Curlew Croft.

Mary was just folding up the skirt she planned to wear on Christmas Day, running a regretful hand over its ragged hem, when Iris gave an exclamation. Mary turned to her. 'Something wrong?'

Iris was pulling two letters from the pocket of the cardigan she had just folded. 'Look what I found – the other letters that arrived the same day as Rob's. I forgot all about them.' She glanced at the first envelope and her face gleamed with pleasure. 'This is from Aunt Sybil.' She packed it with the cardigan. 'I'll save it for later.' Then she looked at the second letter and her expression froze. She sank onto the bed still holding it. 'It's from my mother.'

Mary dropped her skirt and went to sit beside Iris. 'That's good news, isn't it? You've been hoping she'll write.'

Iris made no attempt to open the envelope. 'What if it's just to tell me to stop writing to her?'

'There's only one way to find out.'

'I suppose.' Iris picked up her writing case from her bedside cabinet and pulled out her letter opener. Holding her mother's letter as though it might explode at any moment, she slit open the envelope and drew out a sheet of monogrammed notepaper. One side was covered in elegant handwriting, and Mary drew hope that Letitia Tredwick was reaching out to reconcile with her daughter.

'Shall I leave you alone to read it?' Mary rose as she spoke.

Iris clutched her arm and pulled her back down. 'Please stay. I'll need your courage to help me read it.'

Mary, painfully aware that she had yet to reply to the letter from Owen's parents, wasn't sure if she had any courage to spare. Nevertheless, she sat back down and waited while Iris perused the letter.

'Well?' she prompted when Iris put down the letter and gave no sign of speaking.

'She doesn't say much. No apology, nothing to show she regrets blaming me for Daddy's death.'

'But she did write. What did she say?'

'She wishes me a happy Christmas, hopes I'm well and even says she'd enjoy a visit from me next time I get a long leave.'

'That's encouraging.'

Iris gave a faint smile. 'It is. It's a start, anyway.' Her expression clouded. 'Rob and I had discussed taking leave together and visiting the Scottish Highlands, but I suppose that's impossible now. I might as well spend a few days of my next leave at home and see if we can put things right.'

'Do you think she'll reinstate your allowance?'

'I doubt it. Not unless I break up with Rob, which I have no intention of doing. She'll try and dangle my allowance over my head to manipulate me, but it won't work. Anyway, I've realised I won't need an allowance after I leave the Wrens – I'm going to be a dressmaker. According to Elspeth, all her friends are asking where she got her stylish coat from, and where they can get one like it. She reckons I'd have more than enough customers if I set myself up in business. I'll carry on making clothes as gifts while I'm here, so everyone will know who I am if this damn war ever ends and we can return to a normal life.' Iris bit her lip and looked down at the letter in her lap for a moment before saying, 'Anyway, that's quite enough about me. What about you?'

Mary looked at her in surprise. 'What about me?'

Iris nodded at the card propped up beside Mary's bed. 'When are you going to write Owen's parents a proper letter? I can see it's bothering you.'

It had been bothering Mary, although she hadn't been aware she'd made it that obvious. Several times that week she'd picked up pen and paper to write; so far she hadn't got past 'Dear Mr and Mrs Thomas'. The unfinished letter was lying on the chest of drawers beside the card, giving her a pang of guilt every time she saw it.

'It can wait until after Christmas. I've already sent them a card.'

With a shake of the head, Iris went to fetch the letter and Mary's pen and handed it to Mary, together with Iris's leather writing case to rest on. 'Don't let it hang over you and spoil your Christmas. You'll feel a whole lot better once you've written it. What's the problem, anyway? Afraid to tell them about Joe?'

'There's nothing to tell.'

'Then why is it giving you so much trouble? Go on – if you write it now, we can post it before we have to go on watch.'

Mary unscrewed the lid from her pen and under the greeting wrote: *Thank you for your lovely card*. Then she stopped, aware of the peculiar weight of guilt. She reread the card, and her eyes fell on the message saying how proud they were of Mary joining the WRNS in Owen's memory. That's when it hit her.

She must have made a noise, for Iris asked, 'What's the matter?'

'This.' Mary showed Iris the message. 'I didn't realise before, because I was reading it when you told us about the *Kelpie* leaving.'

Iris read the message then looked at Mary, eyebrows raised. 'Realise what?'

'That's why I haven't been able to write the Thomases a proper letter. Because I joined the WRNS to make up somehow for Owen's loss. I thought I was filling his place. And… and maybe I do feel more for Joe than friendship.'

'And you didn't want to upset them by thinking someone had replaced Owen in your heart.'

'No one could ever replace him,' Mary said. 'Joe's found a place in my heart I never knew existed until now. But I'll never forget Owen.'

'Then that's what you should tell his parents. I'm sure they'll understand. And they'd rather hear it from you than someone else.'

Mary couldn't argue with that. However, she still found it hard to write more than a few pleasantries – the same worn-out phrases she'd always used in previous letters. 'I don't know,' she said. 'What do I have to tell them? I think

I've messed things up with Joe. We're not even a couple and not likely to be now he's leaving.'

'It's not too late,' Iris said. 'I still can't work out why you turned him down. Have you thought about it any more? Maybe if you think back over what happened it will give you a clue why you pushed him away.'

Maybe it was something to do with having the Thomases' message on her mind, but when she thought back to the moment when she and Joe had nearly kissed, pieces of the puzzle fell into place. It hadn't been the near kiss that had made her push him away but his words. That was when she had felt uneasy about being with him. 'He said he would take any punishment for my sake,' Mary said now. 'But I'm not worth it. I don't want anyone else to suffer because of me.'

'Anyone *else*?' Iris frowned. 'What do you mean? No one's taken punishment because of you before, have they?' Then her eyes widened. 'Oh no, don't tell me you blame yourself.' She leaned forward and forced Mary to meet her gaze. 'Please don't tell me you blame yourself for surviving Martha and then Owen? Their deaths can't possibly be your fault.'

Mary couldn't answer. She opened her mouth then closed it again, her throat feeling strangely swollen.

'That's it, isn't it,' Iris said. 'I remember you saying no one expected you to survive diphtheria, then you recovered and Martha died unexpectedly.'

Tears blurred Mary's vision. She felt as though Iris had written her deepest secrets on a banner and was holding it up for the world to see. 'I should have died, not Martha,' she managed to say. She had never truly acknowledged that belief until Iris had said it, forcing her to face the truth.

Iris was shaking her head, and Mary was surprised to see tears in her eyes too. 'Oh, Mary. It wasn't your fault Martha died. It was a terrible tragedy, and a blessing that you survived. You don't deserve punishment.'

Memories were flooding back. Memories Mary had not known she possessed. Of being tucked up in her parents' bed, drifting in and out of sleep, distantly aware of the low murmur of voices in the next room. Then an animal howl had jolted her from her dreamlike state; Mary sat bolt upright, clutching the blankets and gazed wide-eyed into the darkness, shivering, every nerve in her body vibrating from the raw scream of a creature in agony. Then, unbelievably, Mary had heard words in the cry, and it wasn't an animal but her mother. 'No, no, no! Please, not Martha! It isn't fair.'

'It isn't fair,' she repeated now, forcing the words through dry lips. She wiped tears away with the heels of her hands. 'That's what my mam said when Martha died.'

'And you thought she meant you should have died instead? Oh, Mary.' Iris pulled Mary into a hug, heedless of the letter and ink pen on her lap. 'She would have been grateful you survived. I'm sure she'd be horrified to know you'd taken her words, spoken in grief, to mean she thought you should have died in your sister's place.'

Then Iris released Mary and sat back, frowning. 'I can't believe you've been carrying this guilt all these years. You must have thought Owen's death was some sort of punishment, and when Joe said what he did about punishment for your sake being worth it, it made you feel guilty all over again.'

All Mary could do was nod and wipe away her tears. None of this had occurred to her before, but it made sense.

Iris sighed. 'It is unfair. So unfair. Just as it's unfair my father died, and I seem to remember you lecturing me that it wasn't my fault. Or were you lying to make me feel better?'

'Of course not. How could it be your fault?'

'Exactly. And neither were Martha nor Owen's deaths your fault. They were a complete tragedy and wholly unfair. So please make me this promise.'

'What?'

'Promise me you'll start believing that you do deserve happiness.'

'Easier said than done.'

'I know, but we all have to start somewhere. And you can start by writing to Owen's parents and telling them about Joe.' When Mary opened her mouth to protest, Iris silenced her with an impatient gesture. 'And tomorrow, when you see Joe, you can explain everything to him. He's crazy about you, so I'm sure he'll understand.'

Seeing that Iris wasn't going to take no for an answer, Mary picked up her pen.

Chapter Twenty-Four

Christmas was for family. Mary knew that. It had certainly been true of her life growing up. It was why, after her sister had been ripped from them in the cruellest way, her family had never had the heart to celebrate it with the enthusiasm they'd put into it when Martha was still with them. But now she realised that her ties to her family were what had been holding her back. Her parents had never got over the grief of losing Martha. She'd thought she had, but now she saw that her relationship with Owen had not so much healed the hole in her heart as masked the wound. On Martha's death she had turned to Owen for companionship. She had genuinely loved him, there was no denying that, but she had never really faced up to Martha's loss. And maybe, just maybe, there had been the possibility that had Martha lived, Owen would have fallen in love with her, not Mary. Only now was she able to admit to the nagging sense that perhaps she and Owen would never have been a couple had not Martha died. While she had no reason to believe it – Owen had never shown a preference for Martha when they had played together as children – it was one of those unanswerable 'what ifs' that would never truly leave her.

But Joe, if she let him, would be wholly hers. Was that why she hesitated? Joe had never known Martha or Owen.

In being with Joe, she would be forming a bond that was completely new, with no link to Martha or Owen.

She did feel guilty. Guilty that she had survived when those most precious to her hadn't, and that was why she clung to the past and couldn't move on to a future without them in it. Now she saw that, she knew how foolish she was being. Had their positions been reversed, she wouldn't have wanted Martha or Owen to languish in the past, passing up all chances of happiness in the mistaken belief it was somehow keeping her alive. The trouble was, she was so used to living this way, she didn't know how to let go.

She hesitated, her pen poised above the paper, waiting so long a blot dropped from the nib. If she didn't get a move on, she would ruin the paper, and she didn't have much to spare. In the end, she let the words pour out, without worrying about grammar or construction.

I wish I could be with you this Christmas to tell you my news in person, but I don't know when I will get leave next, and I don't want to put this off any longer. I've met someone who I think I could fall in love with. I've made some mistakes, and I don't know if he will still want me, but he's important to me, so I wanted you to know about him. I don't know quite how I can put things right but I'm determined to try. The important thing I want you to know is that, whatever happens, I will never forget Owen. He will always be my first love and I'll always miss him. But now I've found a man I could be happy with, and I wanted you to hear it from me.

She kept the letter brief, only adding a few more lines to enquire after their health and wish them a happy Christmas. When she sealed the envelope the sense of relief was profound.

'Excellent,' said Iris once Mary had sealed and addressed the envelope. 'Now we'll get that to the post, and you can start to work out how you can make it up with Joe.'

–

Handing the letter in to be censored and posted was a weight off Mary's mind. The emotions of the morning had left her feeling hollowed out and light, as though she might be blown away on the slightest breeze. In the afternoon, she and Iris walked to Kyeness for their last watch before Christmas. Mary was quiet, still trying to process what she had discovered about herself, and Iris let her be. As their watch progressed, Mary's initial embarrassment that Iris had seen her break down was gradually replaced with gratitude. Iris had forced her to confront her past, and now Mary understood why she had recoiled when Joe had tried to kiss her.

Joe. She felt a thrill of anticipation knowing she would see him soon. They only had one day together before he was due to leave with the *Kelpie*. Would that be enough time for her to let him know how she felt? Because she knew now that she loved him, and she hoped with all her strength that Joe still felt the same way.

When Mary and Iris got back to the Wrennery after their watch, Sally was waiting for them. 'It's Christmas Eve and we're all on leave at last!' Sally cried, bouncing on her toes.

Faced with Sally's infectious enthusiasm, Mary forgot her worries. 'I thought you'd be up at Curlew Croft,' she said.

'Oh, I couldn't go without you. We have to start Christmas together.' Sally chivvied them up the stairs to their cabin. 'Hurry up and get changed. I don't want to wait a minute longer than I have to. Imagine – a whole three days at Curlew Croft. Won't it be lovely to drift off to sleep listening to the animals?'

'As long as we can't smell them,' Iris said, but she was smiling.

Mary and Iris quickly changed to the accompaniment of Sally's happy chatter, then they grabbed their bags and set off for Curlew Croft by the light of their dim torches and the sparkling stars overhead; the snow crunched underfoot as they walked.

'This feels like proper Christmas Eve now we're all together,' Sally said. 'We should sing some carols.'

So as they tramped up the hill, they sang 'We Three Kings,' which Iris declared the appropriate song, since they were bearing gifts.

When they reached the signal station, the moon had risen, so bright it cast the girls' shadows on the snow ahead of them. A movement on one of the cliff-top paths caught Mary's eye. Even before she looked, she had a feeling she knew what she would see. Sure enough, there was Stewart, edging around the perimeter of the signal station as though trying to keep out of sight of the Wrens on duty inside. He didn't appear to have seen the girls, and Mary hastily grabbed the others' arms and dragged them to a position behind a hillock, out of Stewart's line of sight. 'There's Stewart again,' she said, keeping her voice low.

'What's he doing up here in the dark, on Christmas Eve of all times?'

She inched around the hillock until she could see Stewart, aware of the others doing the same thing. Thankfully Stewart had his back to them. Beside her, she heard Sally gasp.

'I've just remembered something,' she said. 'The day I had my accident, Stewart was on the cliffs.'

'I know,' Iris said. 'He came to help when he saw you'd been hurt.'

'No!' Sally's voice was sharp and her eyes were wide. 'I... we've got to get out of here. Hurry!'

Mary glanced back once at Stewart, who was now heading away from the cliffs at a rapid pace. Then she followed Sally who was hurrying towards Curlew Croft as though a mad dog was snapping at her heels. She and Iris exchanged glances; Iris shooting her a bewildered look that must surely mirror her own.

'What's going on, Sally?' she asked when they caught her up.

'Where is he?' Sally asked, not slowing her pace.

Some of Sally's obvious fear had rubbed off onto Mary; with a racing heart she looked back, half expecting to see Stewart in pursuit. But no – he was heading away from them, a dim shape in the darkness. She released a shaky breath. 'He's gone,' she said. 'Now for goodness' sake, tell us what you've remembered.'

'It was Stewart,' Sally said. She darted a glance back towards the signal station. Mary could see she was clutching the St Christopher medallion she usually wore concealed beneath her clothes. 'It's all come back. Seeing him like that, when I wasn't expecting it, must have jogged my memory at last.'

'What did you see?' Mary was tempted to shake her until she started making sense. However, seeing how upset Sally was, she tried to remain patient.

Sally released her pendant and rubbed her forehead. Mary had the feeling she'd been grasping the St Christopher so tightly, its imprint would still be in her palm. 'I remember seeing him on the cliffs. I remember thinking it was strange on a stormy day like that.' She seemed to be speaking as her memory returned, for her eyes suddenly widened. 'The lid of the coal bunker broke off when I opened it, but it didn't hit me.'

An icy lump settled in Mary's stomach. When Iris had found her, the broken lid had been beside her, so Iris had naturally concluded that she had been struck by it. 'Are you saying it was Stewart?'

Sally nodded, shooting another fearful glance along the path where Stewart had disappeared. 'Let's get inside,' she said. 'I know he's gone, but I don't feel safe all of a sudden.'

The others had picked up Sally's unease by this time, and they set off as fast as the snow and ice allowed. As they walked, Sally described what she could remember. 'When I saw Stewart that day, I thought I ought to warn him – tell him the cliffs weren't safe.' Her fingers crept back to the St Christopher. 'I can't believe I didn't remember this until now.'

'But what did you see?'

Sally turned to face them, her expression grave. 'He was signalling with a torch.'

Mary's mouth went dry. 'Who to?'

'I don't know. I didn't see. Someone at the foot of the cliffs, I think.' She shook her head. 'I was such an idiot. I should have left without letting him know I'd seen him, but I had no reason to suspect him. I thought he was sending a signal to a friend in a fishing boat.'

Mary could picture it all too well. Sally had had no reason to suspect Stewart then. Her dislike of him had only come later, when she'd met Aldo at the hospital and heard about his misdiagnosis. And Sally was way too trusting and optimistic for her own good. 'Don't tell me you just strolled up to him and asked what he was doing?'

Sally had the grace to look embarrassed. 'Well, I didn't walk up to him. I wasn't going anywhere near the cliff's edge with that storm brewing. But I called out to him and warned him not to get too close to the edge.'

'Well, don't stop there,' Mary urged when Sally paused. 'What did he do?'

Sally shrugged. 'I don't know. That's all I remember.'

'He hit you. He must have done.' Iris looked grim. 'And to think I asked him for help.' Then she blanched. 'Oh my gosh! What would he have done if I hadn't come out looking for you?'

The three girls exchanged scared looks but didn't answer Iris's question. As far as Mary was concerned, it didn't bear thinking about. It was a good thing Sally had forgotten Stewart's presence on the cliffs that day. Not only that, but she had told everyone she had lost her memory of the events leading up to her supposed accident, which might well have saved her life. Mary shuddered, thinking how easy it would be for Sally to have taken an 'accidental' tumble over the cliffs.

'But you don't remember him hitting you?' Mary asked Sally.

'No. But it definitely wasn't the coal bunker lid, because I remember that breaking off when I shovelled out the first bucket of coal.'

Mary could have screamed with frustration. Although she would have bet her life Stewart was up to no good, they still had no proof. Nothing they could take to the authorities. By this time they were nearly at Curlew Croft. Before knocking on the door, Mary cautioned them, 'I don't think we should tell Elspeth or Archie. They've got enough to worry about.'

Iris nodded. 'Agreed. What about Rob? I don't like to keep it from him.'

'We should tell him.' Mary paused, then added, 'I think we should tell Joe, too, once he gets here.' She felt another prickle of anticipation.

Once they were inside Curlew Croft, the lamplight, warmth and enticing scent of spices drove away Mary's worries. There must be a perfectly rational explanation for Stewart behaving as he did, and it couldn't possibly involve a traitorous plot. It was the cold, the dark and the long hours spent in the lonely signal station – she had been letting her imagination get the better of her common sense.

'Come along in and make yourselves at home,' Elspeth said. 'You girls are going to share Don's room, and the boys will take Jim's. You'll have to share the bed, I'm afraid. It's a nice big one so you should all fit.'

The girls assured her they didn't mind, although Mary couldn't help grinning at Iris, certain she had never had to share a bed before. They followed Elspeth up a creaky wooden staircase to the upper floor and into the first bedroom. A lamp was already lit, casting its golden glow across the room, showing them a large bed with a candlewick bedspread, a shelf with a few books, and pictures of steam engines tacked to the wall. In the far corner stood a chest of drawers with a large earthenware jug full of water and a basin. It was strange to think that the boy who had once slept in this room was now a prisoner. She took Elspeth's hand and gave it a squeeze. 'You're very kind to put us up. I know it can't be easy, coming in here at the moment.'

Elspeth pressed her lips together, seeming to struggle to maintain her composure. She finally regained control and patted Mary's hand in return. 'I knew it would be difficult, but you young things have really brought some cheer into the house. I can't imagine spending Christmas without you.' She moved to the bed and straightened the bedspread that was already perfectly smooth. 'Now, you lasses freshen up, and come down to the parlour when you're ready.'

The girls didn't need long to get ready. They changed from their warm outdoor clothes into skirts, blouses and cardigans, Mary casting a mournful glance at her much-worn skirt. As she gathered her discarded clothes to put into the wardrobe, she couldn't help noticing a chamber pot tucked under the bed. There was no way she would be using a chamber pot in front of the others, so that would mean a night-time trip to the outhouse if she needed the lavatory at night. Thankfully it was just outside the back door, so she wouldn't need to pick her way across the yard in the dark. Even so, she vowed not to drink past seven each evening.

Iris must have been thinking along the same lines, for she said, 'I never thought I'd miss the freezing cold ablutions in the Wrennery.'

The others nodded and filed out of the room, Sally collecting the box containing her nativity scene.

'What's all this?' Elspeth asked when Sally started to unpack the carved figures in the parlour.

'A present from Aldo, the prisoner of war I told you about.' Sally handed over a donkey and one of the Wise Men for Elspeth and Archie to inspect.

'Bless me, aren't they lovely?' Elspeth said, turning the figures this way and that.

'I thought they'd look good on the mantelpiece,' Sally said.

'Aye, well, there are a few folks who would frown at them as popish nonsense but I think they'll add to the decoration.'

The girls unpacked the little models and arranged them on the fireplace, with the crib in the centre and the shepherds, kings, animals and angels on either side.

'And look,' said Sally, waving the last two tiny people in Mary's face. 'Mary and Joseph belong together, just as our Mary and Joe belong together in real life.'

Mary felt her face burn and, despite her protests, both Sally and Iris took great delight in making comments about Mary and Joseph at regular intervals throughout the rest of the evening.

Chapter Twenty-Five

Mary was lazing in a rowing boat, feeling the sun on her face as she watched Joe pull on the oars. The day had started warm and tranquil; now, inexplicably, the boat started to rock so hard, Mary had to grab the gunwale to stop herself from tumbling into the water. Only the wooden boat suddenly turned into a bolster, and Sally's voice yelled in her ear, 'It's Christmas Day!'

Mary flung back the blankets covering her head. The last tendrils of the dream dispersed, leaving her gazing along the length of the bed to see Sally and Iris, whom she'd been top-and-tailing with, at other end. The lamp was lit, filling the room with its hazy golden glow. By its light, she could see that while Iris had her face buried in her pillow, Sally was wide awake and bouncing in her excitement.

Iris peeled her face from her pillow and squinted up at Sally. 'It's still dark outside,' she said.

'It's seven o'clock. The sun won't be up until past ten, you ninny. We need to get up early because we need to make breakfast and prepare the veg for Christmas dinner before Elspeth does it all. We're supposed to be cheering her up, remember, not making more work for her.'

The bed dipped as Sally sprang out of bed, and the icy air the blankets let in galvanised Mary into action. She rolled out of bed and staggered to the wardrobe to collect her clothes. It was nice to feel a warm rug beneath her feet instead of the icy lino that covered the floor in their cabin. From the grumbling behind her, she could tell Iris was also getting up.

After a quick wash in the cold water, Mary pulled on her clothes, eyeing her skirt with disfavour. A tap on her shoulder made her turn, and Iris thrust a parcel into her hands. 'I thought you'd like this now. Happy Christmas.'

'Thank you,' said Mary, taking the newspaper-wrapped present. Whatever was inside was soft, and Mary guessed it contained clothing. While she opened it, she saw Iris give a similar package to Sally.

'What is it?' Sally asked, her eyes shining.

'Open it and find out,' Iris said.

Mary was already tugging at the paper. She peeled it back to find a stylish tweed skirt in a black and white dogtooth check. It was the one she'd seen Iris making. She touched the fabric, which was dense and soft, scarcely allowing herself to believe she could own something so beautiful. 'It's really for me? It's lovely,' she said.

'Try them on, try them on.' Iris bounced on her toes, looking, if possible, even more excited than Sally. 'I had to sneak into your wardrobes when you weren't around to get your measurements, but I can easily alter them.'

By this time, Sally had unwrapped her gift and Mary saw she also had a skirt. Mary pulled hers on, marvelling at the expert cut that hugged her waist and flared over her hips. The hem fell to just below her knees, and Mary admired the perfect lines. She had always struggled to get the hems straight on her own skirts, and admired Iris's skill.

Iris led them both to the mirror, where Mary could compare her skirt with Sally's. While they clearly followed the same pattern, Sally's was made from a green and brown tartan tweed with a beautiful teal stripe running through it that brought out the colour of Sally's eyes.

'They fit even better than I'd hoped,' Iris said. 'Those colours will go with practically anything.'

Sally's eyes shimmered with tears. 'I've never had anything as beautiful as this,' she said. 'Thank you.' Then, looking as though it pained her, she unfastened the hook and eye at the side. 'I'd better not wear it this morning. Not when I'm cooking.'

As much as she hated taking off the wonderful new skirt and putting on the hated old one, Mary could see the sense in Sally's reasoning. As she folded the black and white skirt and put it away, giving it one last stroke, she couldn't help imagining Joe's reaction when he saw her wearing it. Planning which of the tops she had brought would look best, she opted for a white blouse and powder-blue cardigan, and placed them with the skirt. For the morning, she pulled on a red cardigan with slightly frayed sleeves, thinking she wouldn't mind so much if it got stained while she was cooking.

When they got down to the kitchen, they found Elspeth had already beaten them to it and was stoking the fire in the range. Porridge bubbled in a pot on the top. 'Happy Christmas,' she said in reply to the girls' greetings. 'Archie's already out, checking on the animals. Breakfast will be in half an hour.'

Without waiting for instructions, Mary unhooked an apron from the back of the door, put it on and set to scrubbing potatoes for dinner, determined that Elspeth wasn't going to take all the work onto herself. Iris made the tea while Sally set the table, and by the time Archie had returned, washed and changed, the breakfast was ready.

'What's the weather going to be like today, Archie?' Mary asked. Archie had a knack for predicting the weather, claiming he could always feel approaching storms in his teeth.

'A bonnie day, I reckon,' Archie replied. 'Cold and sunny. The stars are out now, lovely and bright. I'm a bit late returning because I saw Malcolm Spence walk by. He said he's taking the *Puffin* out this morning.'

'On Christmas Day?' Sally asked, looking horrified.

'Aye, I told him the weather was set fair for today, but I can feel bad weather on the way. So he's going out today. Anyway, Christmas isn't such a big deal up here as it is for folks away south.'

'I suppose he has to put food on the table, same as any other day,' Mary said. Life here wasn't so different from life in her home village, and she understood how holidays meant little when you lived hand to mouth.

'Here's the plan of action, then,' she said after a moment. 'We prepare as much of the dinner as we can while it's still dark, then when the sun comes up we head out for a walk and get some fresh air while it's light. Once we're back we can get changed, exchange presents then put the finishing touches to dinner.'

'Good idea,' Sally said.

'If we walk along the cliffs towards Stromness, we might meet Rob and Joe,' Iris suggested.

That possibility had not escaped Mary, and she agreed it was a good idea. Meeting him on a walk, in the company of her friends, might help relieve the inevitable awkwardness. Also, considering Joe was due to leave on Boxing Day, she wanted to spend as much time as possible in his company.

As soon as they'd cleared away the breakfast dishes, they set to work. Archie went to check on a cow with an infected ear, and Sally offered to feed the hens and milk the cows and goats. The others spent the remainder of the dark hours scrubbing, peeling and chopping vegetables, stuffing the chicken and putting it in the oven to roast, and setting the table.

By the time they had got everything ready that could be done early, the sun still had not risen, although a salmon-pink dawn glow lit the sky. Elspeth and Archie declined a walk, saying they would have a rest by the fire in the parlour. Mary noticed Elspeth slip the postcard from Don and a long letter from Jim into her pocket, and knew she would use her quiet time to be with her sons in thought and peruse every last word of their letters, even though she probably knew them by heart. Mary had always done the same with Owen's letters.

As she pulled on her boots, it hit her then that although she had all of Owen's letters in her bedside cabinet in the Wrennery, it hadn't occurred to her to bring them here.

'Is everything all right, Mary?' Iris asked. 'You've been tying your laces for about two minutes.'

Startled, Mary straightened to find Iris and Sally both ready to leave, watching her with expressions somewhere between puzzled and amused. 'I didn't bring Owen's letters,' she said. 'I never go anywhere without them.'

Sally's face clouded. 'Shall we go back to the Wrennery to get them?'

'No, that's not what I meant. I don't need them. I only just realised.'

'Are you sure you're all right?' Sally asked.

'I really am. It's exactly what I put in my letter to his parents. I suppose it's taken this long for it to truly sink in. I'll always miss him, and there will always be a place in my heart that belongs only to him, but I'm ready to...' She closed her mouth before the words escaped. *Ready to love again.* She hesitated to say it, not knowing if Joe still felt the same way, or if he had lost all patience with her. 'Ready to move on with my life,' she said finally, hoping the others wouldn't read too much into her pause. 'Shall we go?' she added, hoping they would take the hint and change the subject.

Iris and Sally exchanged glances then they nodded. They called a goodbye to Elspeth and Archie, then went out into the Christmas dawn.

'Oh look, there goes the *Puffin*.' Sally pointed out to sea.

Sure enough, there was the familiar fishing boat, rounding the headland. The water was as calm as Archie had said. It reflected the sunrise, the vee-shaped wake behind the boat slicing through the reflected glow, splitting it into fractured lines of gold, pink and purple like scattered jigsaw pieces.

Mary glanced at her watch. 'If her skipper sticks to routine, she'll be back past this point at about 1330.'

They walked on, laughing at the *Puffin*'s predictable skipper. They had hardly taken a dozen paces when they saw Joe and Rob striding along the path from Stromness; both had bags slung over their shoulders. Iris broke into a run and flung herself into Rob's arms with a happy cry. Mary felt a lump in her throat as she watched Rob swing her round.

Her gaze slid from Iris and Rob to settle on Joe. She had the feeling he had been looking at her a moment before.

This was ridiculous. They had the whole day to get through in each other's company. If they didn't clear the air, they were in danger of making Christmas uncomfortable not only for them but for everyone else at Curlew Croft. And the whole point of this day was to keep Elspeth and Archie entertained and help them have a good Christmas.

Drawing a deep breath, she approached Joe and waved. 'How did you survive galley duty?' she asked.

In response, Joe removed his gloves and held out a pair of reddened, chapped hands for her inspection. 'Worth every minute,' he said, and the look he gave her set her pulse hammering.

She turned her face to the sea, willing her face to stop burning. More than anything, she wanted to ask if he still wanted to go out with her. However, it wasn't a conversation they could have when everyone else was around to overhear. There was something else weighing on her mind that she needed to ask, though. 'Is it true you're leaving tomorrow?'

Joe nodded, sending Mary's heart thudding to her boots. She had scarcely realised until then how much she had been hoping Iris had been mistaken. 'We sail for Harwich tomorrow, but the rumour is we'll be going overseas from there. Possibly the Med.' A pause, then, 'I'll miss you.'

'Me too.' This was too good an opening to miss. Mary glanced over her shoulder to see how close the others were. Too close for her and Joe to have a private conversation.

She was about to turn back, cursing inwardly, when something caught her eye. She gripped Joe's arm, forgetting her embarrassment in her excitement.

'What's the matter?'

Mary made frantic signs for him to keep his voice down. The others had noticed something was wrong and gathered round. Speaking in a low voice, she said, 'I think I saw Stewart. He was just bobbing behind those rocks over there.' She indicated the outcrop with a subtle jerk of her head, not wanting Stewart to see her pointing in his direction if he was looking their way.

'What was he doing?' Joe asked.

'I don't know. I only saw a quick glimpse of him before he disappeared.'

'Do you think he saw us?'

'I don't know how he could have missed us. We were hardly being quiet.' Mary looked up the path in the direction they had been walking and was struck with an idea. In another hundred yards or so, the path curved back on itself where the headland of Kyeness jutted out into the sea. She pointed it out to the others. 'If we carry on and don't look back, Stewart should think we haven't noticed him. But we can hide behind the rocks over there and get a clear view back to where I saw him. We'll be able to watch what he's doing.'

Joe frowned. 'Why would we want to watch him?'

It was only then that it dawned on Mary that Joe and Rob wouldn't know about what Sally had remembered and the conclusions Mary had drawn over the past few days. 'I'll explain later. Come on – it's important.'

Joe and Rob exchanged glances, then Joe shrugged. 'Fine. Lead on.'

Chattering away as though they didn't have a care in the world, they walked on, towards the outcrop Mary had pointed out. It was at the point where the path curved again, so if Stewart was watching them, he would think they had disappeared around the bend instead of hiding and watching what he was doing. It took Mary a moment to notice that she hadn't let go of Joe's arm. She didn't want to let him go. His arm was solid and comforting beneath her hand, and she had to admit she felt as though nothing could go wrong while he was close by her side.

It was easier than Mary expected to slip behind the rocks when they reached the tip of the headland. There were some low, scrubby gorse bushes that would hide them from Stewart's gaze if he was still there.

'Can you see him?' Sally asked.

Mary, whose face was closest to a cleft in the rocks, peered through. She was standing between Joe and Iris who also edged into positions that allowed them to look across the expanse of water to the place where they had seen Stewart. 'Hold on. And for goodness' sake, take off that hat, Iris. I don't know what possessed you to wear a scarlet bobble hat. If the lighthouse ever stops working, we could always stand you up there.'

Iris snatched off the hat and stuffed it inside her coat. 'I wore it because it's warm,' she said, a plaintive note in her voice. 'And festive. Sorry for not realising we'd be spending our Christmas walk crawling around behind rocks.'

Mary, conscious that her own dark head would probably be visible against the white snow, took care to keep out of sight as she looked through the gap. Although there was a clear view across to the spot on the cliffs where she had last seen Stewart, she couldn't see him, and she wondered if he had run off when he had seen them. Then she saw it: a blur of movement in the rocks, immediately stilled. 'I see him,' she murmured, keeping her voice low even though there was no way Stewart would be able to hear her over the noise of the crashing waves.

'Where? I don't see him?' Joe asked.

'There, on the ledge.' Mary pointed out a ledge on the cliffs a little way below the path. Stewart lay flat on the rocks, facing away from them. His arms were outstretched in front of him, and he had something in his hands, although Mary couldn't make out what it was. A low shrub growing from the ledge shielded it from view.

'What's he doing? I can't see.'

This was from Sally who was at the back of the group.

'I can't make it out. I...' Mary's voice trailed off when she saw a flash of light. 'I don't believe it. He's signalling.' She followed the line of his arms, trying to work out who he was messaging, but there was nothing but water in the direction he was pointing.

'What's he saying?'

'I don't know. I can't see. I only saw one flash. A gust of wind must have blown those bushes aside for a moment, but they're hiding the light again. It doesn't make sense. There's nothing out there.'

Nothing they could see. And then it hit her. 'My gosh, it must be a U–boat.'

Chapter Twenty-Six

The others stared at Mary, showing her expressions ranging from confusion to disbelief.

'You're joking,' Iris said.

Mary shook her head. 'I'm deadly serious. If it's just below the surface, it could see the signal through the periscope if it knows where to look.'

'That's a huge assumption,' Joe said.

It was time for Mary to explain what she had learned. 'No it's not. Listen.' And she told the men about Stewart's notes and Sally's returned memory. 'What do you think?' she asked when she finished, keeping half an eye on Stewart in case he started doing something different.

Joe grimaced. 'Now you put it all together, it does start to make a horrible sense.'

Rob was gazing at Mary, white-faced. 'If he's a spy, do you think he had anything to do with the *Royal Oak*?'

Mary had almost forgotten Rob had been on the *Royal Oak* when it had been torpedoed. Now she recalled what Iris had told her some time ago, that Rob found it difficult to talk about the events of that terrible night, which was why he had tried to avoid Mary when she had first arrived in Stromness and been set on trying to learn as much as she could about Owen's final hours. She stared at him, unsure what to say, not knowing how he would react.

Iris laid a hand on his arm, gazing at him in concern. 'We don't know. It's possible. I think Stewart was in Orkney by then.'

Rob scowled at Stewart's distant figure, his fists clenched. 'I dismissed talk about a spy when I first heard it, didnae want to think anyone on these islands could do such a thing.'

This was so close to Mary's feelings, she nodded.

Iris, however, still looked tense. Her hand tightened on Rob's arm. 'You're not going to do anything stupid, are you?'

Rob tore his gaze from Stewart long enough to give Iris a faint smile. 'If you mean, am I about to tear down the path to him and throttle him with my bare hands, then no.'

Iris relaxed, looking embarrassed. 'I didn't really think you would do anything like that. I just…'

'You just blurted the first thought that crossed your mind. Ah, dinnae worry, lass. That's one of the many things I love about you.' Rob's gaze shifted back to Stewart and his expression hardened. 'But I can't stand by and watch him sell out any more of our ships. If only we could be sure what he's doing, we could report him. As it is, if we carry a tale about him lying on the cliffs, people would just say he'd started his Christmas celebrations early and the cold would soon sober him up.'

'He's right,' Sally said. 'Unless we get some proof, what can we say? We don't even know that he's signalling to a U-boat.'

'And even if he was,' put in Iris, 'what would it achieve? The U-boat couldn't get past the loop without being detected.'

'It did before.' Now it was Joe's turn to look grim. 'Don't forget what happened to the *Snow Queen*.'

There was a moment's silence.

Then the last piece of the puzzle fell into place as Mary recalled seeing the *Puffin* earlier. 'I've got it. If the U-boat crosses at the same time as another ship, when Lower Skaill contacts Kyeness Signal Station, whoever's there would tell them it was the ship.'

Joe looked dubious. 'I suppose that would work, but how would the U-boat know when to cross? The navy doesn't exactly run to a timetable.'

'The *Puffin*!' Mary exclaimed. It was so obvious. Why couldn't anyone else see? 'She *does* run to a timetable of sorts. She always returns at 1330. You can set your watch by her.' She paused to give full weight to her next statement. 'And Stewart has the times written down in that notebook of his.'

Comprehension dawned in Joe's face. 'That's what he's doing now. He's seen the *Puffin* sail out earlier, and he's telling the U-boat what time to cross the loop. I expect the U-boat would have technology similar to our Asdic. They could use it to place itself close enough to the *Puffin* once it knows what time she'll cross a certain position. Close enough to create only one signal from the loop.'

'Why now, though?' Sally said. 'I mean, we've seen him up on the cliffs loads of times. How do we know anything's going to happen today?'

'Because this is the first time he's rendezvoused with the U-boat since confirming the *Puffin*'s regular timetable,' Mary said. She had no real proof but was certain she was right. 'You know the circled number in his notebook that we couldn't work out before? "25-12" – Christmas Day.

I bet they thought if there was any day they might catch the navy hopping, it would be at Christmas.'

Mary felt a sinking sensation. Suddenly it all seemed horribly real. There had been a strange sort of excitement when discussing Stewart's activities with Iris and Sally, almost as if they were playing out a spy story from a film or book. Now, however, it was all too real, and if they didn't act, something terrible could happen. She would never forget the helplessness of watching the *Snow Queen* go down, knowing the *Royal Oak* had suffered a similar fate. She couldn't let it happen again. 'We have to stop him,' she said.

'But how?' Sally asked.

'Go to the police,' Iris said. 'They knew what to do last time, didn't they?' She was referring to the time Rob had discovered the German plane dropping mines. Iris had ended up riding a motorbike through a storm to carry a warning to the police.

'What's the time?' Mary asked.

Iris checked her watch. '1305.'

Mary thought fast. 'Then we have less than half an hour until the *Puffin*'s due back.' She did a quick calculation. 'I don't think that would be enough time for us to get a message through and for the navy to scramble a squadron of Swordfish to intercept the U-boat.' Her heart lurched. 'Don't you remember hearing those Wrens complaining about having to spend Christmas repairing the anti-submarine nets? That means the only defence apart from the loop is the minefield.'

Iris turned a look of horror onto the others. 'But the U-boat will be tracking the *Puffin*. If the navy activates the mines, the *Puffin* will be destroyed too.'

Mary nodded. 'I don't see the navy sparing a U-boat for the sake of a small fishing boat, do you?' It would be a heart-wrenching decision, but they wouldn't risk another *Royal Oak*. Over eight hundred men had died on that terrible night. The *Puffin* and her crew would have to be sacrificed to prevent much greater loss of life. She turned to Joe and Rob. 'You know more about that side of things. What do you think?'

Rob and Joe exchanged glances. 'I think you're right,' Joe said.

'It's up to us, then,' Mary said, feeling sick. 'Or, in under an hour, there could be another U-boat in Scapa Flow.'

Iris glanced at her watch. 'We're running out of time. What are we going to do?'

Joe glanced at the waters of Hoy Sound, looking back towards Scapa Flow. 'I know we said there would be no time to scramble a squadron, but we need to try.'

'The signal station.' Mary said. 'We can use the telephone.'

Joe nodded. 'You three girls should go. You know the Wrens on duty. They'll believe you faster.'

'Why – what are you going to do?' Mary couldn't see why they didn't all go.

Joe exchanged glances with Rob, and a look of understanding passed between them. 'I'm not going to let Stewart walk away from this one,' he said.

–

Trying to make as little noise as possible, Mary hurried along the track to the signal station, aware of Iris and Sally following. They soon rounded a bend that would take them out of Stewart's line of sight; even so, she felt an itch between her shoulder blades as though unfriendly eyes were upon her and she quickened her pace, ignoring the stitch in her side.

'I wish we hadn't left Rob and Joe to their own devices,' Iris said. 'What if Stewart's got a gun?'

Mary hesitated, her foot slipping on a loose stone. 'Oh my gosh, I hadn't thought of that.' She strained her ears, trying to hear over the sounds of their own laboured breathing and the crashing waves, listening for sounds of a struggle. 'Do you think we should go back?'

Sally shook her head and tugged her arm. 'Come on. They're relying on us to get the message out. The best thing we can do to help is get to the station as fast as possible.'

They jogged on, scrambling up a steep path that was the shortest route to the signal station. 'At least the phones won't be down this time,' Iris gasped.

There being no sign of the Wrens on watch on the balcony, they burst into the signal station without being able to warn the current occupants. There was a cry from above, and a white-faced Wren peered down through the open hatch above them. 'Oh, it's you three. What on earth—?'

'No time to explain.' Mary scrambled up the ladder, pushing aside the shocked Wren. 'Are there any naval vessels within signalling range?'

'No. Why?'

Mary ignored her and snatched up the phone receiver connecting the signal station with their base. Within moments she was speaking to the duty officer. Still gasping for breath, she managed to convey what was happening in a few short sentences.

'If this turns out to be a wild goose chase,' the officer began.

'I hope it is,' Mary replied, the urgency of the moment making her forget all protocol. 'Because if we're right, there's a U-boat heading for the anchorage, and there's nothing we can do to stop it.' Then she added as an afterthought, 'Sir.'

The silence that followed probably only lasted about two seconds. For Mary, however, it seemed to stretch out for an eternity, nothing but the faint hiss and crackle of static on the line telling her they were still connected. She could almost see the expression of outrage on the lieutenant's face, and mentally waved goodbye to any chance of promotion. She couldn't help wishing she'd left Iris to make the call, because although Iris was exactly the same rank, her upbringing gave her an air of authority that people seemed to accept without question.

'Very well,' the lieutenant said finally, 'leave it with us.' And he broke the connection.

Mary stared at the receiver in shock.

'What did he say?' asked a voice from the hatch.

Mary replaced the receiver and saw Sally at the top of the ladder, peering through the hatch.

'He said to leave it with him.'

'What are they going to do?'

'I don't know. He didn't say.' Mary knew she shouldn't feel aggrieved. She had hardly framed her report in a logical fashion, only gasping out that there was a U-boat off Western Mainland, and begging them to do something about it. She was a mere ordinary Wren, thus not deserving of any explanation in the eyes of the navy, but simply there to follow orders. 'Get off the ladder,' she added. 'I'm coming down.'

'What should we do?' Sally asked, once Mary had offered a brief apology to the Wrens on watch and descended.

'I'm not kicking my heels here,' Mary said. 'Anyway, the lieutenant didn't tell us what to do. We should go back to Joe and Rob and tell them what's happened.'

'Agreed,' Iris said, her face grim. Mary knew she was as worried for Rob as Mary was for Joe. Together they flew out of the station and retraced their steps along the rocky path, taking care, once they were on the section of path that would be in Stewart's line of vision, to stay low so as not to attract his attention. All the while, Mary's senses were stretched to their limits, and she expected to hear a shout or a report from a gun at any moment.

When they reached the spot where they had left Joe and Rob, they found no sign of them. She knew without a doubt that they must have gone after Stewart.

Chapter Twenty-Seven

Joe watched Mary and her friends walk along the path. Once they were out of sight, he turned to Rob. 'Any ideas?' In all the films he had seen, the hero had instinctively known how to fight. However, he was rapidly coming to realise that his career as an accountant and then as a visual signaller wasn't the best training for overcoming a spy. Neither was Rob a trained fighter. On the other hand, it was two against one, and wasn't Stewart supposed to have a heart condition? At least, that was the reason Stewart had always given for being unable to join the armed forces.

Rob looked as though the same thoughts were going through his mind. Then he squared his shoulders. 'I'm pretty sure Mary's right, but he should have a chance to explain himself. For all we know, there could be a perfectly innocent explanation for what he's doing.'

'But if we just stroll up to him and he *is* a spy, he'll just run for it and we won't have any proof.'

Rob grinned. 'I'm not suggesting we give him the option of bolting. If we cut across the headland, keeping low, he won't see us until we're on top of him. I'd rather question him when we've got the advantage.'

Joe couldn't think of a better plan, so set out with Rob, picking his way across the rocky headland. All the while he kept low, trying not to make an obvious silhouette for

Stewart to notice should he look their way. In the event, he could have saved his spine, for Stewart didn't once take his gaze from the seemingly empty patch of sea where he was signalling. Annoyingly, from his position behind Stewart, he couldn't see the light of his torch so couldn't see the message. Whatever he was sending, he seemed to be taking a long time over it. Joe could only conclude that he wasn't a properly trained signaller. Not like him and Mary, with the shorthand they had developed. There was no returning signal, either, although if he was signalling to a U-boat, there would be no way its crew could respond without surfacing and sending a signaller out to the conning tower. Joe guessed this must be a prearranged place and time for Stewart to signal.

As they got closer to the place where Stewart was stretched out, Joe's pulse sped up. To begin with, the unreality of the situation had helped him to act without feeling any nerves. It was only just starting to sink in that it was actually happening. He and Rob were about to tackle a suspected spy. They were close enough for Stewart to hear them now. Joe slowed his pace, taking care not to kick any loose stones, and placed each foot with care so it didn't crunch on any ice. They were only about twenty paces away now. Surely Stewart must hear them. Ten paces. Joe held his breath.

A tap on his arm made him jump. It was Rob, holding up three fingers, before beginning a silent countdown. Joe nodded, showing he understood: on the count of three they would both charge, hoping to overcome him with the advantage of surprise. Three... two... one—

At that precise moment, Joe stepped on a patch of ice that gave a crack Stewart couldn't have failed to hear. And nor did he. He twisted around, and there was no mistaking the look of shock and fear that briefly showed on his face before he schooled his expression. 'It's Rob Sinclair, isn't it, and Joe Pallant? What brings you here?' He buried his hand in his pocket. Joe guessed he was trying to hide the torch.

Cursing himself for giving them away, Joe took a step closer, blocking Stewart's access to the path and escape. 'We could say the same about you. We were out for a stroll before lunch and wondered what you were doing, lying in the snow and ice. Or, should I say, we wondered who you were sending that signal to.'

There was a real flicker of fear in Stewart's eyes now. He looked from Joe to Rob as though looking for a way out. He affected a laugh. 'Signal? I don't know what you mean. I thought I saw a Great Northern Diver, so I stopped to look. I'm interested in birds, you know.'

This came out too pat; to Joe, it sounded like an excuse Stewart had prepared for just such an eventuality.

'Then perhaps you'd like to show us what you're trying to hide in your pocket?' Rob spoke, his voice holding a threatening edge Joe had never heard him use before.

'I'm not hiding anything.'

'It was you, wasn't it?' Rob said. 'It was you on the cliffs the night I saw that plane dropping mines. What did you do – throw a rock in the sea to make the police think you'd fallen into the water?'

Stewart's eyes widened for a fraction of a second. He recovered his composure quickly, but it was enough for Joe to be certain Rob had hit the mark. 'I don't know what you're talking about,' Stewart said.

Joe had had enough. 'This is getting us nowhere.' Scarcely knowing what he intended to do, he took a swift pace forward, fists raised. Whether he would have actually landed a blow, he never knew, for at that moment, Stewart's hand darted to his pocket. He drew out a thin leather case from which he produced something that glinted silver. Joe instinctively stopped before his brain could grapple with what he was seeing. A knife. Or, rather, a surgical scalpel.

Stewart sneered, throwing the empty case onto the ground. 'Not so brave now, are you? Now, why don't you let me past?'

'So you can bring more U-boats into these waters? You've got to be joking.' Joe held his ground, never taking his eyes off Stewart's face.

'You might want to rethink that.' Stewart punctuated his words with a slash of the knife in the air in front of Joe's face. Joe couldn't help jerking his head back, and Stewart gave a nasty laugh. 'You're right to be afraid. I know exactly where to strike to make you bleed to death in a matter of seconds.'

It took all of Joe's willpower not to raise both hands to his throat in a protective gesture. He wouldn't give Stewart the satisfaction. He couldn't help wishing he'd remembered to put on a scarf that morning, though.

Then he heard a step behind him, and Rob's solid hand was placed on his shoulder. 'I see you've given up the pretence of innocence,' Rob said. 'There's that to be thankful for, at least.'

Rob's support gave Joe the strength to go on. 'It's over, Stewart. Give yourself up.'

'To face a firing squad? I don't think so.'

Stewart's eyes narrowed, his gaze darting from Joe to Rob, and Joe feared desperation would make him attack. 'Don't be an idiot. You can't get past both of us.'

'Want to bet?' Stewart made another feint towards Joe's throat. Or maybe it wasn't a feint, Joe didn't know, for at the crucial moment, Stewart's foot slipped on the ice, and he staggered. Before Joe could take advantage of his momentary lapse of concentration, however, Stewart recovered his balance and brandished the scalpel again.

Joe held up his hands. 'All right. What do you want?' He had no intention of letting Stewart go, but had the idea of keeping him talking until Mary and the others could fetch help.

'Let me go, and I promise to leave the islands.'

'What guarantee do we have that you'll leave?'

'You really think I'd stick around now you know what I am?'

Rob must have picked up on Joe's plan, for he said, 'What I don't understand is why you would betray your country. What made you do it?'

'Perhaps I thought there was nothing left to live for after your precious girlfriend made it clear she preferred an oaf like you to an intelligent, educated man like me.'

'Really?'

Stewart laughed. 'I always thought you were soft in the head, and that proves it. Of course not. I've always supported the Nazis, and have done ever since I was sent to a German school for a year. There are more of us in Britain than you might think. I applied for the post in Orkney, knowing how valuable my services could be to the Führer there. And you can't believe how I laughed at you idiots, so certain everyone in Orkney shared your faith in your fellow countrymen. So sure no one could have betrayed the *Royal Oak*; that it was just a bit of luck on the part of the U-boat captain.'

Stewart hadn't finished, but Joe had heard enough. He heard Rob give a snarl beside him, but Joe was in front, and got to Stewart first. He didn't care about the knife or the waves pounding on rocks as sharp as teeth far below. All he cared about was the loss this traitor had caused. Not only that, but his glee at the hurt he had caused. At the last moment he dodged the slashing blade directed at his throat and flung himself upon Stewart, his hands around Stewart's throat. They crashed down upon the stony ground together, and Joe managed to get a knee on Stewart's chest to stop him rising. Something warm trickled down his arm, but he ignored it, ignored Rob grappling the scalpel from Stewart's flailing hand. He gazed into Stewart's hate-filled eyes and aimed a punch at his face. 'That's for the *Royal Oak*,' he said, meaning Mary's pain. At this close range he couldn't get much force behind the blow. It didn't matter, though. 'And this is for Iris's father and this for the *Snow Queen*.' He landed two more blows before Rob caught his arm.

'That's enough. We need to leave him in a fit state for questioning. We've got him. Be satisfied with that. He won't cause any more deaths.'

Stewart spat blood. 'That's what you think. There's a U-boat out there with all the information it needs to get into Scapa Flow.'

Joe went cold. In his rage he'd forgotten all about the U-boat. 'Tell us how to stop it.'

Stewart grinned. 'You can't. It's too late.'

Joe felt strangely tired. Seeing that Rob had Stewart in a secure grip, he sat on the ground beside him, all his strength drained from his limbs. 'Have you got something we can tie him up with?' he asked Rob. 'We can hand him over to the police when they get here. Maybe Mary and the others have been able to convince the navy to send out some planes to hunt the U–boat down.'

Rob used the only tie he had to hand, which happened to be Stewart's belt. He trussed Stewart with his hands behind his back and then stood guard to stop him from throwing himself over the cliffs. Joe would have helped, if only he didn't feel so weak all of a sudden.

Rob nodded at Joe's upper arm. 'Better let me take a look at that. We could be here a while.'

'What?' Then Joe followed Rob's gaze and saw the neat tear in his coat sleeve. He put his hand to it, puzzled when it came away wet. It was only when he looked at his fingers and saw they were covered in blood that it dawned on him that he had been stabbed. As though prompted by the sight, his arm started to throb. He couldn't seem to drag his gaze away from the glistening blood on his fingertips. 'Well, that's not very clever,' was all he could say, wondering why his voice seemed to be coming from a great distance. He pressed his hand to his wound and hunched over, letting his head drop between his knees. He had the horrible feeling he was about to faint, and where would that leave Rob? He hoped help reached them soon, or Stewart might be able to overpower Rob and make his escape yet again.

–

With a sinking heart, Mary gazed across the cliffs towards the spot where they had last seen Stewart. Sure enough, there were now three figures on the path where before Stewart had been alone. 'The idiots have only gone and tackled him without waiting for help,' she said.

Sally squinted at the place where the men were grouped. 'What are they doing? I can't make it out.'

'Two of them are just sitting down. Joe and Stewart, I think. Rob's standing next to them.' She shook her head, unable to work out what was happening. 'What do they think they're doing – having a picnic?'

'We should go over there. They don't seem to be fighting,' Iris said.

The others agreed, and they set off at a brisk jog down the path, taking care not to slip on the ice. When they reached the others, they found Stewart perched on a rock, glowering, his hands tied behind him. Rob was bending over Joe while trying to keep an eye on Stewart.

'Thank God you're here,' Rob said. 'Joe needs help, and I can't look at him at the same time as stopping this traitor from getting away.'

Mary went cold and pushed past Rob to see to Joe. 'What happened?' she asked, wincing when she saw the blood welling through his fingers where they were pressed against his upper arm.

Rob answered for him. 'Tried to play the hero and got sliced for his pains.'

Joe gave her a weak grin. 'I stopped him, though, didn't I?'

'Aye, I'll give you that,' Rob replied, scowling at Stewart.

'Here, let me take a look,' Mary said, stooping over Joe.

But Joe shook his head. 'It'll start bleeding again if I move my hand. Anyway, is help on the way?'

In her anxiety, Mary had almost forgotten about the U-boat. 'I got through to base but the lieutenant wouldn't say what they're going to do. Or even if they believed us and are going to do anything.' As she spoke, she pulled her handkerchief from her pocket – thankfully clean – and folded it to make a pad for Joe's arm.

'What's the time?' Joe asked.

Iris pushed back her coat sleeve to look at her watch. '1325,' she said. 'Dash it – Elspeth will be wondering where we are.'

'They'll understand,' Joe said. 'But the *Puffin* will be crossing the loop in a few minutes. We can't wait for help. We have to do something.'

Stewart gave an unpleasant laugh. 'Too late. You might have got me, but at least I'll get to enjoy some special Christmas illuminations as a reward. The U-boat already has its instructions.'

Mary felt sick. 'There's got to be something we can do.' She couldn't let it happen. Not again. Not another *Royal Oak* or *Snow Queen*.

But even as she spoke, she saw a tiny dot out to sea that slowly resolved itself into the familiar outline of the *Puffin*. She was torn between running to the cliff edge to gaze at the *Puffin* and see if she could make out the outline of the U-boat, and tending to Joe's arm. She couldn't leave him to bleed, though, so after a brief hesitation, she asked for another clean hanky and Iris handed over hers. It was just large enough to tie the pad in place. She was relieved to see that although a little blood seeped through, the improvised bandage seemed to have controlled the bleeding.

'There you go,' she said. 'I managed to push the pad inside the sleeve, through the tear, so the sleeve will help hold it all in place.'

Then she thought of the U-boat, lurking underwater. What could be done? There was no sign of any destroyers, nothing to stop the U-boat using the *Puffin* as a decoy. Even now, it was probably following the *Puffin* as closely as possible.

She looked at Stewart, her heart full of rage.

Stewart was gazing across the water, a look of triumph on his face. He laughed. 'I wonder how the *Puffin's* skipper would feel if he knew he was leading a wolf into the sheep pen?'

And in a sudden moment of clarity, Mary knew what to do. 'Where's the torch?' she asked. 'I've got an idea.'

She looked around and saw it lying not far from Stewart's right foot. He saw it at the same time and the triumph faded from his face. He aimed a kick at the torch, sending it skittering towards the cliff edge. Mary lunged for it, and nearly screamed in frustration when it reached the edge before she could get there. She made a desperate grab for it and closed her fingers around the loop of cord around its base. With a wail of frustration, she felt it slip through her fingers before she could gain purchase. Then she heard it strike the rocks below.

Stewart grinned. 'Now what are you going to do?'

Mary glanced at Rob. 'You know the *Puffin's* skipper. Does he know semaphore?' She was pulling off her coat as she spoke.

'Aye.'

'Good thing I chose my red cardi this morning. Give me your hat, Iris.'

'What are you going to do?' Iris asked, pulling her bright red hat out of her pocket.

'Semaphore,' she said. 'I can use these as flags.' Heedless of the chill, she pulled her cardigan over her head; there was no time to fiddle with the buttons.

Iris handed over her hat. 'But what can you do?'

Mary snatched the improvised flag. 'Just watch. No time to explain.' Holding the cardigan in one hand and the hat in the other, she scrambled to the highest point on the cliffs. Wishing she was a little taller, she raised her arms and started her message. 'Look this way. Please look this way,' she muttered as she formed each letter, standing on tiptoe, trying to make herself as visible as possible. She could only pray the skipper didn't think it was a hoax and ignore her. If it hadn't been for Stewart's comment about the skipper's innocence, she wouldn't have thought of it, worrying that he was complicit in the scheme. Now, knowing he would be horrified to know what his predictability had led to, she signed: 'Danger. U-boat following you. Steer for shore.' For the *Puffin* was, at present, following the main channel taken by all shipping, which was protected by the minefield. The skipper would be blissfully unaware that the mines would be activated. If the *Puffin* steered for the shore, she hoped the U-boat would part ways with the fishing boat now it was across the loop and continue through the minefield alone.

She didn't stop after finishing the message but repeated it, her arms aching, never taking her eyes off the fishing boat as she chugged through the water. She didn't seem to be changing course but was following her usual route.

'Look this way, please!' She didn't know how visible she would be to anyone on the boat, who would surely be eagerly anticipating their lunch and probably not paying too much attention to anyone up on the cliffs. If she was Sally, she would pray for a miracle or make a Christmas wish or something. But there was no such thing as miracles.

Even as the thought crossed her mind, she thought of all that had happened recently – how she had rediscovered her ability to draw; the Heddles' joy on learning Don was alive; how her frozen heart had come back to life; the Northern Lights doing their best to make her date with Joe the most romantic evening ever. It was she who had messed that one up, not fate or any higher power. Perhaps magic or miracles were true after all, and it was how you acted on them that made the difference in the world. Well, if there was room for another miracle in her life, she needed it now.

'Please,' she said, 'make the skipper see me. Stop the U-boat getting through.'

And whether it was an answer to her prayer or just coincidence, the sun came out from behind the clouds, and she was standing in a pool of light. With fresh hope in her heart, she signalled again, the breeze catching her improvised flags, so they trailed like banners from each hand.

Five seconds… ten… the *Puffin* continued without altering course. Mary could have screamed in frustration. Then she frowned. Was it closer to the shore than it had been before? She watched the boat, dry-mouthed, and repeated the message. By the time she'd finished, she knew it was working. The wake following the boat was definitely showing a curve towards an inlet. All she could do now was pray the U-boat was stopped by the mines. There was no way of telling from here, as the mines were on the other side of Graemsay. She had done all she could. Now she had to trust the navy to finish the job.

Sally and Iris had scrambled up the rocks to stand beside her. They would have been able to follow the semaphore so would understand her plan.

'You genius,' Iris said. 'I was terrified we would watch the *Puffin* sail to her doom.'

'But will it work?'

'We'll have to wait and see.'

As if in answer to prayer, she heard the sound of running feet, and saw a contingent of soldiers appear, probably sent from one of the camps outside Stromness. At the same time, Mary heard the distant throb of aero engines. Looking up, she saw faint specks in the sky which gradually resolved into five Fairey Swordfish. The last of her fears fell away. Even if the U-boat managed to evade the minefield, it wouldn't escape the Swordfish.

'That was a bit of luck,' said a young lieutenant, eyeing the *Puffin*, which now bobbed gently in the inlet. 'We were all sure the fishing boat was going to be blown up by the mines – the order's gone out to activate them.'

'Luck had nothing to do with it.' Joe, looking pale but smiling, approached, clutching his arm. Behind him, Mary could see a pair of soldiers taking custody of Stewart. 'It was this Wren's quick thinking that saved the *Puffin* and her crew.'

Mary felt a flush of pleasure at his praise. 'And Joe caught the spy for you,' she said, feeling a blush heat her face as she caught Joe's eye.

'So I think it's only fair that we leave the clearing up to you lads,' Joe said. 'We've got an urgent appointment with a Christmas dinner.'

It was clear that the danger was passed, and the fate of both Stewart and the U-boat was now out of their hands. Undoubtedly they would all be called upon later on to give evidence, but for now they were content to let others take over.

Mary's first thought was for Joe. A glance at his arm showed her that the temporary bandage was stained with fresh blood, so she spoke to the lieutenant. 'My friend is hurt,' she said, pointing at Joe. 'He needs a medic.'

The lieutenant nodded and hailed a private, giving him instructions to drive Joe to a doctor. Joe tried to protest, but Mary told him not to be an idiot. 'You're bleeding right through the bandage,' she said. 'You're probably going to need stitches.' After watching Joe stumble with the private towards where the trucks must be parked, she turned to the others. 'You'd better get back to Curlew Croft,' she said. 'Elspeth and Archie must be wondering what on earth we're doing. I'll catch you up.'

Now the panic was over, she couldn't help feeling disappointed that it looked like she wouldn't be spending Christmas with Joe after all. There would be no cosy evening by the fire. No chance to put right what had gone wrong that night when it seemed like the heavens had conspired to bring them together. The least she could do was try and clear the air before he left. She ran after Joe. Catching him up didn't prove too difficult, as he soon abandoned his attempt to walk unaided across the rocky headland and accepted the private's arm to help him to the vehicle.

She took Joe's other arm. 'I'll come with you to the truck,' she said.

They didn't talk much until they got to the trucks, but when the private went to crank-start the vehicle, Mary turned to Joe.

Joe got there first. 'I'm sorry I spoiled the celebrations. I'll come back to Curlew Croft as soon as I can.'

'Don't be silly,' she said. 'You couldn't help getting hurt. You stopped Stewart. You should be proud of yourself.'

Joe didn't look comforted. 'I was trying to prove to you that I was good enough for you.' He looked at his feet. 'I made a mess of that, didn't I?'

Mary took his good hand. 'How can you say that? You put yourself in danger. You're the biggest hero of the day.' *And I love you.* She wanted to say it, but the words died on her lips when the roar of the motor split the air. Then there was no chance to say what was in her heart, for the private opened the truck door for Joe, saying, 'Hop in. We'll have you down in Stromness in two shakes.'

'I'll be back as soon as I can,' Joe said.

'We'll wait for you before we start dinner,' Mary said.

But Joe shook his head. 'I could be ages. Don't wait. Save me a bit of everything.'

With that, the truck lumbered off and all Mary could do was wave, leaving unsaid all the words she longed to say.

Chapter Twenty-Eight

Mary returned to Curlew Croft, and although Christmas dinner was a merry affair, she kept glancing towards the door, wishing Joe would return. What if he didn't come back and she never got the chance to apologise for pushing him away? She only half listened to Iris, Sally and Rob as they filled the Heddles in on the events of the day.

Elspeth and Archie had listened to their tale in amazement, asking them to repeat it several times. 'I cannae believe it,' Elspeth said for what seemed like the hundredth time as they took their places at the table. 'Stewart Irvine a spy, and working here in Orkney all this time with no one realising!'

'I always said I didn't like him,' Sally said, 'but I still can't believe he was a spy. All those deaths. And him a doctor. How can he live with himself?'

It was on the tip of Mary's tongue to say he wouldn't have to live with himself for much longer, but she stopped herself. It was hardly a suitable comment for a festive dinnertime. Although, judging from the expressions on the others' faces, they were thinking along similar lines. This was supposed to be a day for cheering Elspeth and Archie, however, so she hitched a bright smile upon her face and said, 'I've been looking forward to this meal for so long. Merry Christmas, everyone.' She raised her glass, containing some of Archie's parsnip wine, and said, 'Here's to us, and to all our loved ones, whether near, far or no longer with us.'

She took a sip, thinking of Owen. Then she glanced at Iris and saw a shadow of pain cross her face. Mary knew she must be thinking of her father and feeling the pain of celebrating a first Christmas with him no longer in the world. She was probably thinking of Rob, too. Who knew where he would be next Christmas? Mary couldn't regret mentioning those they had lost, though. Their loss would always be a presence in their hearts, the pain waxing and waning but never completely fading.

However, her thoughts soon drifted from Owen to Joe. How was he? Would he really be able to get back to Curlew Croft that afternoon? If there was still any Christmas magic left, her one last wish would be for a chance to put things right with Joe before he sailed with the *Kelpie*.

The afternoon turned to evening. After the girls and Rob had cleared the kitchen, they listened to King George's Christmas message, and still Joe didn't arrive. The Christmas presents beneath the tree remained unopened, as everyone wanted to wait for Joe before handing them out. 'I hope they haven't admitted him to hospital,' Mary said as they fixed the blackout curtains and lit the lamps. 'That'd be a miserable way of spending Christmas.'

'He'll be here,' Sally said. 'And because it's Christmas, I won't tease you for saying "him" when you meant Joe, making it obvious you've been thinking about him non-stop.'

'I'm worried about his arm,' Mary said, bending over the last of the lamps so the others wouldn't see her blush.

'Of course you are,' Iris commiserated. 'Now, let's play some parlour games.'

They were in the middle of a noisy game of charades, presided over by Iris, when they heard Joe arrive in the kitchen, calling out a greeting. Mary rose, smoothing her new skirt with trembling hands, hoping to meet him in the kitchen for a private word. However, she met him in the parlour doorway and couldn't think of a reasonable excuse to take him away from the others. He had his arm in a sling and was still pale but shook off their concerns with a grin.

'Doc said it was a good thing I was wearing my thick coat and a jersey – it meant the cut in my arm wasn't as deep as it could have been. He gave me eight stitches and a tot of brandy, and now I feel grand.' Joe sat in the chair Mary had vacated, and Mary, resigned to the fact that she wouldn't get a moment alone with him, went to fetch his meal.

'Did you hear anything about the U-boat?' Iris was asking when Mary returned with Joe's dinner on a tray.

Joe gave a curt nod, looking grim. 'It was stopped by the mines before it could do any damage to the fleet.'

'That's a relief. I was so worried it would manage to get through.' Iris bit her lip. 'Although I hate to think of the poor submarine crew. They were only following orders.'

'Their deaths are on Stewart Irvine's head,' Joe said, his voice harsh, 'just as much as all the other deaths he's had a hand in over the years.'

Mary couldn't help eyeing him in concern as he ate his somewhat dried meal, which had been kept warm in the oven. Once he had eaten, Sally clapped her hands. 'Time for the presents,' she said.

While Mary usually loved the gift-giving at Christmas, she couldn't help wishing she and Joe could have some time alone. All that remained unsaid hung heavily between them as she sprang to her feet to fetch the presents she had prepared. Still, she couldn't help picking up Sally's excitement and handed out her presents with a tingle of anticipation, receiving others in return. Soon the room was full of the sound of tearing newspaper, and Mary had a pile of treasures building up beside her chair. In addition to the skirt from Iris, which she had changed into before dinner, she was given an embroidered lavender bag from Sally, a pair of pretty mother-of-pearl hair clips from Elspeth and Archie and rose-scented soap from Rob. She hadn't received anything from Joe and presumed he hadn't had time to get anything, having been confined to the *Kelpie* for a week. She had kept her present for him aside, hoping for a chance to give it to him privately.

'Oh, Mary, this is beautiful!' Iris had opened her gift from Mary and now gazed at the framed sketch from her diary. 'How did you know this was my favourite?'

'I thought the picture of a ship at sea might make you think of the *Kelpie* and Rob.'

'It does. It's perfect.' Misty-eyed, Iris gazed at Rob, and Mary knew she must also be painfully conscious of how little time they had before the *Kelpie* was due to leave, taking Rob and Joe away from Orkney.

Sally, too, was delighted with the picture of Solva harbour that Mary had given her, and Elspeth and Archie admired the Ring of Brodgar picture.

'You've got real talent,' Elspeth said, placing the drawing in pride of place on the mantelpiece. 'This is equal to anything I've seen in the art galleries in town.'

'What do you say, Mary?' Iris said. 'We could set up a shop after the war, selling my clothes and your art.'

Mary hardly knew what she said in reply. *After the war.* How long would that be? Would she see Joe at its end? It was hard to smile and admire her gifts with everyone when all she wanted to do was spend some time alone with Joe and make it clear to him that she wanted to be with him. Was falling in love with him. She couldn't bear for him to leave without knowing.

The evening wore on, and Mary was on the point of giving up in despair and retiring to bed when Archie said, 'I'd better check I remembered to bolt the door on the shed. The catch is a bit loose, and with the wind blowing up again, I don't want it slamming open.'

'You stay here,' said Joe. 'I'll go.' And he shot Mary a look that was an unmistakable plea.

Mary leapt to her feet. 'You can't fasten that heavy bolt one-handed. I'll come with you.' She snatched up the parcel containing his present and followed him out into the darkness.

It was the work of a moment to see that the bolt was indeed drawn and there was no risk of the door swinging open in the night. Mary couldn't imagine Archie forgetting to do it, and wondered if he hadn't made it up to give her and Joe the opportunity to be alone.

'I got you a Christmas present,' she said. Anything to delay their return to the crowded parlour. 'Shall I open it for you?' Without waiting for a reply, she tore off the newspaper, placed the hat on his head and wound the scarf around his neck, thrilling at the excuse to be near him. 'I've got that drawing of the barn you asked for, too, but I left it inside. There's a frame for it I wanted to get but I couldn't afford it.' She hardly knew what she was saying.

She was only conscious of the need to keep talking, to stretch out this moment alone for as long as possible. 'I promise to get it as soon as I can, though.'

'That sounds suspiciously like you plan to see me again. Does that mean you want to stay in touch?' His teasing tone couldn't quite disguise a note of hope.

'Of course I do. I can't bear the thought of you leaving.' Her voice hitched, and her vision blurred as tears welled in her eyes.

'That's good, because I feel the same way.' Joe fished in his pocket and pressed a slim rectangular package into her hands. 'I got you this present, hoping you'd want to write. I had to get Rob to buy it, seeing as I was stuck in the galley all week.'

Mary opened it to see an elegant fountain pen. She drew a shaky breath. 'I love it. Thank you.' She dared to kiss his cheek. 'I'll write as often as I can.' The knowledge that Joe wanted to stay in contact gave her the courage to ask, 'Do you feel up to a bit of a stroll? I... don't feel like going in quite yet.'

'Nor do I.' Joe offered her his good arm, and Mary took it, snuggling against his side. The clouds had all cleared, revealing a breathtaking array of stars overhead. The moon was just past full, lighting their path with its silvery glow, meaning there was no need to use torches. Mary hesitated to speak. She had messed it up once and didn't think Joe would have the patience to wait for her any longer. What if he had already changed his mind and decided he didn't love her after all? The sudden fear closed her throat, and they walked out onto the cliffs in silence.

'I wanted to say I'm sorry,' Joe said finally.

'You? What for?'

'For moving too fast. Pressuring you for more when you weren't ready.'

'I—'

'I bet you're relieved that I'll soon be out of your hair.'

'Don't be an idiot. I… I'll miss you.'

'Really?'

'Of course.' Mary broke off, blinking back more tears. She was running out of time and now she was terrified of getting it wrong; terrified that Joe would leave tomorrow and she would never get the chance to tell him how she felt. It seemed her last and most heartfelt Christmas wish wouldn't be granted.

Then Joe gasped. 'Would you look at that!' He pointed up.

Mary had been so busy looking at Joe, she hadn't seen what was happening in the sky. Now she couldn't understand how she had missed it. The sky was ablaze with dancing light, turning from green to red to deepest mauve. The Merry Dancers were out again, and Mary swore she would never again laugh at Sally's belief in miracles. This could only be in answer to her wish – a chance to relive the night when she should have said yes to Joe but had let her fears get the better of her.

'Do you believe in second chances, Joe?'

'Second, third, fourth. As many as it takes.'

Gathering her courage, she said, 'I'm sorry, Joe. I made an awful mistake the other night, and I want to put it right.' She plunged on before Joe could speak, wanting to get it all out before she lost her courage. 'I've been such an idiot. I had this crazy idea that I couldn't be happy because of what had happened to my sister. It took Iris and Sally to make me see how wrong I was. What happened to

Owen… well, I had this stupid belief that it proved that I didn't deserve to be happy.'

'Deserve? Mary, do you think bad things happen because people deserve them? The world doesn't work like that.'

'I know that now. But when you told me how you felt… well, I thought I needed to earn it or something.'

Joe pulled her to him in a clumsy one-armed embrace. 'My love for you is a free gift. I don't expect any return.'

'I'm starting to believe you.'

'How can I convince you?'

Mary looked up at his face, crowned with dancing light. 'I can think of one thing.' And she raised herself on tiptoe and pressed her mouth to his, and it felt as though all the charged air surged through her flesh, and she could swear she felt a snap of electricity between them.

'That's a method of persuasion I rather like,' Joe said, when they parted. 'Do you feel more convinced?'

'I think so, but we'll probably need to do it again to make sure I remember,' she replied, laughing.

After another lengthy kiss, Mary rested her head on Joe's shoulder. 'I love you,' she said. 'I should have said that to you before, but I was too scared. I'm not scared any more, but I'm sorry I wasted all that time. You're leaving soon, and we could have been together for much longer.'

Joe pulled her closer. 'We're together now, and that's all that matters. I can leave with a light heart, knowing I have your love. We can write, and I'll come and see you when I get leave.' He pointed up at the Northern Lights. 'We've got the heavens on our side. We'll be together again.'

–

It was much later when they returned to the parlour, where they were greeted with good-natured laughter.

'I always did say that bolt was a tough one to draw.' Rob raised his glass to Joe in a silent toast. 'Good thing you had Mary with you to help.'

'It must have been quite a struggle.' Iris's eyes danced. 'Your faces are quite red.'

Mary took the joking in good humour, and she and Joe sat in the only space available, which happened to be on the rug in front of the fire. Joe leaned his back against Rob and Iris's shared armchair, and Mary rested her head on his good shoulder, in the circle of his arms. It felt so right to sit like that. She wouldn't allow herself to think of the parting to come. Some words from the king's Christmas message returned to her: *Though severed by the long sea miles of distance you are still in the family circle, whose ties, precious in peaceful years, have been knit even closer by danger.*

Everyone in this room, from different places and backgrounds, were as close as family, and would continue to support one another. They had seen loss and grief and experienced danger, but their close bond had seen them through. Looking around the dear faces, she knew that nothing, not even distance, could truly separate them. They would help each other through whatever trials lay ahead.

She beamed at them all. 'Merry Christmas, everyone,' she said. 'Who's for another game of charades?' Because it was still Christmas Day. For as long as the day lasted, they could forget their worries. They were together, and that was all that mattered.

Author's Note

When I started researching wartime visual signallers, I was fascinated to learn about the abbreviations they used, in much the same way they are used in textspeak today. For example, '4' was used instead of 'for', 'U' for 'you' and 'R' for 'are'. As soon as I read this, I knew I had to have Mary and Joe use this form of shorthand as they embarked on their tentative courtship via their signal lamps. I have no idea if the real-life visual signallers turned it into as much of a game as Mary and Joe, challenging each other with ever more obscure abbreviations, but I like to think they did!

Although I've tried to write about real locations as much as possible, Kyeness Signal Station and the headland it stands on are completely fictional. The anti-submarine indicator loop was real; however, the work of monitoring the vessels crossing it was carried out by visual signallers based at the Ness Battery.

The sinking of the *Royal Oak* did, tragically, happen in real life. On 14 October 1939, *U-47* managed to navigate the supposedly impassable channel between Mainland and Lamb Holm. It got into Scapa Flow and torpedoed the *Royal Oak*, causing the deaths of 835 men and boys. Later, there was speculation that there was a German spy in Orkney who had guided the *U-47* into Scapa Flow. This is now believed to be untrue, but the tale was too good for me to ignore and it formed the basis of the spy story thread running through this book and *A New Start for the Wrens*, the first book in the series.

Acknowledgements

Thanks to the easing of Covid restrictions, I was able to travel while writing *A Wrens' Wartime Christmas*, so I was finally able to take the research trip to Orkney that had to be postponed from the year before. I would therefore like to thank the staff at the Orkney archive in Kirkwall for going out of their way to dig out the information I needed. Thanks also to Andrew Hollinrake whose excellent and informative guided walk around the Ness Battery gave me a much greater insight into how Hoy Sound was protected. Needless to say, any mistakes in the book are entirely my own. Another Orkney resident I must mention is author Lynn Johnson who gave me a warm welcome to the island and not only gave me helpful advice on places to see but also showed me where to find the best cake in Stromness!

As ever, a huge thank you to my wonderful editor Emily Bedford and the whole team at Canelo for helping me make the book the best it can be. Finally to my brilliant agent, Lina Langlee for all her hard work and support.